*Books by C. A. Newsome*

SNEAK THIEF
MAXIMUM SECURITY
DROOL BABY
A SHOT IN THE BARK

# Sneak Thief

A Dog Park Mystery

## C. A. Newsome

TWO PUP
PRESS

This is a work of fiction. All of the characters, places and events portrayed in this book are either products of the author's imagination or are used fictitiously.

SNEAK THIEF

*Julia* by Carol Ann Newsome
Cover design by Elizabeth Mackey
Copyright © 2015 by Carol Ann Newsome

**ISBN-13:** 978-0-9963742-0-0

Published by Two Pup Press
1836 Bruce Avenue
Cincinnati, Ohio 45223-2060

*To my readers,*
*For supporting me in this great adventure*

# Prologue

"Come back here, you little sneak!"

Clad only in panties, arms waving, Desiree lunged across the top of her unmade bed. She grabbed for the baby-blue underwire dangling from her Beagle's mouth.

"Julia, I mean it!"

Julia reared back as Desiree's fingers brushed her muzzle in a failed attempt to reclaim the frilly wisp of satin. Desiree slipped on the covers, burying her face in a pile of throw pillows. She lifted her head. For a moment the pair froze, Desiree's murderous eyes boring through the bedclothes to meet Julia's mutinous ones.

Julia tilted her head and considered her options. The Beagle jumped off the far side of the bed and dashed out the door with the saliva-stained bra streaming behind her like a medieval battle standard. Desiree shrieked and raced after the reprobate. Her lush body disappeared into the living room, leaving only the rumpled bedclothes behind.

The monitor screen winked out, turning the tiny room into a black void populated with a faint scattering of metallic reflections like faraway stars.

"Whew." The Watcher leaned back in his chair with a dazed grin on his face. If Desiree only knew there was a spy cam in her bedroom. He couldn't believe his luck the week before, when she said she'd been late to work because her alarm clock died. Easy enough to say he had a spare an aunt had given him for Christmas. Overnight shipping for the clock with the hidden surveillance camera had been astronomical, but worth it. She'd been so appreciative when he handed it to her, thanking him with a coy smile that made his knees wobbly. *No, thank* you, *Desiree. Thank you, thank you, thank you.*

When he went to her apartment earlier that day, The Watcher expected the difficulty to lie in retrieving the clock's data card and swapping it out for a new one. He'd never been to her house and hadn't known where she lived until he snuck a GPS monitor—purchased at the same time as the clock—under the wheel well of her car. Monitoring her movements from his cell phone gave him her location without the risk of discovery. Today he'd been unable to resist his urges any longer and had gone after the tiny card.

The two-family Victorian Desiree lived in lurked behind hedges that hadn't seen clippers since the turn of the millennium. The Watcher walked up to the porch as if he belonged and looked at the mail boxes. *Just checking to see what floor my friend lives on, nothing going on here, nothing to see.* He didn't *really* believe in Jedi mind-tricks, but he mimicked Obi-wan Kenobi's signature hand gesture anyway.

The Watcher fake-rapped on the door and turned around, hands on hips, as if waiting for someone to answer. While he was doing this, he scanned the sidewalk and the houses across the street. A circular saw whined next door and he could hear a hammer pounding, but no one was outside.

He walked around the side of the house and ran into a six-foot privacy fence. *Damn. Shoulda kept up with the chin-ups.* He eyed the rolling garbage bin next door, wondering if it would hold his weight, then dragged over a lichen covered-Adirondack chair instead. The Watcher straddled the chair, one foot on each broad armrest. Grabbing the top of the fence, he set one foot on the top of the backrest and boosted himself up. Once over the fence and away from prying eyes, discovery of a large dog door in Desiree's kitchen door surprised a snort out of him. He tipped the door with one cautious toe. It swung in easily, unlocked. *Piece of cake.*

It was a tight fit, eeling through the low opening. He'd had a rough moment when, his head through the hole and his arms pinned to his sides, a barking dog raced into the kitchen to confront him. *Dog door. Dog. Duh.* The mutt stopped a few feet away and curled its lip, growling. Having no other options, The Watcher stilled. *Think possum. Think possum.* The mutt spent a full minute asserting her property rights, then advanced to the door, sniffed The Watcher's nose and started licking his face. The Watcher slumped, the breath he'd held gusting out of him like a deflating balloon. He continued worming his way through the pet door and rewarded the incompetent watch dog with a marrow bone from a package on top of the fridge.

The Watcher hadn't expected the dog. But Julia—her tag said her name was Julia— only wanted to play. It looked like Julia was going to make his pursuit of Desiree Willis even more entertaining than anticipated.

Desiree, lovely, lovely Desiree, with the magnificent breasts. Desiree of the smoky voice that whispered to him in dreams where she lay in his bed, the pale green tips of her spiky hair like a verdigris crown against his shoulder and her pearly, pale blue eyes adoring beneath long sooty lashes. Sweaty dreams that woke him night after night. He'd known about the barb-wire tattoo wrapped around her biceps. Now he knew about the Celtic trinity symbol on her shoulder blade and the sweet, winged heart on the small of her back. He had to learn everything about her. When he made his move, he wanted it to be perfect. Perfect for her would mean perfect for him.

So Julia liked to steal underwear. That could come in handy. Desiree wouldn't think anything of it if a pair of her panties went missing. He marked that last segment of the video file and exported it as a looping clip. The Watcher leaned back in his chair to see it again.

## Chapter 1

**Friday, April 18**

Lia leaned over to peer at the odd squiggle on Desiree's monitor. "Is that supposed to be a bicycle?"

Desiree sighed. In the vast array of computers that was Scholastic Scoring Systems, it was an insignificant gesture.

"I guess so. A bicycle in a wreck with a tree. I think he's trying to say, if he were riding the bike at the speed they said in the question, he wouldn't have been able to stop. Proficiency testing is whack. Fourth-graders think they're so cute. After grading the same question 5,000 times, they're a freaking riot." She rolled her eyes.

Lia tilted her head sideways to get a better look. "I don't know, I like the added touch of the body on the ground. The broken arm really makes it. What's that blob?"

Desiree squinted. "Blood, maybe? But I can't give him any credit for this, can I?"

Lia shrugged. "You're asking the wrong person." She shot her hand up in the air to grab their Team Leader's attention. She already knew what the answer was, but Eric liked to feel needed. And he'd get a kick out of the little sketch.

Eric bopped over to their row—he was much too energetic to merely walk—and stood behind the women.

He stroked a trim red beard and raised his eyebrows as he examined Desiree's screen.

"What should I do with this?" Desiree asked. "This kid clearly knows the answer."

"He doesn't state it directly, and he doesn't show his work. We can't give points for artwork. No matter how creative it is." Eric folded his arms and gave her a mock-stern look over his glasses. "You know the rules."

Desiree slumped back in her chair and twisted her mouth. "I guess. You're no fun, Eric."

"I'm not supposed to be fun. Just consistent."

"You're fun on Fridays, when you bring us chocolate." Lia toasted him with her half-eaten Nestle's Crunch bar. "Do you get an allowance for all the treats you give us?"

"What? No, of course not."

Eric's head popped up, his attention caught by a waving hand two rows up in the expanse of monitors.

Lia watched as Eric bounced off to settle another question. "You know, he's kinda cute for a short guy."

"I'm so over that whole shaved head thing," Desiree said. "I ran into it a lot at The Comet. I thought you had a boyfriend?"

"I was thinking for you."

"You think so?" Desiree made a moue and tilted her head. "I don't know . . . I usually go for bad boy types. Eric is just so . . . chipper. And I usually like them taller."

The two women considered Eric Flynn as he bent over a retiree's monitor. He was actually taller than he looked, since he tended to lead with his head, leaning forward as if he couldn't wait to get where he was going. Lia pegged him in his late twenties. Blue eyes, the shade of the sky on a crisp autumn day, hid behind heavy, black-framed glasses.

Lia wondered if his shaved head was due to early male pattern baldness, style or politics. Perhaps inspired by a bout with cancer? She thought his Batman hoodie

6

showed just the right amount of humor. Desiree's coppery hair with its blue-green tips would look cute next to Eric's Buddy Holly glasses and baggy—not saggy—jeans.

What guy wouldn't go for Desiree? Lia always caught men staring at the shorter woman's packed, curvy figure. She looked up to see Avery, the room supervisor, watching them from the corner of his eye as he strolled down the center aisle separating the computers like Moses parting the Red Sea. His eyes flicked away when Lia caught him ogling her scoring partner. Case in point.

Desiree seemed oblivious. Or maybe she was just used to it. Though it was probably self-defense. Still, Lia couldn't imagine any woman wanting to encourage Avery. The guy was a prissy tyrant in Ralph Lauren his mother bought at a factory outlet. Ugh.

She nudged Desiree. "Back to work. Avery is looking over here."

Lia and Desiree were hunched over their monitors when Eric came back. They looked up at him with wide, owl eyes.

"Why do I think you girls—excuse me, *women*—are plotting something?"

"Who, us?" Desiree blinked, a suspiciously blank expression on her face. "We're just scoring away here. Was there something you wanted, Bwana?"

Eric's lips twitched. He leaned over and tapped a little figure made of crumpled aluminum foil that was sitting on top of Desiree's monitor. "Who's this funny little guy?"

"I found him clinging to my car antenna yesterday. Cute, isn't he?"

"I think Desiree has an admirer," Lia said.

Desiree rolled her eyes and huffed. "Whatever."

"Just be sure to take him with you when you leave tonight," Eric said. "First shift gets wiggy if the work stations aren't pristine when they show up."

"Yeah, yeah, yeah. Some people have no sense of humor."

"First shift sure doesn't," Eric agreed. "Back to work. We've got the best stats in the room. You don't want to ruin that for us, do you?"

Avery looked up at the clock. "Be back by 7:33," he announced to the room.

Lia and Desiree grabbed their bags and joined the crowd heading for the break room. "You seem a bit off tonight. Didn't you get any sleep?" Lia asked.

Desiree smirked. "No, but it was on purpose."

"Brian?"

"Brian is so last week. This was Claude. Remember, I told you about him."

"The guy with the sexy accent?"

"That's him. Too bad he's only going to be here for a few more days."

"I don't know where you get the energy. Oh, look, there's Terry. I want you to meet him." Lia waved at the chunky man sitting at a far table in the break room and pointed to the kitchen. She mouthed, "Be right there," before she and Desiree joined the line at the coffee machine.

"I hate drinking coffee this late," Desiree said, "but that last hour is murder without it. Damned if you do, damned if you don't. If I drink it, I'll have a hard time making it to the shop in the morning." She sighed and the line inched forward. "I've got to get through tonight. Tomorrow will have to take care of itself."

"You never mentioned what your day job was," Lia said.

"I make jewelry for this place off Ludlow."

"Really?" Lia reached for a cup and filled it under the coffee spigot. "What kind?"

"I'm assembling stuff. It's monkey work, but it's a step up from the beading I do at home. Al has a line of

8

jewelry that he sells wholesale. He promised to teach me real jewelry making—casting and setting stones and stuff—if I stick around long enough."

"Sounds fun." Coffees in hand, the pair snaked between tables to the back of the room where Terry sat. "Hey Terry, this is Desiree. She lives in Northside and makes jewelry."

"Indeed?" Terry Dunn tilted his head back so he could see Desiree clearly through the mid range portion of his trifocal lenses. He was a rudy-complected man of average height in his early sixties. He sported a white, bushy mustache and a buzz cut. His tee shirt read "GUN SAFE-TY - Until You are Ready to Fire, Keep Your Booger Hook Off the Bang Switch." Lia thought he looked like Teddy Roosevelt.

"Terry spent last Christmas singing Cthulhu carols by the light of TV snow. He says the static contains remnants of light from the Big Bang."

"We were chanting. One does not 'sing' to honor the ancient one."

"How nice to meet you. What's a cachoola?" She flashed her best smile at Terry.

Terry preened. "Why, have you never heard of H. P. Lovecraft?"

Lia mentally shook her head, amused. *Good thing I have a sense of humor. A girl could get an inferiority complex hanging out with Desiree. She has Terry wrapped around her pinky and she's only practicing.*

Lia Anderson stood several slender inches over Desiree's scant five feet. Chestnut hair was messily twisted into a knot on the back of Lia's head, held in place with a ruined paintbrush serving as a hair pick. High cheekbones and tilted moss green eyes gave her a slightly exotic look. Always casual about her appearance, she usually wore jeans and men's tee shirts. And she felt like a bag lady next to Desiree.

9

"… so you like guns. People here are so interesting. What brought you to Scholastic?"

"Lia," Terry volunteered, "is a painter. She decided to donate her time creating murals for the Belmont Convalescent Care Center this spring, so she works evenings to pay the rent. When I told her I was looking for a part time job, she referred me."

"Wow," Desiree said, looking at Lia. "You never told me you were a real artist. I only play one on TV. What about you, Terry?"

"Alas, my lady love moved back to Idaho to be near her grandchildren. I retired, but I am now stuck with paying all the bills until I find a room-mate."

Lia pulled a plastic container out of her tote, pulled the lid off, and dug her fork in.

Desiree leaned over, wrinkled her nose. "What *is* that?"

"Curried carrot and lentil salad," Lia said, munching.

"But the lentils have little tails."

"Raw lentil sprouts," Terry explained while Lia ate.

"Raw?" The look of horror on Desiree's face had Lia hiding a grin. *People can be so squeamish about food.*

"I have a wonderful recipe for a lentil salad," Terry said. "Cooked lentils, of course. You have to be careful with lentils. There is a very small window between buckshot and total mush—"

"Raw food is the best kind to eat, and lentils are extremely healthy. I am determined to find a recipe for lentil sprouts that I like," Lia said.

"And do you? Like that, I mean," Desiree asked, pointing at Lia's salad, which resembled a compost heap.

"Like is such a funny word. It's edible and it gives me a lot of energy."

Desiree shuddered and turned to Terry. "How do you and Lia know each other?"

"I was just an innocent lad—" Terry began.

"Don't listen to him," Lia said, pointing at Terry with her fork. "We've known each other for years from the dog park."

"Is that the Mount Airy Dog Park? I've wanted to go there since I got Julia."

"You should join us," Terry said. "Oops, time to get back to work. Lia, I'll see you tomorrow morning."

Desiree watched Terry exit. "He likes guns and worships monsters. You're friends with this guy?"

"I figure he'll be useful during the coming zombie invasion."

A trio of black noses forced the front door open as Lia unlocked it. Lia bent down to pet Honey, her Golden Retriever and Chewy, her Miniature Schnauzer. A medium-sized dog with plush black fur shoved between her and the others, whimpering excitedly as she shimmied her butt and licked at Lia's hand.

"Look at you, Viola. If you're here, your daddy must be here, too. Where is he?"

Detective Peter Dourson stretched his rangy, six-foot-two frame on the couch, watching basketball on the flat screen TV he'd given Lia for Christmas. Lia said hello to the dogs and let them out the back door, then sat down beside him on the edge of the Mission style couch and brushed the hair off his forehead.

"Chief Roller's going to be after you to get it cut any day now. Shame. The retro Beatle bangs are cute."

Peter grunted and kept his eyes on the screen as LeBron James faked out a pair of Celtics and made a dash for the basket. The Cavaliers made the expected two points and Peter clenched his fist in a modified fist-pump.

"You break into my place and all you're going to do is grunt at me?"

"Sorry, Babe." Peter turned his head to look at her. While Eric's eyes reminded her of autumn, Peter's were a luminous indigo exactly the shade of twilight in a Parrish print.

"I spent the last several hours deciphering handwriting on thirty-year-old reports that were never entered into the system. I'm exhausted and my eyes are bleeding. This case has me stumped as a preacher in a whore house."

"Considering what some preachers get into, not very then."

"This preacher was my Uncle Clarence on my mother's side."

"Okay, that's different. Why does Roller care about 30 year old crimes?"

"This came from higher up. One of our esteemed state supreme court justices is an ancient gentleman named Wilber Hatch. He was once the very proud owner of a lovely little Renaissance bronze of the goddess Diana, rumored to have belonged to King Louis the something of France. The statue and numerous other family heirlooms disappeared while Hatch's 17 year old grandson was visiting. The grandson was doing drugs at the time and Grandpa let him stay while he sorted his head out.

"Hatch has always been convinced his grandson did it. James Hatch, the grandson, continues to maintain his innocence. There's been a rift ever since. James Hatch is now an assistant district attorney.

Last week the statue showed up at Christie's and Wilber nearly had a stroke. He and James are both anxious to discover the truth."

"Why can't they just ask the person who put it up at Christies?" Lia asked.

"He was in kindergarten when it was taken. He's the executor of his uncle's estate, and uncle can't enlighten us unless Bailey can get some help from one of her pals."

Peter sat up, the vertebrae in his back audibly popping as he stretched.

"We pulled Cynth in to do some computer analysis. She ran some statistics just for fun and discovered a pattern. High-end burglaries. Antiques, fossils, jewelry, small stuff, very selective. It's been going on for years, right under our noses. One every 12 to 18 months, going back to the '80s. They were spaced so far apart, no one realized they were connected until Diana made her debut in New York.

"Roller assigned me to this mess."

"You couldn't turn him down?"

"I could, but Heckle and Jeckle were chomping at the bit to work it and Cynth begged me to save her."

"I owe the pleasure of your company to Cynth?"

Peter tilted Lia's chin up, leaned in for a brief kiss.

"You owe the pleasure of my company to being gone every night this week. Can't I miss my best girl?"

"Your best girl is in the back yard, peeing on the azaleas."

"How about my best green-eyed girl?" he asked, toying with an escaped tendril of hair while he looked into her eyes. Lia felt a pleasant thrum inside. Peter loved to play with her hair and he was always so serious about it. He pulled the paint brush out of her Boho bun, letting the knot unwind over his hands, running his fingers through to the ends to fluff it out. He leaned closer, inhaling the scent of her freesia shampoo. "How's the job going?"

"Could be worse." Lia tilted her head to one side, exposing her neck for a nibble. "The working conditions are good. It makes up for the way they nit-pick over the answers on these standardized tests. Sometimes I think a room full of drunk howler monkeys came up with the grading criteria, but I'm sure I'll get the hang of it. They give us chocolate."

"Well, then, that's okay. So you like it?" Peter traced an index finger around the outside of her ear, giving her chills.

"Scoring the same question a thousand times in a night gets to be a grind, but for a side job, it's better than I expected. The people are really nice. My team leader is cool, and the girl who sits next to me is fun. It's like having another sister. Her name's Desiree."

"That's a name you don't hear often."

"Oh, it fits," Lia said. "Every time I turn my head, I catch some guy staring at her. If it's not the room supervisor or one of the team leaders, it's one of the other scorers."

"I wouldn't stare at her."

"How do you know?"

"I've got you to stare at. You're all I can handle." He tapped the slight dent in her chin with his index finger, then traced down her neck, over the collar of her tee shirt, halting when he hit a bump. "You never wear it out where anyone can see it. Don't you like it?"

Lia fished an opal pendant out of her shirt. The gem retained a layer of stone matrix and nested in a fluid gold setting, the polished face flashing color as it swayed on the gold chain. It reminded Lia of an egg, life glowing through a hole in its shell, something mysterious about to be born.

"I love it. I'm afraid of losing it or damaging it somehow. If it's inside my shirt, I can always feel it and I know where it is."

They were interrupted by the sound of scratching at the back door. Lia let the dogs in and grabbed a Bass Pale Ale and a glass of herbal ice-tea before she returned to the living room. Viola sat on the couch next to Peter, sneering at her as Peter scratched behind her ears. Honey and Chewy watched from their beds across the room, waiting to see what Lia would do.

"See, she's your best girl. I'm not allowed to sit next to you when she's around."

"Now that's just silly." Peter patted the couch. "I can pet you both at the same time."

"Oh, yeah?" Lia sat down, handing Peter his beer. A low rumbling noise emerged from Viola's throat. Lia stood up. It stopped. She sat back down. The rumble grew louder. She stood up. It stopped. "See?"

"I don't get it. When did this start?"

"She would get like this when Luthor had her. It comes and goes." Lia sat down on the other end of the couch, next to Viola, and stroked her fur. "She's perfectly happy for me to give her attention. I'm just not supposed to give you attention when she's in this mood."

"How, exactly, are we supposed to deal with this?"

"She'll prove her point, then go off to lie down. We just have to wait."

The Chow mix looked up and grinned, showing canines on either side of her lolling tongue. Chewy huffed and put his head down on his paws. Honey began chewing a tennis ball, deliberately ignoring the drama on the couch.

"This is ridiculous," Peter said, shooing Viola with his hands. "Off!"

Viola gave him a wounded look and slunk away to sulk under a chair in the corner. Lia swore Honey was laughing.

Peter took a swig of his beer. "Does it bother you, having Luthor's dog around? I never asked."

"I love Viola, even if she has her perverse moments. I'm glad you kept her."

"That's good to know. Seriously," Peter said, changing the subject, "you don't have to donate all your time to Alma's murals. She wasn't expecting the Sistine Chapel. She just thought you could paint a few flowers in the hall and it'd cheer up the residents."

"I don't put out inferior work. If I'm going to do it, I'm going to do it right. My name goes on this, regardless whether I get paid or not. I . . . " She struck a pose. ". . . am an artist. I have a reputation to think of."

She shrieked when he goosed her in the side, causing all three dogs to pop their heads up.

"I hate to think of you painting all day and working all evening. I wish you'd let me help you out."

"We talked about this, Peter. I like things just the way they are, and I'll get by, just like I always do. It's only for two months, and it could open up larger projects for me."

"And I'll never get to see you."

"You're seeing me now."

"That's true. I am. We could do kubotan practice."

"You're in a masochistic mood tonight."

"Okay, weapons practice is out. You up for a little illegal search and seizure instead?"

"Depends. What do you plan on seizing, Kentucky Boy?"

"What do you think?" He stood, pulling Lia with him, and tossed her over one shoulder in a fireman's carry. When he kicked the door to her bedroom shut, she was laughing.

# Chapter 2

**Saturday, April 19**

A bell tinkled as Lia pushed her way into the dimly-lit storefront on Telford Avenue. She studied the barrister cases lining the walls. Lights inside the cases illuminated semi-precious gems, giving them an unearthly glow. An older man with a hooked nose and dour expression ignored her from his desk behind the counter. Desiree emerged from the back, her green highlights visible before the rest of her features took form.

"Lia, you came! Let me show you around. Are you looking for anything special, or is this visit strictly for drooling?"

"Just checking everything out. I don't know why I've never been here before." The stacked cases in the dim light reminded Lia of the snake exhibit at the zoo. She almost expected to see eyes staring from behind a heavy serpentine necklace. It was a trick of the light, she decided, and of the decision to display the jewelry draped across carefully positioned tree branches. The shop's resemblance to a serpentarium was heightened by the informational cards on the cases explaining the metaphysical properties of the different gemstones. "I'd love to see the jewelry you make."

"That's over here. We sell a ton online." Desiree lowered her voice. "It's not exactly Tiffany's, but I suspect it keeps the doors open."

She led Lia to a large display case on legs, like a table. The interior was lined with folds of gun-metal gray Ultra-Suede. Long strands of stones pooled and spiraled across the cloth. The effect was a dizzying kaleidoscope of color that shifted and flashed as Lia moved around the case.

"Do you like it?" Desiree asked. "Al let me do the display." She glanced over her shoulder at the man at the desk, then lowered her voice. "Al designed the spacer beads and has them mass produced. I'm not supposed to tell people I assemble this stuff. Ruins the mystique."

Lia grinned. "I won't rat you out. How did you wind up working here?"

Desiree shrugged. "I wandered in one day and asked Al—that's short for Alfonso—about buying some unmounted stones for my grandmother's necklace. I wanted to try to fix it. So he asked me some questions and said he could use a helper."

Lia looked back at Al. His nose was still buried in his papers, a scowl on his face. She couldn't imagine him warming up enough to be congenial. "How do you like working here?"

"It's great. Hardly anyone comes in, so it's nice and quiet and I just sit in the back and play with the stones. Al looks like a sourpuss, but he's really sweet to me." She leaned in, confiding. "His son is really hot and he's a big flirt. He's been hitting on me a lot when Al isn't here, but I don't want to mess with the boss's son. This is the only job like it that I've found and I'd hate to lose it over sex. I console myself by flirting with the guys rehabbing the house next to mine.

"Anyway, the jewelry is really easy to make. I feel like I'm one step up from Hobby Lobby."

"A few more steps than that. The spacers are lovely and I'm sure the quality of the stones is better."

Desiree looked back at her boss. "Not that much better," she said. "I think it's a hoot that people are willing to pay hundreds for a strand of beads that can't be worth more than twenty."

"I feel the same way about art. Twenty bucks worth of canvas and paint, and if you have a name, you can sell it for a hundred times that."

"Oh, but painting takes skill. This is easy."

Lia thought about pointing out that the value was in the design, but decided to keep her mouth shut. In this case, she didn't see much that was extraordinary about the pieces, so maybe Desiree wasn't far from the truth. It wouldn't be the first time the world of fashion repackaged the ordinary as classic and sold it at premium prices.

Lia strolled by the cases, examining the different stones. "I'm familiar with garnets and moonstone, but ametrine, celestite, peridot? I've never heard of them before."

"Most people haven't, unless they're rock hounds or crystal freaks. We've got an encyclopedia of minerals and stones that's four inches thick. Al tells me they discover more gems every day, many of them rarer than diamonds. Diamonds aren't even in the top ten, unless you're talking about the Pink Star Diamond. It's 60 carats. Sotheby's sold it for 83 million."

"Wow, that's almost as much as Christie's got for Van Gogh's *Sunflowers*. So when are you bringing Julia to the park?"

# Chapter 3

**Monday, April 28**

The Watcher thumped back in his chair and scowled at the offending monitor. He should have expected this. He *had* expected this; he'd overheard Desiree talking about her date on her cell phone. He'd been in agony, forcing himself to wait until the optimal time to retrieve the SD card from the camera, all the while hoping the date was a bust. Obviously not, as their ghostly, grappling bodies demonstrated on his monitor.

The quality of the infrared was excellent. It tortured and titillated him as he watched the rude hand shove up under Desiree's bra. The sound quality was fine as well, capturing her breathy moans and his grunts.

"You make me crazy," the unknown Lothario rasped, "making me work so hard to get you alone."

"That's how I like my men," Desiree gasped, "sweaty … and crazy."

The Watcher clicked the mouse, freezing the wrestling match. He swiveled away from the monitor and tapped angrily on the armrest. The guy's hands looked like he hauled hay bales. And talk about no finesse!

*Is that what she wants?*

He should trash the file. Watching the video was making him nuts. But how could he *not* look? He scrubbed at his face with his hand and kicked at the floor, slewing the chair back to face the screen. A jab at the trackpad set the figures back in motion. Elbow on armrest, The Watcher propped his chin with his fist and glared, wishing death to his rival and aching for Desiree.

The loathsome Lothario wrestled Desiree's bra off, then levered himself off the bed and unbuckled his belt. Desiree moved towards the spy cam—had she realized she was being videoed? As she leaned over, her necklace swung out towards the clock, obscuring the lens. When it passed by, Desiree had blurred into a white mass filling the screen. He heard the sound of a drawer opening, then the white mass receded and morphed into his Venus again. She held a small packet out to her date. "You'll need this," she said, honey in her voice. "I'd love to put it on you."

He took it, snorted, and tossed it aside. Then he unzipped his pants.

Desiree reached out and zipped them back up, and pointed to the floor. "Pick it up, jerk-face." No longer cajoling, her tone warned that honey would no longer be part of the equation if he didn't comply. Not Venus. Sekhmet, the Egyptian goddess of war in her lioness form. Her arms crossed, barring her chest from further exploration.

"Ah, man, you can't be serious?"

"As a heart attack."

"I don't take showers with a raincoat on, and I don't do rubbers."

"Well, then. Looks like I don't do you."

The Watcher snorted. Things hadn't gone so well after all.

"You don't mean it," Loathsome said, disbelieving.

"Okay, you don't have to use a condom."

"That's better." Loathsome leered and leaned forward.

"You can leave."

He stood there. "Hey, I deserve a little something."

"Now!" She grabbed up a pillow and flung it in his face, then shoved his chest. Loathsome stumbled back. She scooped a shoe up off the floor and hurled it at his head.

The Watcher pumped his fist. "Yes! Atta girl! Woo hoo!" He spun around in his chair, laughing, then leaned forward, to watch Loathsome's degrading departure.

"Bitch!" Loathsome spat over his shoulder.

"You'd better believe it, asshole!" Desiree yelled.

Julia, disturbed by the commotion, started howling.

The Watcher cheerfully bayed with her as Desiree flung her necklace at the slamming door.

# Chapter 4

**Tuesday, April 29**

Lia was letting Honey and Chewy out of the back of her Volvo when Desiree pulled up in a neon green Honda. A Beagle with huge, gorgeous eyes stood in Desiree's lap and propped her paws on the half-opened window, head hanging out, quivering with excitement.

"Hey, you made it!" Lia called out.

Desiree opened the driver's door and Julia exploded off her lap and proceeded to run figure eights in the parking lot.

"Julia! Come back here! Oh, she drives me insane."

"The park will be good for her. She'll run some of that energy out," Lia said.

"You don't know the half of it." Desiree trotted after Julia, who stayed ten feet in front of her and headed for Westwood-Northern Boulevard.

"Hold up, I know this game," Lia yelled. "Come back this way."

"But she'll run off," Desiree insisted.

"I don't think so. If she was going to run off, she'd be gone already. She's playing keep away. I bet if you ignore her and go on up to the park, she'll follow. Trick is, don't look back."

"You sure?"

"I'll keep an eye on her, but I bet she wants to play more than she wants to run away. She'll stick around my dogs, and she won't want to be far from you."

The two women headed up the service road to the dog park entrance. Julia continued to stay back, then as the women were 20 feet away, she ran up behind them, still out of reach. She halted and barked. Lia and Desiree ignored her and continued up the hill, though Chewy strained his lead toward her and yipped shrilly. Julia danced at Chewy and dashed away.

"Don't look now," Lia said, "but we're being followed."

The service road ended at the top of the hill, in front of a picnic shelter. The Mount Airy Dog Park consisted of six acres along the top of a narrow ridge at the former High Point picnic area. The picnic shelter separated two fenced enclosures. Lia nudged Desiree to the right, toward the one-acre enclosure for small dog breeds, which was empty.

"Take Chewy and Honey and go on through the entrance corral. I'll hang back and hold the first gate open. You stand on the other side of the corral. Hold the inside gate open, but don't look at her. When she runs through, I'll shut my gate."

Desiree did as directed. Lia held the outside gate to the corral open while Julia ran circles in the picnic shelter. She stopped when she realized no one was paying attention to her. She spied the open gate and the dogs inside the fence. She zoomed through both gates and into the middle of the enclosure. Lia let the gate swing shut with a loud clang. Startled by the noise, Julia stopped and turned around, gaping in betrayed disbelief. Desiree unclipped Honey and Chewy. Chewy made a beeline for the beguiling Beagle and the pair ran off together.

"How did you know she'd follow?" Desiree asked.

"It was a hunch. Peter's dog does that, stays just out of reach when she could easily outrun me, and I've been able to catch her by tricking her into following Chewy and Honey into a fenced yard. Taking advantage of their social instincts is the easiest way to nab loose dogs, so long as they're friendly."

After a brief period, they crossed to the other fenced area. The dogs shot into the larger enclosure, dashing across the acreage. This side of the park was populated with old picnic tables and older trees.

They passed by two men perched on top of a picnic table, smoking cigarettes. A pair of black labs and a buff-colored Mastiff sprawled in the mulch beside them.

"Hey, Lia, who's your friend?" a handsome white-haired gentleman called out.

The women turned around and joined the men at the table.

"Charlie, Jose, this is Desiree. She works with me at the scoring center."

"You like doing that, Desiree?" Charlie asked.

Desiree tilted her head and batted her eyes at Charlie. "It's okay for seasonal work. I like reading all the answers. The kids can be really funny."

"Hey, Lia, I got a joke for you."

Jose groaned and shook his head.

"Really, Charlie, you don't have to." Lia leaned over. "Run," she whispered to Desiree. "Do not pass go."

"I like jokes," Desiree said, smiling at Charlie and waving Lia off.

Charlie nodded at Desiree with an amused twist of his mouth, took a drag from his cigarette, blew out the smoke.

"What do you say to a woman with two black eyes?"

"Excuse me?" Desiree blinked.

"Nothin.' You already told her . . . Twice," Charlie concluded, slapping his knee as he roared with laughter. "How's that for politically incorrect humor?"

Desiree's face turned stormy. "What are you pigs laughing at? Domestic violence isn't funny."

"Did she just call us what I thought she called us?" Charlie asked Jose.

"And you wonder why you can't get a date." Jose turned to Desiree. "Hey, it's his joke. I didn't say nothin'."

"And I suppose you think domestic violence is a laughing matter?" She zeroed in on Charlie.

"Whoa, now, it's just a joke. I would never hit a woman."

"No, you just condone an atmosphere of intimidation against women. Do you have any idea how many women are beaten every day by their husbands? Do you know that one out of three murdered females is killed by a husband or boyfriend?" Desiree was in tears.

"Hey, you guys have Lorena Bobbit," Charlie said.

"And only one in 25 murdered men is killed by a domestic partner?"

"Whoa," Charlie protested. "I'm just a dumb redneck. I don't mean nothin' by it. All you have to do is tell me I'm not funny. You don't have to make a federal case out of it."

Lia tugged on Desiree's arm. "Let's go find the dogs before they get into trouble."

Desiree stumbled after Lia. "Ignorant assholes like you are what's wrong with the world!" she shouted over her shoulder. "Some friends you've got," she accused Lia.

"Here, let's climb up on this picnic table. I'm sorry about that. I should have warned you about Charlie."

"What, that he's a misogynistic son of a bitch?"

"Charlie likes to tell me the worst jokes he hears. He doesn't believe that stuff. I won't excuse him, but if you were broken down by the side of the road, he'd be the first person to stop and help you."

"If he pulls up while I'm stuck on the side of the road, I'm going to taser him."

"You meet all kinds up here, conservatives, liberals, hipsters and rednecks but they all care about their dogs. They at least have that as a redeeming quality."

"I guess," Desiree grumbled.

"This is my table." The table was identical to four they'd passed by. "We sit on top so the dogs don't slam into our legs while they're running around."

Desiree laid her key-fob down and climbed up to join Lia.

A tall, willow-thin woman walked up, followed by her lanky Bloodhound. Chewy and Julia tagged along, dancing around the dignified dog. There was a certain strength about the woman, perhaps in the lift of her chin and the firm set of her shoulders. She waved a long graceful hand. "What's with Charlie and Jose? They said we had a crazy woman in the park. Are you the crazy woman?" she asked Desiree.

"Desiree, meet Bailey. Kita is the poor hound trying to ignore Chewy." Lia turned to Bailey. "Charlie just told her a domestic violence joke," Lia said.

Bailey shook her head and rolled her eyes, her chin-length red hair swinging around her face in emphasis. "If it makes you feel any better, Charlie says stuff like that when he thinks you're cute."

"Gee. He likes me. I'm thrilled," Desiree deadpanned.

Lia laughed. "I see you've met Julia," she told Bailey.

"Is this your dog?" Bailey asked. "She's adorable. I've never seen such big eyes."

Julia bounced up on the table and wiggled around Desiree. Chewy, who had never figured out how to jump up on the table, whined.

"Looks like Julia's made a conquest," Bailey said.

Desiree hugged Julia. "All the guys are after you. It's a curse."

"I hope she's spayed," Bailey said.

"Desiree works at the scoring center with me and Terry," Lia said.

"I wish they scored in the winter, when I'm not working," Bailey said. "I could use the extra income then. Nobody wants their yards mowed in January."

"Bailey has a gardening business," Lia explained.

"Thus the grass stains," Bailey said, gesturing to her knees with a graceful hand that should have been turning letters on TV.

"Desiree has a secret admirer. Did you ever find out who left that little man on your car?"

"No, and a couple days ago, I found a shoebox with a scene in it on my steps. A little foil boy and a little foil girl sitting on a bench, holding hands. There was a tiny little Beagle sitting next to them."

"That's so sweet! Have you figured who it is?" Lia asked.

"No, and I've been looking."

"Doesn't it creep you out, just a little," Bailey asked, "knowing that someone is sneaking around you like that?"

"Bailey, you have no romance in your soul," Lia said. "Anyway, I think Desiree can take care of herself. You should have seen her handing Charlie his rump on a plate. She's small, but she's mighty."

Lia looked at her phone. "I've got to run. I'm meeting Alma in an hour."

"I've got to go pick up plants," Bailey said.

"Don't leave me here," Desiree said. "I'm coming with you." She felt around on the table top for her key-fob, finding nothing. She turned around, searching. "Where are my keys? They were right here." She climbed off the table, looked underneath. Still nothing.

"You're missing something else," Lia said. "Where's Julia?"

"Julia!" Desiree jumped up and scanned the four acre enclosure. "That dirty little sneak thief, I bet she has them. Julia! This isn't funny!"

"She has to be inside the fence, at least," Bailey said.

"I hope she still has the keys," Lia said. "Otherwise we'll have to get Terry down here with his metal detector."

"Oh, no," Desiree moaned. "Where *is* that dog?"

Lia looked towards the front of the park. Several dogs were playing together. Julia wasn't one of them. "Let's walk to the back fence. If we don't see her, we can head back up front. We need to pay attention to the side slopes. It's easy to miss dogs down by the fence-line."

They were almost to the rear of the park when they heard a hollow clanging.
"What's that?" Desiree asked.

"The agility tunnel," Bailey and Lia said in unison.

They veered towards a set of enameled steel agility equipment that had been donated to the park.

"Bailey, get on the far side, in case she tries to run off." Lia and Desiree waited until Bailey circled around the eight foot long tube, then approached the opening. The clanging continued. Lia bent over and peered inside. Julia grabbed up the fob and headed for the opposite end. She found Bailey cutting off her escape and turned back around. She sat in the middle of the tunnel, stymied.

"Whatever you do, don't yell at her," Lia advised Desiree.

"She's my dog, I can yell at her if I want to."

"True, but she's not likely to come to you if you're yelling."

"Oh. I guess you're right." Desiree knelt at the mouth of the tunnel. "Here, baby doll, come to Mommy. Who's the prettiest little Beagle girl in Cincinnati? Come, Julia! That's a *girl*!"

Julia came out but struggled to maintain her grip on the keys. Desiree wrested them away, then wiped a drool-drenched hand on her jeans.

"Ugh! Look at this! Teeth marks! I can't believe you did this!" Desiree shook the key-fob at Julia, who responded with a mutinous expression. "And don't look at me that way."

"Maybe it will still work," Bailey offered.

"It had better. It costs a fortune to replace it."

They headed for the front gate, a recalcitrant Julia in tow. Honey, Chewy and Kita trotted along with smug looks on their faces.

"I bet *your* dogs never do stuff like that," Desiree said.

"Does she often take things?" Lia asked.

"Underwear, TV remotes, phones, kitchen utensils, you name it, she'll steal it. She likes to hide stuff, too."

"You ever try distracting her with toys?" Bailey asked.

"She had a squeaky toy, but it drove me crazy. I threw it out when she chewed it up. She still wants Mommy's stuff. It tastes better than dog food, doesn't it, Julia?"

"Try hiding her kibble around the apartment instead of feeding it to her in a bowl. Finding her food will keep her Beagle instincts too busy to get into your stuff," Lia said.

"Won't the kibble leave crumbs everywhere?"

Lia shrugged, holding her hands out with the palms up. She lifted her left hand. "Kibble crumbs." Her right hand. "Hundred dollar electronic key fob and your sanity. You choose. Besides, I bet she won't leave any crumbs."

"Truth," Bailey said.

As they were loading their dogs into their respective cars, Lia glanced over at the windshield of Desiree's Honda. "What's that?" She pointed to a small silver figure propped up by the driver's side wiper, leaning on the glass. It was peering into the car with its tiny hands shielding its eyes.

The women gathered around the offering.

"How did that get here?" Desiree asked. "Did either of you see anyone around the car?"

Lia and Bailey shook their heads.

"I didn't notice any strange cars, but I wasn't paying attention to the parking lot," Lia said. "Maybe Charlie or Jose saw something. I'll go back up and ask around."

"Oh, don't bother," Desiree said. She plucked the figure off her car and held it up to look at it closer. "He is kind of cute." She tossed it onto the passenger seat.

"How many of these have you gotten?" Lia asked.

"This is the third one that's just by itself. Then there was that box scene—what do you call those?"

"Diorama," Bailey and Lia said automatically.

"That's it. Just one of those," Desiree said. "Whoever he is, I wish he'd show himself. This is starting to get weird. I mean, I was right here. Why didn't he just give it to me?"

"He's shy; he's unattractive or otherwise inappropriate and thinks you'll reject him; or he's a deranged serial killer who wants to drive you bonkers before he finishes you off by carving his initials into your heart with an ice pick." Bailey ticked these options off on her fingers.

"Gee, thanks for putting that in my head," Desiree said.

"Why don't you talk to Peter?" Bailey asked Lia. "Maybe he could get fingerprints off this stuff."

"Unlikely," Lia said. "He says "CSI" has given everyone unrealistic expectations about what can be done with forensic science and police budgets. And they'd never do it for a case where there is no obvious threat.

"Desiree," she continued, "have you noticed anything out of place at your house, anything strange? If this guy's a stalker, he may be breaking into your apartment. Check your underwear drawer, see if anyone's been in it. Pay attention to your laundry basket. He could be stealing your dirty undies."

"Eeeewww." Desiree grimaced. "You think he's snorting my panties? I'd rather he was a deranged serial killer."

"I don't know about that," Lia said, thinking about the deranged serial killer she'd confronted not so long ago. She let Honey and Chewy back out of her Volvo. "But I'm going back up to ask around about strange cars. I'll call you if I find out anything."

The Watcher sat in his car in McFarlan Woods, mesmerized by the blinking light on his smart phone as he monitored the GPS device on Desiree's car. He toyed with the lock of hair he'd painstakingly collected from her brush, flicking the ends across his lips as he considered his next move.

McFarlan Woods sat next to the dog park. He'd stashed his car there and followed one of the trails to the dog park. The Watcher originally planned a quick dash to her car to plant the doll, then back into the woods where he could see her reaction to the little offering. Once he got there, he realized there was a chance a loose dog in the parking lot would smell him in the woods and expose him. So he sat in his car to see where she was going. Probably home, since she had Julia with her.

The Watcher felt a gaping hole in his chest as her car pulled further and further away from him, a plunge from the heady excitement of leaving his offering on her car.

He'd taken a huge risk this time. Anyone at the park could have seen him, had they chosen to look down at the lot from the ridge where dogs and their owners gathered. His heart pounded in his ears when a meandering Schnauzer yipped at him from behind the fence. Now the capricious organ dropped into his stomach, resuming the familiar dull ache that kept him listless and depressed unless she was around. He could barely eat and was losing weight.

His only relief came when he reviewed his surveillance videos, or when he broke into her apartment to swap out SD cards. He found himself spending more and more time at her place during these excursions. He knew it was dangerous, but it was such pleasure being where she spent her nights, touching the towels she dried her creamy skin with, inhaling the essence of her lingering on the sheets.

Desiree was an indifferent housekeeper and left her bed unmade. This made it easy for him to lay on her bed, share her pillow. He liked to close his eyes and imagine her lying next to him.

The blinking dot stopped moving, pulling him out of his revery. She wasn't home. The dot was miles away, in the parking lot behind Ludlow Avenue. What would she be doing there? It occurred to him that patrons often took dogs into Om Cafe, the metaphysical restaurant above the lot. If he hurried, he could bump into her there. He could do that, couldn't he? It would be an accident. At least, she would think it was.

"I'm worried about Desiree," Lia told Peter.

They sat in her kitchen, sharing an Edgar Allen Poe pizza from Dewey's while the dogs watched and drooled. Peter ripped a crust into three pieces and tossed them to the dogs. Honey snatched hers out of the air, Chewy snapped at his and missed, then snuffled around the floor looking for it, and Viola sat with a look of disbelief on her face that he would assault her with flying food.

Peter picked up the offending bit of crust and offered it to Viola on his open palm. "Here you go, your highness." Viola sniffed at the crust, then delicately nibbled it out of his palm. She laid it on the floor and licked it twice, then ate it in one gulp.

Lia shook her head. "When are you going to stop trying to get her to act like a regular dog? It's beneath her."

33

"I keep hoping. Why are you worried about Desiree?"

"Someone's been leaving her these little dolls made out of foil, and she has no idea who's doing it."

"How do you make a doll out of foil?"

"I'm not sure, but it looks like one piece of foil crunched up so that it holds its shape. I bet it's easy if you figure out how. I thought it was cute at first. Now it's getting creepy."

"What is it that's disturbing you?"

"The dolls are cute and they look harmless. It's just that one popped up while we were at the park today. Someone knew she was at the park or went to the trouble of following her there, and they chose to leave something on her car instead of saying something to her. Why doesn't he just ask her out on a date?"

"I seem to recall leaving plants outside your studio door," Peter rubbed the back of his neck and gave Lia a wry twist of his mouth.

"That's different. I knew it was you. And it was very sweet. Desiree doesn't have a clue who's doing this."

"Has anything else happened to make her feel like she's being stalked? Hang up calls, harassing emails, anyone following her?"

"Not that she's said."

"Anyone showing interest in her lately, someone who may be more into her than she realizes?"

Lia laughed. "That could be anyone. She dates a lot. Strange men are always looking at her."

"That could be the problem. Some guy probably thinks she's out of his league and doesn't have the stones to approach her. Could be a case of erotomania."

"Eroto-what?"

"Erotomania. Usually erotomaniacs are convinced that the person they're in love with secretly loves them back but for some reason, has to deny it publicly. They feed off unrequited love."

"That's crazy."

"It is, it's a mental disorder. Erotomaniacs usually aren't dangerous. There are lots of reasons for stalking. If she doesn't have an angry ex, or if she doesn't feel threatened by the behavior, it could be someone who's fixated on her but for some reason, doesn't know how to have a relationship. In most of those cases, he doesn't mean her any harm. It could just be a case of terminal shyness and poor judgement."

"How do you know so much?"

"Part of the job. Stalking can be hard to define. We have to be able to assess whether or not an actual threat is involved."

"So, in Desiree's case, it may be weird but harmless?"

"I can't say. I don't want to make light of it. She should definitely pay attention to the people around her and write down anything strange, document when and where these dolls pop up. What you've told me is not a lot to go on."

"I guess I shouldn't worry about her too much. She threatened to taser Charlie today."

Peter barked a laugh that made all the dogs jump. "I bet he deserved it."

"He did."

"You can give her Brent's number. If she's worried, he'll be happy to talk to her."

"Why not give her your number?"

"Unsolicited attention from the opposite sex is more his territory than it is mine."

Lia snorted.

"Claude left town and it can't be Al, he's married," Desiree said as she dipped a plastic spoon into her tub of artichoke hummus. She made a face. "I've got to start bringing my own silverware. I hate the idea of wasting resources. Does anyone realize how much garbage this country creates *every day*?"

"Focus, Desiree. Maybe that's why he can't say anything. Maybe he's pining away for you. What's his wife like?"

"I've only met her a few times, but she always gives me the evil eye."

"You, the evil eye? What could be the cause of such a phenomenon?" Terry eased down into the chair next to Lia and gingerly tugged his bag of popcorn open, letting out the steam before he offered it to the two women. Tonight he wore "Subduction Leads to Orogeny" splashed across his tee shirt.

"Popcorn, ladies?"

"No thanks." Desiree waved off the treat. "Al's wife is just spooky. She never talks to me. She just keeps staring at me like she thinks I'm going to pocket the silver." Desiree shuddered. "At least she's not around much. But I can't imagine a goldsmith impressing a woman with aluminum foil, can you?"

"Maybe he wants you to appreciate his artistry instead of his materials." Lia turned to Terry. "We're trying to figure out who's leaving the foil men for Desiree. She went out to her car at the beginning of break and found this on her dashboard." Lia indicated a little silver man sitting cross-legged in the middle of the table, elbows on knees, chin in his cupped hands. "Looks kind of glum, doesn't he?"

"I knew I should have locked my car," Desiree said.

"I wish you would ride with me," Lia said.

"Me, too, but I can barely make it on time leaving directly from the shop. We've got to get this big order out before next week. Things will slack up after that. Maybe then."

Terry eyed the little man. "Curious and curiouser." He rocked the figure back with his index finger, examining the face. "Not much detail. I'm not impressed."

"It's in the posture," Lia said. "It's very expressive. I think it's charming."

36

"If I'm going to have a secret admirer," Desiree said, "I'd rather have roses. Or jewelry."

"Ah, the avarice of women . . . so like a serpent's tooth. Wait, wrong quote," Terry said.

"Maybe art is all he has to give you. Maybe he's poor," Lia said.

"Yesterday you said he was a stalker, now he's charming?"

"Peter said you should pay attention to anything weird, but he's probably harmless. Speaking of weird . . . ." Lia jerked her head in the direction of Avery Simmons, their room leader.

Despite his affection for Ralph Lauren, Avery would always be an Ichabod Crane of a man, prematurely balding with pasty skin. His features spoke of sensitivity and intelligence, but Lia just knew that inside he was a snotty little brat whose mother had sung lullabies to his superiority when she tucked him in at night. Lia bet she still did.

He was the sort of man her aunt always pushed on her. "He has a job, and a house, and he has such nice manners. You can tell he's good to his mother. You can't do better than a man who loves his mother."

Her aunt always said that while pointing out some boring guy who looked at Lia as if she were an exotic jungle beast. Aunt Connie wouldn't stop there. Next it would be, "Forget the cop. A man who chases after criminals all the time, it's going to rub off on him—I saw that Nicholas Cage movie about that awful lieutenant. He'll get himself shot, and where does that leave you? That nice tush of his isn't going to last forever.

"Art is no kind of living. You have to think about your future. Four husbands, and your mother never learned to find a nice, stable guy who pays the bills. You want to end up like your mother?" She popped out of the memory and found herself staring at that night's lentil sprout concoction. She shuddered. *No wonder I never talk to my aunt.*

37

Avery was still talking to Eric. Eric's head bobbed in response to whatever his supervisor was saying as the pair walked over to their table. Simmons put on a greasy smile and spoke to Desiree's chest while Eric shrugged an apology for his boss's boorish behavior.

"Ms. . . ah . . . Willis, is it? And Ms. Anderson? Eric here," he nodded at their team leader, "was just telling me that you're his most accurate scorers on this project." Desiree looked down, an affectation of modesty. "We try."

"You're doing a great job. We have a tricky project coming up. I hope you plan to stay with us for the next contract?"

"Sure, I can always use the money. You coming back, Lia?"

"Wouldn't miss it."

"Good, good. I'm going to request that you both be in my room again." He glanced up at the clock. "Looks like time to get back."

The two men walked off. Desiree waited until their backs were turned, then shook her hands as if she'd touched something disgusting. "Eeeeeewww."

"Your not-so-secret admirer?" Terry inquired.

"Ha. Ha. You should do stand-up."

"We'd better get back," Lia said, sliding her chair back. "And if Avery is your secret admirer, shoot yourself now."

## Chapter 5

**Friday, May 2**

"Yuck! Julia, get away from there!"

Julia had her nose in the plastic wading pool someone had placed under the water pump for the dogs to play in, which many did. She lapped away at brown water peppered with floating bits of the mulch which the park service laid down to prevent soil erosion. Julia was sucking bilge like she'd just stumbled out of the Sahara.

Desiree grabbed her up. "No! Bad!"

"I don't know what it is about dirty water," Lia said. "I guess if people enjoy drinking that toxic waste they put in soft-drinks, then it makes sense dogs would enjoy some flavor, too. They can get giardia from standing water, but the pool gets dumped several times a day. I doubt it will make her sick."

"I don't care, I don't want her drinking it." Desiree set Julia down and grabbed the edge of the pool and tugged at it without success. "Geez. Why does it have to be so big? There has to be at least 50 gallons in here. That's over 400 pounds."

"You sure? How do you know how much water weighs?" Lia asked.

"I used to fill water jugs to use for hand weights. It's over eight pounds for a gallon."

"Hold on, I'll give you a hand. Good thing we only have to tilt it, not pick it up. You pull on top and I'll get my hands underneath and lift."

Together the women leaned over the pool. Lia's opal pendant popped out of her Tee shirt and swung over the muddy water, hitting Desiree in the nose.

"Watch it, your jewelry is aiming to kill."

"Sorry."

With effort, they slid the pool sideways to uncover the drain, then dumped the water. It formed a dark puddle on the concrete pad, spilling over the edge onto the surrounding apron of gravel. They stepped back to avoid getting their feet wet and watched the water retreat.

Desiree examined Lia's pendant. "I remember this. Al made it. He let me buff the setting before he mounted the opal. That's such a sweet piece. It's one of my favorites."

"Small world. I never asked Peter where he had it made."

The water gone, the women set about refilling the pool. Lia leaned on the pump handle, holding it open while mentally calculating how long it would take to refill.

"So your Peter is Detective . . . wait, it's on the tip of my tongue . . . Dorsey?"

"Doursen. I can't believe you remember a customer you had months ago."

"Oh, well, that's not where I met him. I can't believe we've been hanging out for weeks and I never made the connection."

Julia sniffed at the now sanitized water and stuck her nose up in the air. She ambled over to the edge of the ten-foot concrete pad and began licking water off the surrounding gravel.

"Julia, stop it! Bad!" Desiree chased Julia away from the gravel. Julia gave her a hurt look and wandered off.

"Honestly!" Desiree huffed.

"Dogs are designed to eat rotting dead things. I've been coming here for years and I've never known a dog to get sick from the water. Julia's more likely to get sick from the awful stuff they put in commercial dog food than she is from eating stuff she finds outside."

"Maybe. It's still revolting."

"I still can't believe you know Peter," Lia probed.

"It's not something I like to talk about. He questioned me once. I'll never forget it."

"Really?" Lia encouraged.

"He was really nice, but it was such a shock. I'd been seeing this guy. I really loved him, but he had this bitch of a girlfriend who wouldn't let him go, you know? So I told him not to come back until he'd worked it out."

Desiree's face crumpled. A tear rolled down her nose and clung to the tip before dropping onto her chest. Lia let go of the pump handle and rubbed Desiree's back in comforting circles. Tears poured down Desiree's face. Lia pulled Desiree into her arms, and she proceeded to blubber into Lia's tee shirt. Honey, Chewy and Julia gathered around, worried looks on their faces. Chewy sniffed at her leg while Julia whimpered. Lia led her over to the nearest picnic table and steadied Desiree as she climbed up. Honey and Julia jumped on the table and snuggled around Desiree to give comfort. Chewy propped his front paws on the bench and head-butted her leg. Desiree stroked the dogs and cried herself out.

"Sorry." Desiree wiped her nose with the back of her hand, streaking it with snot. "I thought I could talk about it. It's just . . . I wish I'd never sent him away. Maybe if I hadn't, we'd be together now."

"I'm so sorry. What happened?"

"He . . . he killed himself."

"Oh my God! That's horrible," Lia said. "Look, you can't blame yourself forever. I know what that feels like. My boyfriend was murdered almost two years ago, and it happened because of me. I blamed myself for a long time, and sometimes I still do. I have a good therapist, though, and she helps me."

"So you know what it's like." Desiree sniffled.

"It's a rotten place to be."

"I know I shouldn't blame myself. Part of it is feeling like I lost out on the love of my life. Luthor was so perfect for—"

"Luthor? Luthor Morrisey?"

"How did you know?" Desiree looked up at Lia, blinking.

"Luthor was *my* boyfriend. And he didn't kill himself. He was murdered."

"What are you talking about?"

"Don't you read the papers? Geezelpete, it was all over the news!"

"You're *her*? *You're* the bitch?"

"Excuse me?"

"Oh, I heard all about you. How he was trying to get away from you, but *you* wouldn't let him go. Too bad you didn't see a shrink *before* you got him killed."

"What are you talking about?"

"Luthor used to tell me stories about you, how he was worried because you were unstable, how you needed him too much. Well, I needed him too!" Desiree hopped off the table, shouting in Lia's face.

"Yeah, he told you stories, all right. I'd dumped the bastard for the third time the night he died. He always hounded me until I took him back. If he wasn't with you, Honey Boo Boo, it was because he didn't want to be. I would have handed him to you on a gold-plated platter. I'd have served him up with hollandaise sauce and a sprig of parsley!"

Lia felt the crack of Desiree's palm on her face. Years of self-imposed guilt exploded into rage. She leapt off the table before she realized what she was doing and watched herself shove Desiree as if she were watching another person. Desiree stumbled back several feet. She threw herself at Lia, knocking her on her ass. Lia's mouth gaped in shock.

"Are you *serious*?" She stood up, deliberately planting her feet, looming over Desiree. They glared at each other. She grabbed the front of Desiree's shirt and yanked it towards her. "Listen, *Missy*—"

The sound of tearing cloth caused both women to freeze. Desiree looked down. Three buttons had popped and the fabric was ripped straight down the front, exposing Desiree's fuchsia satin bra. She grabbed the hem of Lia's T-shirt and jerked it with the force of a respectable round-house punch. The ancient cotton parted at the seam.

"Atta girl, Lia! You show her whose dog park it is!" Charlie yelled from the sidelines. Lia jerked her head up to see Jose elbow Charlie violently.

"Best entertainment I've had since Jesse Ventura went into politics," Charlie hooted.

Lia looked around her to realize her debacle with Desiree had attracted a crowd. During the course of their pushy-shovey, she and Desiree had worked themselves onto the concrete pad. Lia narrowed her eyes. Desiree glared back.

Now in full possession of herself, Lia clenched her fist, slowly drew it back, then planted it in Desiree's face. Desiree stumbled back several feet, then toppled into the wading pool, drenching her jeans and spotting her expensive lingerie. Julia jumped into the pool and began licking drops of water off Desiree's exposed midriff.

Lia stormed off to the sound of clapping and cheering dog-parkers, Honey and Chewy racing after her.

A muddy tennis ball thumped her in the back. She kept going.

Lia rubbed at her latest chalk lines with a damp rag, smearing the offending shapes. She huffed in frustration. Nothing she drew this morning worked.

"Would you like a break, dear?" Alma asked. "I brought you coffee."

Lia turned away from the nursing home wall to accept a cup from a bird-like octogenarian with a feathery cap of stubbornly black hair. She glanced across the resident lounge to check on Honey and Chewy. They were happily entertaining the attentions of a trio of women in wheel chairs.

"Alma, how is it that you've never gone gray?"

"It's all the greens, dear. Kale, chard, spinach." She ticked these off on her fingers. "They keep color in your hair while they keep your brain sharp. Are you okay?" The tiny woman nodded at the scuffed-over drawing above the wainscoting. "You seem to be having trouble making up your mind today."

Lia sat down in an over-stuffed armchair. "Oh, Alma. I probably shouldn't have come in today." She looked up at the chalk drawings lining the lounge walls. "I wanted to finish up the drawings today so I could start painting in here tomorrow, but everything I've done so far stinks."

"Want to talk about it?"

"I had a fight with someone I thought was my friend."

"I'm so sorry." She patted Lia's knee. "I saw Peter this morning. He said he was bringing you pizza tonight. I know he'll make you feel better."

"I'm sure you're right." Lia lifted a corner of her mouth in a pitiful attempt to smile that fell, doomed. She changed the subject. "What's with Henry?" She nodded towards the sixty year old widower who sat moping in the corner.

Alma scowled. "Damned Nurse Ratched."

"Excuse me?" Lia blinked. Alma rarely used what she called 'salty language.'

"She cancelled book club."

"A book club seems pretty harmless. Why would she do that?"

"Well, half of the people who come to the meetings can't read because of strokes. The rest of us wanted them to feel included, so the person who selected the book for that meeting would read their favorite scene for everybody. A few months ago, we decided to make it a group affair. We would assign parts and read the scenes like we were doing a play, with one person as narrator."

"I don't see anything wrong with that. Why would that be a problem?"

"We had Henry's book for our last meeting. Henry loves to read, but with his stroke, he can only read very light fiction. His daughter left behind a romance novel one day, and he got so excited because he could follow the book. He began reading all the romances he could. He brought his favorite to our meeting yesterday."

"Oh, no."

"Oh, yes. He was thrilled about playing Jaime Mac-Dougall, clan laird in *Highland Hostage*. He was doing this wonderful Scottish brogue, so we didn't understand that it was the wedding night scene. When we figured it out, everyone was having such a good time, I didn't have the heart to stop it. Then Jaime gave the mighty thrust that rent the veil of innocence from his captive, and ninety-three-year-old Agatha Mabry, fully in the spirit of the virginal Colleen, gave a maidenly shriek that could be heard down at the nurses station.

"I'm sure you can guess the rest. Funny thing is, at least a dozen women have offered to play Laird and Captive with Henry in his room since then."

"I don't understand. Why is he moping?"

"Well, I'm not sure, but the rumor is, his doctor won't allow him to have his Viagra."

"Poor Henry." Lia didn't know whether to shake her head or start laughing. "And they say seniors don't know how to have fun."

The Watcher leaned back in his chair, swiveling absently, the twelve-inch square of aluminum foil in his hands reflecting the glow from his monitor. He lightly creased the sheet in thirds, then unfolded it. He folded it in half in the other direction, creasing one end up to the first of the faint folds. He opened the sheet back up and split it along the fold, stopping at the middle third. He flipped the sheet around and made two creases in the opposite side, splitting this section into thirds, again stopping at the middle section. Once these creases were split, he had his doll template.

He held the foil up so that the section split in two was at the bottom. This would be the legs. The middle section was the body and the top would be the head and arms. He carefully brought his hands together, causing the foil to crumple inwards, stopping when his fingers touched. He moved to the legs and the arms, working slowly so that the foil would crumple in different directions, creating volume as he brought the edges closer together.

He twisted the arms and legs gently to give them strength and help them hold their shape. To make the head, he crunched the end of the foil piece, then slowly rolled it in upon itself, rolling and crunching, down to the body. He left the final bit smooth so he could manipulate it with a dulled toothpick to create features.

He frowned at the blank figure, wondering what he should make it do. Sometimes he let his hands speak and tell him unexpected things. Today his hands were silent, waiting for him to make a decision.

He turned around, looking at the walls of foil dolls playing soccer, hugging, eating, dancing, fighting, making love, lurking in the dark room, their tiny facets reflecting fragments of shattered light from his computer screen.

Desiree wasn't getting his message. It never got through. In the past, he believed the woman wasn't the right one if she didn't understand his messages. It would hurt, but he would say good-bye in his own special way and move on.

He couldn't do that to Desiree. He *had* to make her understand, but how? The tiny multitude of emissaries stared at him, mutely taunting him with their inability to truly speak for him. He looked down at his clenched fist, at the shapeless ball of foil inside. He threw it against the wall, knocking a dozen of his creations off their perches

Lia fixed her eyes firmly on her monitor as Desiree rushed into the scoring room, barely skimming inside the grace period for latecomers. A colorful shiner graced her left eye and cheek. Lia fixed an impassive expression on her face, determined to stand her ground while maintaining the composure she had lost that morning.

Desiree walked past their row to Eric's station. The two conversed in tones too low for Lia to make out what they were saying. The confab ended and Desiree brushed behind Lia on the way to her chair. As her computer loaded the scoring program, she pulled five foil figures out of her tote and arranged them on her monitor and tower.

Lia watched her out of the corner of her eye. Desiree pouted as she fussed with their positions, turning them to catch the light on their foil angles and pretending the entire scoring team was not glued to her in fascination at the moment.

Five figures. One more had appeared that day, then. This one stood in an aggressive pose, chin down while clenching tiny fists in front of his face in a boxing stance. Lia wondered if Desiree's admirer had somehow learned of the scene, or if Desiree had altered the figure's pose. Lia thought not. The foil had been deftly formed. It did not show the crinkling of repeated handling.

Had he been there, clapping and hooting along with Charlie and the rest? She didn't recall any strangers that morning, but she'd been preoccupied. Curious as she was, she was not about to end the silence and ask Desiree about it.

Tension remained thick in the air until break time. Lia waited for Desiree to leave, then grabbed her bag and stood up. The room was almost empty.

"Lia, wait up a sec," Eric called. He caught up with her at the end of the aisle. "What's going on with you and Desiree? She comes in late, sporting a huge shiner, and asks to change seats on some bogus pretext. The two of you haven't said a word to each other all night. Usually, you're thicker than thieves in molasses."

Lia looked in the clear blue eyes and saw only concern. "I don't want to talk about it. If Desiree does, that's her business. Anything else you wanted, Kemosabe?"

"It's affecting your performance. Your count is way up, but your accuracy is down. Not horrible, but not to your usual standard."

"I'll be more careful." She turned away, signaling the end of the conversation.

"Look, are the two of you going to be able to work next to each other? Seating assignments are practically carved in stone. I need something more than a fake cough and a complaint about the AC vent. I can make it happen, but you both would wind up with a tick in your file about not playing well with others."

"No problem on my end. I can't speak for Desiree." She kept going.

She ran into Ted in the coffee line. He was a cheerful, middle-aged man who sat in front of her in the scoring room.

"Who hit Desiree?" he stage-whispered.

"Not talking." She held her palm up and veered off to the other coffee machine.

Coffee in hand, she scanned the tables until she spotted Terry in a back corner, munching on popcorn. The front of his tee shirt read "The answer is 42." Lia knew the back of his shirt said "42 is 54."

"That's a serious mouse you gave Desiree. I'm sorry I didn't catch your boxing debut this morning."

"Not you, too," she groaned, sitting down with a thump. She pulled a baggie of mixed nuts and dried fruit out of her tote. "I didn't realize you'd heard about it."

"You kidding? Charlie was so enthused, he offered to turn the old entry corral into a mud pit for wrestling."

"Charlie is always the gentleman."

"What started it? Nobody at the park knew."

Lia sighed, abandoned her fruit and nuts. "You and I have been buddying up to one of the women Luthor was sneaking around with when I dated him. And she's carrying the romantic notion that if only the bitch, namely *moi*, had let Luthor go, he'd still be alive today and her life would be complete."

"Ah, the delusions of youth. Of course you had to disavow her of such a ludicrous idea."

"Delusions is right. I don't think she got the message. It's the Cold War all over on our row."

"I would sic Napa on her for you, but I couldn't even get her to bite the IRS agent who audited me last year."

"You're a true friend, Terry."

Honey, Chewy and Viola rushed the door when she unlocked it. She bent over to pet them, then gasped when a strong arm snaked around her waist and pulled her against a hard chest. Another arm wrapped around her neck.

"What are you going to do now, little girl?" a hoarse whisper sounded in her ear.

Not in the mood for games, Lia raised her kubotan keychain, grasped it firmly with both hands and drove the end into a pressure point on Peter's elbow.

"Ow!" Peter dropped his arms. He stepped back, rubbing the injured joint. "What did I do to deserve *that*?"

"It's what you *didn't* do." She glared up at him, folding her arms. Chewy nudged her leg. She ignored him.

"Well, that's clear as mud. Mind cluing me in?"

"How about you cluing *me* in? Like how about my *boyfriend* letting me know that my new BFF was one of Luthor's old *girlfriends*."

"Oh, Jesus." Peter sighed and sat down, rubbing his face with one hand. Viola whined and laid her head on his thigh. He patted her automatically.

Lia sat down opposite him, her placid face revealing nothing. The silence drew out.

"You do know the pizza's getting cold?" Peter tried.

Lia raised one eyebrow.

"It's Dewey's."

Lia said nothing while continuing her impassive stare. She was not moved by the worried look on Peter's face. Peter looked away first.

"Well?" Lia prompted.

"I should have told you."

"Yes, you should have."

"I didn't know for sure that it was her the first time you mentioned her, and I didn't want to drag up old wounds."

"Uh-huh, that was more than two weeks ago."

"And I figured you'd go your separate ways when the project was over. I didn't know you were going to invite her into the dog park crowd."

"But I did."

"And you were getting along so well . . . ."

"And?"

"And I'm a big chicken."

"Yeah, you are."

"How bad was it?"

"Before or after I decked her?"

"You *hit* her?"

50

"After she slapped me and tore my favorite studio shirt."

"Jesus H. Christ."

"The guys were entertained. We had quite an audience before it was over."

"Are you okay?"

"*I'm* fine. It's going to take a while for Desiree's black eye to fade."

"God, I'm sorry."

"How could you?"

"I just explained . . . ."

"Not that." Lia swatted the air. "How could you go to one of Luthor's old girlfriends to make a necklace for me? Don't you have *any* concern for my feelings?"

"It wasn't like that—"

"How was it then? Either she made it or she didn't."

"I thought the old man made it. He's the one I talked to."

"So you *didn't* know Desiree was working there?" She folded her arms and leaned back, daring him to deny it.

"Well, no, I knew she worked there, I just didn't re— Look, I went to the place that understood what I wanted. What does it matter who made it?"

"Because." Lia stood up and pulled the delicate gold chain with its glittering talisman out of her pocket, holding it up by two fingers. It flashed color as it swayed between them, reminding Lia of the roof lights on top of a police car.

"It. Has. *Cooties.*" She thrust the necklace at him.

"What are you doing?"

"Take it back. I don't want it."

"Now, hold on—"

Lia flicked her hand, letting the pendant fly. It hit Peter's chest. He fumbled to catch it before it fell.

"Maybe Desiree will want it. She sure seemed to like *you* well enough." Lia stalked into the kitchen.

51

Peter heard the oven door open. "It's not like that. You *know* it's not like that."

She returned holding the Dewey's box. "How can I know what it's like when you don't tell me anything?" She shoved the box in his chest. "Take your pizza and go. I'm not in the mood for company."

Peter stood, gawping. "This is why I never said anything," he called over his shoulder. "I knew you'd freak about it no matter what I said. C'mon, Viola. Looks like you're getting more than crusts tonight."

# Chapter 6

"I just want you to know, I had nothing to do with it," Jose called out as Lia and her horde entered the dog park.

"What are you talking about, Jose?" Jose's Sophie leaned her massive body against Lia's legs. She automatically reached down to stroke the furred boulder that was Sophie's head.

"You ain't seen it yet?"

"Seen what?" Lia ruffled Sophie's ears. "You're such a good girl, aren't you, Sophie?"

"I hate to be the one to break it to ya, but your scrap with Desiree wound up on YouTube."

"WHAT?" Startled, Sophie loped off. "Are you *serious*?"

"As a heart attack. But I didn't do it. I don't know who did."

Lia turned to look at his companion. "Charlie . . . ."

"Don't look at me. The only thing my phone does is make calls. You're real popular. You had over 5,000 hits when I saw it this morning. Must be a lot of guys searching YouTube for girl fights."

Lia closed her eyes, breathing in and out slowly, the way her therapist taught her to stave off anxiety attacks. "I don't believe this."

"Believe what?" Bailey said as she walked up with Kita.

Lia took Bailey by the arm and pulled her towards the back of the park. "Walk with me. You have no idea what's happened."

"That you punched Desiree? I heard about that. Why didn't you call me yesterday? I thought we were friends."

"We are. I was too upset. This is worse."

"What could be worse?"

"Someone put it on YouTube and it's gone viral."

"Wow." Bailey paused to consider. "At least it's not *your* fuchsia underwire hanging out for everyone to see. I hear she has amazing breasts. Maybe that's why it's getting so many hits. Did you really rip her shirt off?"

"I ripped it. I didn't rip it off. Doesn't anyone have anything better to talk about? Everywhere I go, someone has to cross-examine me about it."

"Are you going to tell me what happened? The speculation is rampant and imaginative. The hopeful theory is that it was a lesbian love-spat."

"Oh, that's just dandy." Lia rolled her eyes. "I suppose Desiree's the femme and I'm the butch?"

Bailey looked Lia up and down. "What do you expect with her satin underwear and your bag-lady discards?"

"Remember Luthor?"

"What about him?"

"Desiree is one of the women he was seeing while he was with me. She seems to think he would still be alive *if only* I had been willing to let him go."

"You're kidding."

"Nope. I deprived her of the love of her life."

Bailey sputtered, "*Luthor?*"

"Yep."

"What was she, twenty-one or twenty-two when that happened?"

"What has that got to do with it?"

54

"She's still pretty young. She probably believed everything he told her."

"Bully for her."

"You should consider cutting her a little slack. I know I was pretty stupid about men when I was her age."

"She slapped me first."

"I bet she doesn't know anything about endorphins. I bet she's confusing oxytocin with true love. She's probably convinced Luthor was her soul-mate. I'd hate thinking I had to wait until I died to see my soul-mate again."

Lia rolled her eyes. "Cry me a river."

"This video could get you some attention. You never know. You could get famous. She might have done you a favor."

"I'll be sure to thank her when the Whitney Museum comes calling."

"Do you know who posted the video?"

"Bailey, I haven't even seen the video. And I don't want to."

Bailey pulled her phone out of its belt holster and tapped the Video Tube icon. She hummed the Jeopardy theme while searching, bobbing her head in time with the tune. Lia wondered if she was doing this deliberately to annoy her.

"Here it is, 'Cat Fight at the Dog Park . . .' Hmm . . . this was posted by someone named The Watcher—oooh, spooky." Bailey faked a shudder.

"Cut it out," Lia said, giving Bailey's shoulder a light shove.

"He only has the one video up . . . That's weird. No picture and nothing in his profile. Wow. Look at all the comments."

"Put it away, Bailey."

"Don't you want to figure out who posted this?"

"No."

"Now you're just being stubborn. I'm going to watch, even if you aren't." Bailey turned to face Lia on their picnic table, so that Lia could only see the back of the little phone.

"Is that the soundtrack to *300*?" Lia asked.

"Fun movie. Great music."

"Give me that." Lia reached for the phone.

Bailey turned away, putting the phone out of reach. "You didn't want to watch, remember? Ooooh! She cracked you a *good* one."

"Hand it over."

"Wow, she does have amazing breasts. This guy has a very effective use of zoom."

"Bailey . . . . Wait a minute, how do you know it's a guy?"

"A woman would never focus in on her chest like that. Whoa! You must have knocked her ten feet! Right in the water. Great aim, Lia! . . . And there you go, walking off into the sunset . . . wait a minute, there's Desiree again . . . Beloved Goddess, would you look at that!"

"What?"

Bailey shook her head. "Desiree is sure ballsy. The guys must have been staring at her, because she hauls herself out of the tub and proceeds to remove her torn shirt and toss it in Charlie's face before she picks up a tennis ball and wings it at you. Then she stomps off, with nothing but her jeans and bra on. . . . Oh, it's over. I guess you didn't know about that because you'd already left."

Lia sighed. "May I please see it?"

"All you had to do was ask nice." Bailey extended a graceful hand, offering the phone for Lia's perusal.

Lia hesitated. "Maybe I don't want to see it after all."

"It won't bite. You know you're going to watch it eventually. You might as well get it over with and save yourself the agonizing."

Lia picked up the little phone and examined the still at the beginning of the video. It showed her hugging a weeping Desiree. "Something's wrong with this."

"What do you mean?"

"Someone was recording us *before* the fight started."
She hit play, watched the emotional moment turn into a
brawl. Paused it. Pointed at the little screen. "See? You
can just barely see a slice of Charlie's back on the edge of
the frame, and I bet Jose's standing on his other side."
"So?"

"Whoever shot this was well behind Charlie." She
looked up, scanning the far side of the park. "You said he
used zoom?"

"Uh huh. Start it up again, you'll see."

Lia watched as the video closed in on Desiree's very
expensive brassiere. She hit pause again and looked up,
squinting as she struggled to remember which way Desiree had been facing. She hardly remembered any of it, it
had happened so fast.

"He was in the woods. With the slope on that side, he
had to be up a tree to get that shot. I don't think it was
anyone we know. I bet The Watcher is Desiree's Foil-man.
Can you download and save YouTube videos?"

"I think so. You can use ClipGrab, but you need to be
at your computer. You didn't even want to look at it. Why
do you want to save it?"

"He might decide to delete it. She needs to be
warned." Lia pulled out her phone and tapped out Desiree's number.

"Yesterday you gave her a black eye, now you want to
protect her?"

"This is serious. If this guy is willing to climb trees just
to look at her, who knows what he'll do next."

"Maybe it was you he was looking at."

"It wasn't *my* boobs he zoomed in on."

"You think she'll listen to you? Why don't you let Peter handle it? I mean, it *is* his job."
"Peter," Lia gritted out, "is out of the picture."

Bailey widened her eyes. She made an 'O' with her
lips and said nothing.

The call went to voicemail. Lia left the information about the video along with a plea that Desiree talk to someone at District Five.

"Think that's enough?" Bailey asked when Lia put the phone away.

"Who knows. But it's the best I can do if she won't talk to me."

# Chapter 7

**Monday, May 5**

Desiree was sitting at her station when Lia arrived at the scoring center the following Monday. The swelling had gone down around her eye and the bruise had faded to a psychedelic yellow mess with green and purple blotches. She wore a skin-tight top the same virulent fuchsia as her bra from the park debacle. Lia wondered if she *wanted* people to recognize her from the YouTube video.

Desiree avoided meeting Lia's eyes and even the appearance that she was aware of Lia's presence. Ted came in after Lia. He turned around to drape his jacket over the back of his chair. "You look mighty pretty in pink, Desiree," he said.

"Thank you, Ted. You're sweet to say so."

Blushing, Ted busied himself with his computer.

Eric came by, handing out work folders. He caught Lia's eye, then darted a glance at Desiree in question. Lia shrugged one shoulder and rolled her eyes. Once everyone was settled in, she leaned over and whispered to Desiree, "Did you get my message Saturday?"

Desiree hissed, "I don't see what the big deal is. People video stuff all the time. I just think you're jealous."

"Why would I be jealous?"

"That camera wasn't focussed on *your* tits. That's because he couldn't find them, even with a zoom lens. I bet a microscope and a backhoe wouldn't help."

Lia's jaw dropped. She snapped herself face forward, catching the tail end of a smirk on Avery's face as he walked by.

Why did he do it? He'd never shared any of his women before. The Watcher sat in darkness, turned away from the sightless silver faces of his tiny populace, all attention on his YouTube page. Desiree's brawl with her friend had over 11,000 hits, with new views every time he refreshed the page. And he still didn't know what the fight had been about.

He wanted to share his magnificent warrior woman with the world. Proud, beautiful, ferocious, she was an Amazon queen. It was the crass comments, hundreds of them, that upset him.

Should he delete it? Not from home, that could be traced. Rage grew as he continued clicking through the foul, lurid comments. *How dare they! Defilers!* His mind screamed to respond, flame them all. *Not good, not good. Not now. It can be traced. Maybe later?*

He calmed. He could compose his response, upload elsewhere from a flash drive. He hunkered over the keys and set to work.

Lia's shifts at Scholastic were conducted in an arctic silence that had her wondering why she and Desiree didn't both get hypothermia. Eric shook his head frequently as each pretended the other did not exist. After two days he stopped suggesting that they confer with each other before either of them called him over for a scoring decision.

Desiree's shirts got tighter and skimpier as the week went on and the YouTube hits climbed. She stopped wearing a sweater at her station, despite the over-active air conditioning vent. Lia could see goose flesh on Desiree's arms, if she bothered to look in Desiree's direction. Which she didn't. At least, not very often.

Desiree's creepy foil menagerie grew, spilling off her tower, onto the table the women shared. She cooed over them as she set them out each day, showing them off to Ted . The rest of the team seemed oblivious to the drama, as people kept their conversation to their scoring partners. Lia wondered why Avery never said anything about the aluminum clutter. It wasn't like Scholastic encouraged people to personalize their stations.

Lia struggled to keep her focus while maintaining the Mexican standoff. *So Desiree turned out to be a little trollop without a lick of sense. So what. It's her life. If she likes having some weirdo stalk her as if he's her personal paparazzi, that's her business.*

Terry was entertained by the situation, seeing it as a prime example of cultural anthropology and female psychology. He kept mental statistics on the percentage of flesh Desiree showed each day in relation to the number of YouTube hits the video received, and felt Lia should, as an artist, take some interest in the color-coordination or lack there-of, of Desiree's bruise with her clothing. He talked about writing a paper on his conclusions once the impasse was resolved.

Bailey skipped mornings at the park now that her busy season was in full-swing. Other friends now had day jobs or were away on trips. Lia would not, could not, call Peter. She saw Peter's neighbor, Alma, most days, and caught her giving Lia a puzzled look more than once.

She was lying on the sofa with Chewy on her chest, tugging his ears when Peter finally called. She put her hands around his head and waggled it back and forth, then let it go. Chewy snapped playfully at the air while she waited for the answering machine to click on.

"Lia, I don't know if you're there or not. I guess it doesn't make any difference. Shutting me out is no way for an adult to act, and it's no answer to our problems. If you want to talk, we'll talk. I'll see Asia with you, if you want. But I'm not going to chase you down this time. You know where to find me."

Chewy continued to snap at her hands, though Lia was no longer paying attention. How was she supposed to explain herself when she didn't understand anything except that she hurt? How could she tell Peter what she wanted when she didn't know? She buried her hands in the Schnauzer's overgrown coat, blinking moisture out of her eyes.

Lia had always enjoyed solitude before. Now she felt alone.

# Chapter 8

**Monday, May 12**

Bailey and Lia finally caught up with each other for a late breakfast at the Blue Jay. A Northside staple since 1967, the diner had dark panelling and big booths conducive to private conversation and leisurely meals. Lia was reviewing the menu when Bailey arrived, sporting grass-stained jeans that announced she'd been performing heavy yard work. Bramble scratches covered her long, pianist hands and her swing of red hair was tucked under a faded bandana.

Sarah, one of two waitresses who worked at the diner, came with tall glasses of water. Bailey drank half the glass before she set it down.

"Hi, Sarah," Lia said. "How are you getting along with Tanya on maternity leave?"

"Better than I expected. Her baby is due any day now. Do you ladies know what you want?" Sarah asked.

"I don't know why I bother looking at the menu," Lia said, laying down the laminated sheet. "I always get the same thing. Spinach and feta omelet with rye toast. Water is fine."

"I'm starving. Eggs over medium, wheat toast, Jacob Special on the potatoes. Ice tea to drink."

Sarah gone, Bailey leaned over the table. "Okay, out with it."

"Out with what?"

"Last week you said Peter was out of the picture and you didn't elaborate. I haven't been able to catch up with you since. It's driving me crazy. What happened between you and Detective Hottie?"

Lia sighed. "I just don't know, Bailey. Peter knew Desiree from his investigation into Luthor's death. He failed to tell me about her, even after I met her at Scholastic and started hanging out with her."

"No!"

"Yes. And it gets worse. He had my necklace made at the shop where she works and it never occurred to him that it would bother me. She said she helped make it."

"Ouch!"

"Yeah, ouch."

"What are you going to do?"

"I don't know. So I'm taking a time out."

"That's such a guy thing, you know? Not thinking it mattered."

"Yeah, why should I care if she had her grubby little man-stealing hands all over his love-offering to me?"

Bailey snorted a laugh. "Well, she didn't exactly steal Luthor, she only borrowed him. And you didn't exactly want him at the time."

"That's beside the point."

"What's really bothering you about this?"

"Being blind-sided isn't bad enough?"

"It is, but I know there's more. Have you talked to Asia?"

Lia scoffed. "Like I have time for therapy with my schedule? I thought about it, but I just can't fit it in right now."

"So tell me. That's what friends are for."

Lia ran both hands through her hair and considered her words. Sarah's partner, Tanya, brought their food. Lia used eating as an excuse to stay silent. Finally, she said, "Luthor died because of me. I thought I'd dealt with it, but Desiree brought it all up again. I'm feeling raw. How do you fix something like that?"

"Oh." Bailey pondered this while she chewed her eggs. She pointed her fork in the air for emphasis.

"I have a different take on it."

"Okay, let's hear it."

"You met Luthor at the park, right?"

"Right."

"If you hadn't started dating him, would he have stopped going to the park?"

"Probably not."

"If you hadn't started dating him, would he have still been the same narcissistic, lying deadbeat that he was?"

"I guess so. What are you getting at?"

"Bucky liked to target people she felt contempt for, right?"

"Right."

"She didn't kill Luthor to get him off your back, no matter what she said. She did it because she wanted to. Were you dating any of the other people she targeted?"

"Well, no . . ."

"Luthor still would have landed on her radar, just by being who he is. She may have used you as an excuse, but it was really all about her. No other reason."

"I don't know, Bailey . . . ."

"Look, if she had asked, would you have ever said, 'I want Luthor dead'?"

"Of course not."

"Exactly. It wasn't about you. It was *never* about you. But I don't think that's what's really going on."
"Oh?"

"Don't get your back up. I've just noticed that you take every little excuse to push Peter away."

Lia gaped, speechless, her mug halfway to her mouth.

"Lia, he's not your father. He's not Luthor, He's not anyone else you've ever been with in a relationship. Why are you hanging their baggage on him?"

"I'm not—"

"Sure you are. Stop sputtering. If Luthor had pulled a stunt like that you would have rolled your eyes and moved on. So why are you so hard on Peter when he doesn't measure up?"

Lia set down her coffee mug. She stared at the fake walnut paneling, seeing nothing, blinking as her eyes watered up and threatened to spill over.

"It never mattered with Luthor. I never loved him."

Bailey leaned back in the booth, took a sip of coffee, let Lia process what she'd just said, waiting until her friend had her emotions under control.
"He's not your father."

"You already said that." Lia spoke to the remains of her omelet. Her voice was small.

"Scares you, doesn't it?"

Lia choked out a whisper. "It freaking terrifies me."

"So, are you going to forgive Peter?"

"I don't know, Bailey. I hate it when he doesn't tell me stuff. Every time we have a problem, it's because he decided, in his infinite male wisdom, to keep something from me. How can this ever work if he's going to let me be blind-sided like that?"

"Promise me you'll talk to Peter about it."

"I will, I just have to get my head straight first."

Bailey squeezed Lia's hand and gave it a shake.

"There's hope for you yet, Anderson. Anyway, I had something else I wanted to talk about."

"Oh?" Lia latched onto the change of topic gratefully.

"I had Trees trace the video," Bailey said, referring to the hacker who was her long-distance boyfriend.

"Really? What did he say?"

"Inconclusive. The video was uploaded at the Westwood Branch Library. Chances are Desiree's stalker logged onto their wi-fi. Trees says he may have done it from his car. Did you know he posted a rant a few days ago? That came from the library, too."

"I've been avoiding YouTube and Terry just checks the number of hits it gets. Do I want to know what he said?"

"It was bizarre and kind of poetic. He called Desiree his green-haired Aphrodite and said the Philistines making crude comments about her weren't fit to lick the dung off the bottom of her sandals."

"Wow."

"You get to be a goddess, too. He wasn't specific about which one. Just something about how viewers should 'tremble in awe,' being privileged to witness a 'war between goddesses.' Or something like that."

"Sounds like a non-starter."

"Mostly. But he probably lives near the library."

"That's Terry's neighborhood. Maybe we should ask him to walk around looking for empty Reynolds Wrap boxes on garbage day."

"I know it's not much," Bailey apologized.

"I'm sorry. I shouldn't be cranky with you, you did what you could and I didn't even ask you to get involved. It's going to be a moot issue after tonight."

"How so?"

"The current project is ending. The next one won't start for a couple weeks, and I may not even be in the same room with Desiree. As far as I'm concerned, it's her issue, and she doesn't want my help."

Peter stared at the phone like a terrier waiting for a rat to emerge from it's hole.

"You should practice that look, brother, and use it during interrogation. It would kill all our suspects and we'd never have to take another case to court," his partner, Brent said, sitting his sharply suited hip on the far edge of Peter's desk, the edge away from vintage coffee rings and assorted mystery stains. A southern transplant,

Brent's voice whispered of mint juleps and magnolia trees. "What did that phone ever do to you?"

Peter shook his head and exhaled audibly in self-disgust. "Every time Lia's upset, she runs away and won't talk to me."

"You drew the line in the sand, brother. You need to stand behind it."

"Some creep secretly videotaped her, and I have no idea who it is. He's still out there."

"You did what you could. Cynth traced the file upload to the Westwood Library. That's miles from Northside. We know he's not likely to live in her neighborhood."

"That's something."

"Lia's a big girl, she knows how to dial 911. And from that bruise on your elbow, it looks like she's not shy with her kubotan. Then there's that punch I saw her give Desiree. Damn, I sure wish she would have held off decking Desiree a little longer. That video is too brief."

"You mean Desiree's shirt is too brief. I catch you drooling over Lia on YouTube, and I'll have to hurt you."

Brent nodded at a musclebound officer entering the bullpen. "Lookie here. If it isn't Captain America. Wonder what he wants with Heckle and Jeckle."

"Captain America. That's good," Peter eyed the ex-marine chatting up a pair of detectives across the bullpen. He stood a head taller than his companions, and his build could only be the result of strenuous workouts.

"Think we should tell the new guy that his muscles are certain to squeeze out his brain if he doesn't stop eating factory farm chicken? I hear those birds are pumped *full* of steroids."

"Nah," Peter said. "If he's dumb enough to prefer big muscles and shriveled nuts, his brain isn't worth saving."

"Well, it's nice that H and J have adopted a pet," Brent offered. "I bet our large friend thinks H and J are slumming with a street cop because they recognize his potential and want to benefit his career."

"I'm sure they recognize potential when they see it. Potential to benefit themselves."

"Maybe it's for his willingness to confront a dangerous situation."

"How so?"

"Rumor has it, he was following a car with a burned out bulb over the license plate the other night."

"And?"

"It was near midnight, and he figures the guy is up to no good, maybe has body parts in the trunk or something."

"Driving while black?"

"Nah, an Italian guy. Like Mafia. So he follows this car, trying to figure out what the guy's up to that he doesn't want anyone to know his plate number, and the car keeps heading north. After five miles, they're up past the 275 loop, and the road is turning into one of those two lanes where there are no lights and the semis blow past at 60 miles per hour."

"Great place to dump a body," Peter said.

"Now he's afraid the car is driving beyond his jurisdiction, so he puts on his lights and blasts his siren, but the car keeps going. Not speeding or anything, just not pulling over. So Brainard sits on his ass and in a couple hundred yards, the car pulls into a parking lot for one of those huge corporate offices, one of the banks. He pulls right up under a light, one of those towering parking lot lights like at the stadium? It must have been thirty feet tall. "

Brent paused, took a sip of Peter's coffee. Peter suspected it was a matter of drama more than a dry throat.

"Okay, I'll bite. What did Captain America do?"

"Our intrepid officer parks twenty feet away, gets out of his patrol car and draws down on the guy."

"You're kidding."

"Nope. He takes a firing stance, and yells for the mobbed-up Italian hit man to get out of his car. The guy in the car starts screaming at him, to put the gun away. About that time, Heckle and Jeckle show up. Apparently, Brainard called for back up and they were coming back from an 'adult venue,' one of those places out in the sticks with pole dancers."

"Better and better."

"No joke. So they drive up and see that he's holding a gun on this guy, who still won't get out of his car. So Jeckle calls to the guy and asks him why he won't get out, and he say's it's because Brainard drew down on him. And so he asks Brainard why he drew down on him, and he says it's because the guy wouldn't pull over. And then the guy says there wasn't a safe place to pull over on that stretch of road and he was coming here anyway. Now all this time Brainard is shaking like a blue-tick hound treeing his first coon.

"Finally, the guy agrees to get out of his car because he figures that he won't get shot with witnesses around, even though Brainard is still acting like a one man SWAT team. Heckle and Jeckle have removed themselves from the line of fire and are just shaking their heads. Of course the Italian guy is livid and is screaming right back at Brainard.

"Brainard tells him to assume the position, and it's no longer about checking the guy's license and giving him a ticket for the bulb, he's going to arrest him and take him in for interfering with a police officer. And the guy tells him it ain't gonna happen, and Brainard is still doing his macho thing, and he's got the driver up against the car, arm twisted up behind his back and cheek jammed into the side window. The guy says, 'No, you aren't taking me in. Look up at the light.' Brainard says 'I'm not taking my eyes off you, asshole. What the hell does a light have to do with anything?' and the guy says . . ." here Brent started snorting so hard he almost choked. "Just take a quick peek. See that little box? That's a security camera and I've got you on tape drawing down on me just because I drove

70

in to work the midnight shift with a burned out bulb.
What with the lights and sirens, I bet there's seventy people inside that building, lining up at the windows right
now."

Peter burst out laughing. "Unbelievable."

"Truth. So if Heckle and Jeckle have adopted Captain
America, it's because they want to have a chump on tap if
they ever need one."

"Forget Captain America. Brainard's new name is going to be Brain-dead before the week is out."

"Heads up, brother," Brent said. "The love of my life
is arriving."

Cynth McFadden emerged from her basement computer lab and was headed their way. Peter shook his head.

"Are you ever going to give up?"

"Not as long as she curls her lip at me in that sexy way
she has," Brent said.

"She does that because she hates you."

"Oh, ye of little faith. Her attraction is—Hey, gorgeous, when are you going to marry me?"

Cynth executed a neat turn, sliding deftly in front of
Brent and dropping a thick file folder down on Peter's
desk as if Brent's hand had not been in that precise spot a
nano-second before.

"I finished the printouts," she said, speaking directly
to Peter as if they were alone. "I know you said you'd go
over them, but there's more there than we counted on. I'm
free tonight if you want help."

Peter found it hard to focus on Cynth's pleasantly ex-
pectant face while Brent glared at him over Cynth's
shoulder with an ever-increasing intensity of expression.

The IT officer hid her Baywatch-worthy figure with
shapeless golf shirts that were two sizes too big. A fat,
wheat-colored braid fell to her waist. Wire-rim glasses
obscured eyes that Peter knew to be large and warm as
melted chocolate.

A martial arts expert, Cynth was the most dangerous woman on the force. Ironically, her superior hand-to-hand skills, her lack of interest and her baggy clothes, all intended to put off the advances of men, drew them—Brent Davis being the most persistent among them—like a magnet.

Peter eyed the inch-high stack of paper with apprehension. "Don't you have better things to do? I thought you were teaching that self-defense class."

"Oh, that's over now. We won't start up again until June. Tell you what. I'll bring pizza. And beer."

Peter and Brent watched Cynth exit the bullpen, navigating the jungle of desks with athletic grace.

"I am a sick man," Brent moaned. "The more that woman disses me, the better I like it. It's not right that such a perverse woman should have such power."

# Chapter 9

**Thursday, May 22**

The wall was filled with birds. Birds swooping, birds roosting on branches, birds singing. Blue jays, woodpeckers with red crests, orange-bellied orioles, swallow tails. Little brown wrens. Pearly mourning doves. Mockingbirds. Swallows. A robin feeding her nest of chicks. They chirped, swooped, perched against a lacy backdrop of branches and spring leaves playing peek-a-boo with a blue sky.

" I can almost hear them sing," Alma said.

"Thanks, Alma. I wanted something active and cheerful."

"It fills the bill. And it's a lovely complement to the water lilies lining the hall. You've been putting in a lot of hours to get this done so quickly. I thought you had a job in the evening?"

"I do, but we're off for a couple weeks. It's been nice to focus on this full time. But I go back next Monday." Lia glanced over to see Honey curled up on the sofa, her head in Henry's lap. Chewy was head-butting his hand from his other side, hoping for pets.

"And the dogs love it here. If I left without them, I don't think they'd notice."

"Oh, I doubt that," Alma said.

"Henry looks like he's feeling better."

"I think he's relieved because he finally fessed up."

"What brought that about?"

Alma leaned forward, whispered. "Well, the women kept after him and wouldn't go away, so he broke down and told them about his problem."

"And?"

"His fan club has taken it on as a challenge, and they've become quite competitive about 'stiffening his resolve,' so to speak."

Lia's phone beeped, signaling a text. "Excuse me," she said, pulling out her phone. She frowned at the message on her screen: "Call me! IMPORTANT!!!" It was from Desiree. She rolled her eyes and shoved the phone back in her pocket.

"Where were we?" Lia asked.

"Is everything okay? You got a funny look on your face just then."

"Fine, just a message from someone I don't care to talk to."

"It wasn't Peter was it?"

"Oh, no, not at all—"

"Because he's stopped talking about you, and you never mention him anymore, and I was wondering if something was wrong."

"Oh, Alma," Lia stumbled, not sure what to say.

"Have a seat, dear. Talk to me."

Lia wiped off her brushes and put them to soak, then followed the little woman to an empty couch. Lia hugged a floral chintz throw pillow, resting her chin on the top edge. She set it aside when Honey and Chewy disengaged themselves from their current flirtation and returned to their now-available mistress.

"I don't know where to begin." Lia checked her hands to make sure they were free of paint, then began stroking the dogs, one with each hand. The distraction gave her time to think. "You won't tell Peter we talked?"

"Peter who, dear?" Alma winked.

"Thank you . . . Peter, well, he . . . he acts like my dad sometimes."

"How so?"

"He decides things without consulting me. He'll decide what I do and don't need to know, and sometimes I wind up looking like a fool. He let me get all chummy with one of the women Luthor was cheating with. He *knew* who she was and chose not to tell me. There I was, patting her on the back while she was crying about her boyfriend killing himself over some bitch, when I find out *I'm* the bitch she was talking about!"

Alma patted her knee. "That is unfortunate. I know you and Peter were brought up very differently. I don't think young people take that into account when they get into relationships. They think they're speaking the same language because they both know English."

"How do I get the message across that he needs to treat me like an adult?"

Alma nodded at Honey. "How do your dogs know what you want?"

Lia blinked, not sure where Alma was going. "Uh . . . consistency and clear communication."

"And how many times do you have to repeat a lesson before they learn a command?"

"It depends on the dog, on the reward, and how difficult it is for them to do."

"And once they learn a command, do they always do it perfectly?"

"No, some days are better than others."

"What do you do when they forget?"

"We go through the lesson again to reinforce it."

"Do you yell at them or punish them?"

"No, that would be counter-productive."

"Exactly! Humans aren't much different. I bet you don't give up on a dog that comes to you with bad habits."

"This isn't like teaching a dog to sit, Alma. It's a lot more complicated than that."

"I wouldn't know about that. Gene and I had a good marriage before he died, but we had to figure each other out in the beginning, and it was a while before it took. We both tended to revert to our own ways without thinking about it."

"What kept you from killing him?"

"Well, he was rather hot . . . ."

"*Alma!*"

"You have to keep reminding yourself why you love them, and that you're not perfect. Prayer helps. There were times I prayed for understanding several times a day."

"And that helped?"

"It helped me. Things seemed to work out better when I did. Then there's forgiveness."

"I don't think I'm ready for that."

"Do you love Peter?"

"Mostly. Right now I'm having a hard time of it."

"Either you love Peter or you don't. *How* you love Peter is another matter."

"What do you mean, 'How you love. . . .'?"

"Love isn't in feelings. Love is in action, the choices you make, what you do. You can always choose to do the loving thing. Sometimes that requires tough decisions."

"You mean like when you refuse to enable an addict?"

"Yes, though that's an obvious example. The important thing to remember is that being loving never requires you to do anything that is harmful to yourself, whether it's harmful to your self-esteem or your finances or your body. Self-love has to come first. So many young women throw their lives away on men, treating themselves like they were nothing. That's not love, though I'm getting off topic here. I don't think that's your problem with Peter, is it?"

"No, I don't think so. But what *is* the topic?"

"Love between two is a mutual commitment. The rest is working out the details, like what kind of relationship you have, where you're headed and what the boundaries are. Sometimes when you're learning about each other, you discover a deal-breaker, like he's a violent alcoholic or he sells stray dogs to animal testing facilities. That falls under the 'I could never live with a man who . . .' category.

"Anything less than a deal-breaker requires you to search your heart."

"What am I looking for?"

"First you have to find your part in the problem."

"My part? I'm not the one keeping secrets!"

"Dear," Alma said, "there's *always* a 'my part.'" She patted Lia's knee. "It's about time for recreation. We're showing Elvis movies all week. This afternoon it's *Blue Hawaii*, and I don't want to miss that." She winked at Lia. "You'll figure it out."

Lia ruffled Honey's ears as she watched the birdlike woman bend over Henry and invite him to the movies. She wondered if she would ever tell Alma that the sassy woodpecker was modeled after her.

"Those brushes aren't going to clean themselves," she told the dogs. "Which one of you is on studio duty today? Neither one of you? What do you mean you're both permanently on kitchen duty?" She could swear the dogs were laughing at her as she rinsed her brushes out in the nearby custodial closet.

"Think you're smart, do you?"

She stowed her box of supplies on a shelf, then turned back to her dogs.

"My part? What the hell does she mean, 'my part'?"

# Chapter 10

**Monday, May 26**

Lia checked the roster outside Maple room while the army of graders for the new session swarmed by her. She found her name on the list for Eric's team, then scanned the names of her teammates. Desiree was there as well. *Damn. Really, though, it was too much to hope for, that they would split us up. I'd give anything to be at the other end of the building. Hell, I'd happily work in the parking lot. If Eric seated us together, I'll ask to be moved, and damn the blot on my record. I can't take three more weeks of drama.*

She entered the room, scanning the rows for Eric. The room was alive with movement as other scorers found their assigned stations and settled in. She located her team, indicated by teal card stock placards perched on monitors, designating seating assignments.

She found Desiree's assigned station in the first row. She did not find herself. Eric was standing in the last row, at the station next to his. She started to open her mouth to ask why she wasn't assigned a station when Eric placed one last placard on top of the monitor next to his.

"I'm going to be next to you?" She asked. "I don't know whether to be honored or terrified."

"You'll be fine. I put you and Desiree as far apart as I could. That's the best I can do without requesting to transfer you to another team. Can you handle it?"

"Like you said, I'll be fine."

Lia settled in for Avery's orientation and pretended she was not waiting for Desiree to show up. Her mind wandered as he droned on, explaining Maple Room rules to the newbies while team leaders handed out paperwork.

Desiree had been working longer hours at A. Vasari during their last project and was frequently late, skimming just under the wire of the grace period. She only maintained her attendance bonus through good weather and the kindness of benevolent traffic lights.

*Any minute now . . .* Lia kept glancing up at the door while she filled out the forms. No Desiree. When they trooped to the training room to review the questions assigned to the team for this session, she was amazed at Desiree's gall, that she would be so late on the first day of a project. *She'd better get here soon, or she won't be able to pass her qualification test.*

Lia almost lost herself in the intricacies of assigning points for a complex math problem. The four pointer involved figuring the surface area of a room's walls, minus 3 windows, then deciding whether it would be cheaper to use the inexpensive paint that would require a second coat, or the more expensive paint guaranteed to cover in one coat.

*Any minute now, she's going to burst in, full of excuses, and disrupt everything. Or maybe she'll slink in with that 'I've been a bad puppy' look on her face and somehow grab everyone's attention anyway.*

Desiree did not burst in or slink in or enter in any fashion whatsoever. Break came and went. Worry and inattention had Lia tanking her practice test. She had to refer to her handouts on the qualifier and was the last to finish.

"That's it for tonight, folks. You did great with a very complicated question. Tomorrow's question is only a two-pointer. It looks easier on the surface but it has hidden dimensions."

"What's up with you?" Eric leaned over her computer. "You usually do much better."

"I'm worried about Desiree. Has she called?"

"Not a peep." He shrugged. "If she comes tomorrow, she can qualify on the second question. She misses again, she's out for this session and her ranking drops way down on call-backs. If that happens, you won't have to worry about avoiding her for the next three weeks." Lia gathered up her things and headed for the door.

Somehow, the thought of not having to avoid Desiree didn't make her feel any better. She joined Terry in the lobby. "Hold on a sec, I need to make a call." The army of exiting scorers milled past them, noisily streaming around her and Terry like water around a pair of rocks in a brook. They headed out into the night, leaving her and Terry alone in the sterile corporate lobby.

Lia shook her head and put her phone away.

"No luck?" Terry asked.

"Straight to voice mail."

"Who were you calling?"

"I was trying to get Desiree. She never showed." They headed out the double doors, into the nightly parking lot exodus, cars jammed like the population of Manhattan fleeing alien invasion. Headlights splashed across their legs as they wove through the stalled traffic to Terry's truck.

"I'm sure the winsome lass found something better to do with her time. Or someone. I thought you weren't talking to her?"

"I'm not."

"Clearly."

"I hope she didn't blow off this job because we fought. I'd hate to think she ditched extra income because Peter is a jerk."

"Desiree is not so faint of heart. As for Peter, he's a man. What can you expect of us? We're flawed."

"Hmmph."

"Speaking of your good-hearted but misguided beau, when are you going to let him out of the dog house?"

Lia climbed into Terry's truck. "I don't know. Alma says I need to see my part in the problem."

"A woman admitting fault? That would upset the balance of the universe."

# Chapter 11

**Tuesday, May 27**

Lia peered through the glass into the dim interior of A. Vasari. Alfonso stood in the back, his arms flying about in animated conversation with a younger version of himself. Bells chimed when she opened the door, freezing Alfonso in mid gesture. The men turned in tandem to see who entered. Alfonso waved his son off, shaking his head as he watched Lia approach.

Lia passed by the display cases and stopped at the counter separating Alfonso's bench from the rest of the store.

The old man looked up. "That Desiree, she's not here."

"Do you expect her in today?"

"What do I know? She hasn't been here since Thursday. Today is Tuesday. That makes four days she don't come, she don't call. She's a prima donna, too good to work. You too good to work?"

"Uh, no."

"You leave a job without telling anyone?"

"Umm, no, I can't say I have."

"That's because you're a good girl. You see her, you tell her—" He made a disgusted noise and waved his hand. "Forget it. Don't tell her anything. That girl is not worth my time."

Lia chewed her lip as she drove back to Northside. She took a moment to sneer at District Five before she swooped down the Ludlow Viaduct onto Hamilton Avenue. Where to next? She'd never been to Desiree's place, but Desiree said it was up Hamilton Avenue, a quick walk to The Comet. If she didn't see Desiree's car, she'd stop by the bar and ask.

Desiree's day-glo green Honda sat in the drive between a pair of the ubiquitous dilapidated Victorian-era houses that populated Northside. The car was blocked in by an old truck hauling a jungle of paint-splattered ladders and scaffolding.

Lia parked her car, eyeing the gray shotgun on the right. Two men stood on a narrow platform supported by a pair of 30 foot extension ladders. They scraped loose paint off the front dormer window of the Mansard roof while Z-Z Top's "Sharp Dressed Man" screamed out of portable speakers. She eyed their three-day beards and ratty tee shirts. *Ironic choice of music.*

The house on the left was blocked by bushes tall enough to hide a pair of elephants. The white clapboard was trimmed with large horizontal stripes of bright blue, powdery and intense as poster paint. She hoped the person responsible enjoyed it. *Some people shouldn't be allowed near a brush. Oh, well, different strokes . . ."*
A flash of yellow caught her attention as she crossed the street. She veered left toward the narrow gap between the bushes. Wide yellow tape criss-crossed the front door of the blue and white monstrosity. "Crime Scene" it said. "Do Not Enter."

Lia drew closer, uneasy. A distressed sound penetrated the thumping bass emanating from next door. She concentrated, tuning out the music, listening for something just below consciousness, more felt than heard. She latched onto the sound. Someone or something, some dog, was whining. *Julia?*

Lia's unease bloomed into apprehension, heading for alarm. Her heart pounded in concert with the painter's rock music. She froze like a woodland animal caught in headlights. Lia warred with her anxiety, mentally clawing for Asia's lessons. "People hold their breath when they panic. Exhale, and you will automatically inhale in response." Lia pushed the air out of her lungs and started counting, taking several deep, calming breaths. *Inhale, two, three, four. Hold. Exhale, two, three, four . . . .* Once composed, she approached the ladders.

"Hey up there!" she yelled, hoping to be heard over Robert Palmer's "Addicted to Love."

Tall Shaggy Blond Guy looked down while Stocky Redhead turned down the music.

"Whassup?" he yelled back.

"I'm looking for a friend. You're parked behind her car. Desiree Willis?"

"You talking about the hot chick next door? The one who liked to party? She got shot during a burglary. Nice chick." He shook his head. "What a waste."

Lia felt a punch in her gut. She struggled to speak. "Do you know when it happened?"

He looked at his friend. "What day was that? Friday? Saturday?"

His friend spat over the side of the platform, into the bushes. "Had to be Friday night. Don't you remember complaining about the flashing lights from the cop cars Saturday morning? You said they were making your hangover worse."

"Oh, yeah. Friday night. Damn margaritas," he yelled down to Lia. "Sorry about your friend. We saw them haul out the body bag Saturday morning, but we don't know anything else." Stocky Redhead nudged him and nodded at Lia. Shaggy Blond squinted, examining her more closely. "Hey! Didn't we see you on YouTube?"

"Thanks," Lia said, avoiding the question and turning away. Her stomach twisted into knots, making her want to curl in on herself. She took a few more deep breaths, imagining the sound of a rushing brook, leaves floating on top as the current flowed downstream. It was her favorite of the visualization techniques she'd learned from Asia. She'd walk up to The Comet. Someone there would know more, and it would give her something to do until her stomach settled and she was calm enough to drive.

The Comet resided in a strip of brown-brick storefronts built sometime before World War II. She took a moment to observe the details. The lower portion of the facade, below the display windows, was faced with black ceramic tile. Vertical stripes of blond brick added a linear element. Faux chimneys and decorative peaks created a syncopated roofline. *Not exactly Art Deco. Maybe Art's funky cousin.*

Lia expected the bar to be dark, not closed. She shut her eyes for a moment, swallowing frustration, then read the sign again. Four more hours before The Comet was ready for business.

Peering through the window, she saw a tall, dark-haired man emerge from the back, pushing a mop in a rolling bucket while whistling a credible version of "Can The Circle Be Unbroken." The bar consisted of two rooms. A long bar topped with upended stools ran the entire length of the lefthand wall of the front room, facing a pair of pool tables and two booths. She knew tables, a vintage photo booth and space for a band were in the larger room next door. Collages by an unidentified neighborhood artist decorated the walls.

Lia banged on the door. The man left the mop and bucket, came to the door.

"We're closed!" he yelled through the door.

"I know! It's about Desiree. Please let me in."

He grabbed an enormous ring of keys hanging on his belt and cracked the door. "What about Desiree?"

"The painters said she was shot. Is that true? I haven't been able to reach her, and I'm terrified. . . ." Tears spilled down her cheeks.

He pulled the door open without a word and walked over to the long bar, pulled a stool off the bar, flipped it and set it on the floor.

"Have a seat. I'm Dave Cunningham. This is my place."

As Lia collected herself, he filled a tall glass with ice, splashed syrup in the glass and filled the rest with soda from the gun. He stirred it briefly, squeezed in a lime wedge, popped in a straw and deftly slid a coaster under it as he set it down in front of her.

As he worked, it dawned on Lia that he could be Peter's older brother. He was as tall, but less lanky with it. True, the dark hair was curly (and had probably run riot in his younger days) and his face was longer, more weathered. Still, there was something about the quiet confidence with which he moved that reminded her of Peter. Then he turned to her and his perceptive brown eyes dispelled the illusion.

"Home-made ginger-ale. Good for what ails you. I think I've seen you in here before, but it's been a while."

"I came in here a time or two with Luthor Morrisey. It's been years."

"Yeah, Luthor. What is it with you and gunshot victims?" Lia's face crumpled. "Sorry, my bad. What do you know about Desiree?"

"Nothing. I worked with her at Scholastic Scoring Systems. We had a fight a few weeks ago and weren't talking. Last week she texted me and said it was important. I didn't respond. Then she didn't show for work yesterday and I got worried."

"You're the one who clocked her on YouTube?" He tilted his head, squinted. "Ye-e-a-a-h, now I recognize you. You've got some punch."

Lia turned red. She stared down at her ginger-ale.

"So you're Lia. You were with Luthor when he died - well, not *with* him. You know what I mean."

"Yeah, I get it. I'm the bitch who destroyed Desiree's chance for love and everlasting happiness."

"Oh, hey, nobody but Desiree believed that. We all liked Luthor, but he wasn't exactly a hearth and home kinda guy. It's not your fault Desiree insisted on believing what she wanted to believe. I tried to tell her it was a waste of time to wait for him to leave you."

"Why did you think that?"

"Well, hey, he could do what he wanted, and you weren't looking for a ring. I think it made him a bit crazy. All his other girlfriends wanted a commitment. Like, why didn't you want to nail him down the way they did?"

Lia shook her head in disgust. "I really don't want to talk about Luthor. What happened to Desiree?"

"I heard she interrupted a burglary. Crying shame. She didn't have much worth stealing. Her laptop was junk. Only thing she had worth anything was her iPhone. That and her car. I wonder why he didn't take her car?"

Lia shrugged. "That doesn't make sense, does it?"

"She was in here before it happened. I'm surprised we didn't hear the shot. Guess the music must have been too loud. If it makes you feel any better, she'd stopped sticking nails into her voodoo doll of you by then. Why do you suppose she texted you? She say what she wanted?"

"She just said it was important. You don't think . . . you don't think it had anything to do with why she was shot, do you?"

"I bet she just wanted to kiss and make up. She was all morose and saying how she was an idiot and maybe you weren't a bad person after all. Then she went on about how pretty you were and how talented and of course Luthor would pick you over her. Tell the truth, I was kinda relieved when she left. Too much drama, you know? Makes me feel guilty when I think about it. If she'd stayed, maybe the creep would have been gone before she got home."

"Dourson." Peter continued to page through the auction catalog on his desk as he answered the phone.

"Why didn't you tell me about Desiree?" Lia demanded.

"Hello to you, too," Peter responded pleasantly.

"Don't you act all innocent. You deliberately chose not to tell me about this."

"How can I choose not to tell you something when you won't talk to me?"

"Don't confuse me with technicalities."

"Look, I don't want to discuss this on the phone. Where are you?"

"I'm in the parking lot across the street."

"Wait there. I'll be right out."

"Mount Saint Lia blew?" Brent drawled from the next desk.

"Looks like."

"Good luck, Brother."

"Thanks. I'm going to need it."

Peter stood on the steps to District Five and watched the agitated figure pacing in the lot across the street. *Time to gird your loins, Dourson . . . . What the hell does that mean, anyway?* He checked traffic on Ludlow Avenue and trotted across the street. Lia spotted him. Fists pumping, she bore down on him.

"No hug?" Peter asked. When Lia glared at him, he shrugged.

"Very funny," Lia said. "Let's walk on the viaduct."

"Why?"

"Because I like the view and this lot is dirty, ugly and smelly."

"Lead the way." Peter extended a hand toward the overpass in invitation.

88

Peter trailed behind her as they walked in silence, Lia dragging her hand on the massive steel railing.

"Okay, this is far enough," Peter said as he stopped, resting his forearms on the railing so he could look out over the train tracks below. In the distance, boxcars eased lazily along a side rail. "I didn't realize you didn't know."

"Would you have called me if you had?"

Peter turned his head to look into Lia's accusing eyes. "I don't know. Maybe I would have made Brent do it. I know it's upsetting."

"Upsetting? Peter, she tried to contact me right before it happened! It might have had something to do with the reason she died. I was around her. That weirdo who's been stalking her was spying on me, too, whether he meant to or not. I don't know what that means. Will he come after me now?"

"Doubt it. Whatever this is, it's not Foil Man. Just a burglary gone wrong."

"How do you *know*? You don't even know who Foil Man is!" Lia erupted.

"Calm down. It doesn't fit the profile for a stalker killing. Evidence indicates that she walked in on a burglary and was shot.

"Foil Man has some kind of warped fantasy. He would have tried to play that out. Fantasy stalkers like to abduct their targets so they can spend time with them in private. And stalkers almost *always* make some kind of threat before they turn violent. Foil Man is weird, but he never made any threats that anyone is aware of."

"But—"

Peter held his hand up to forestall Lia's rebuttal. "Our guy trashed the place, looking for valuables before she showed up. He only took her electronics. Stalkers take souvenirs, not portable items they can trade for meth, and instead of trashing the place Foil Man would be more likely to deck it out with candles and rose petals. Probably a junior gangbanger. We think he may have shot her by ac-

cident. Professional burglars don't carry guns. We're looking for a nervous punk, not some warped Romeo."
Lia scowled. "Is this your case? Are you and Brent work-
ing it?"
"Heckle and Jeckle have it."
"I bet they were making lewd comments over her
body. I bet they only went to the autopsy so they could
see her naked."
Peter chose not to mention the remarks he'd overheard about Desiree's flying heart tramp stamp. "They're
better at this type of police work than most."
"That's because they're a pair of neanderthal goons.
What they lack in refinement, they make up for in brute
force."
"They do the job."
Lia narrowed her eyes. "I can't believe you're defend-
ing them. You don't even *like* them. Who's taking care of
Julia? I heard her crying when I was there. Surely they
didn't just abandon the dog?"
"It's not my case. You'll have to ask Jarvis and Hodgkins." "Ramblin' Man" sounded from Peter's phone holster. "Excuse me." He tipped the phone up to look at the
display. "I need to take this."

The barrier created by Peter's lean back did not prevent
Lia from overhearing, or from the annoying urge to reach
out and stroke her hand down his spine.
"Sure thing. Still up for Dewey's? I'll meet you in the
parking lot." Peter ended the call and turned around.
"Sorry about that." He reached out, as if to put his hands
on her shoulders in reassurance, then stopped himself.
"You're going to be okay. Really. Whoever shot Desiree,
they don't know you from Adam. Or Eve. I've got to go."
Lia watched as he strode up the viaduct and crossed
over to District Five. A short, buxom woman with a long
braid came out of the building and took Peter's arm in a

casual gesture of affection. Lia stared, mouth open, as Cynth hopped into Peter's Explorer. She remained frozen until they pulled out of the lot and headed away from her, towards Clifton.

"Dewey's! He took her to *Dewey's*!"

"Calm down, Lia, it was lunch, not a nooner," Bailey said. Damp strands of hennaed hair escaped Bailey's tie-dyed do-rag. Her tee shirt was limp with sweat. Bare knees sported grass stains.

"Dewey's was *our* place. And you didn't see her hanging on him." Lia looked around the empty patio at Barrio Taqueria. The restaurant was located in the now-defunct Painted Fish. "This was a bad idea." She nodded at the tiny outdoor stage. "I can't stop thinking about the time he sang karaoke to me right there. Maybe we should leave."

Bailey picked up a fish taco. "Can we stay long enough for me to eat? I left Cruella's beds half planted. I have to get back and finish up this afternoon or she'll breathe fire and all the plants will die from the fumes. Besides, if you're going to get all weepy on me, you might as well do it where there's no one around to see you."

"*I* do *not* get weepy." She slumped back in her chair. "Thanks for interrupting your work day, Bailey. I didn't know what I was going to do. Today has gone from bad directly to the seventh circle of Hell. I don't know what I expected from Peter, but it wasn't this!"

"You don't know it was a date. Didn't you tell me that Brent had his eye on her? Do you really think Peter would poach on his partner?"

"Gee thanks. Not 'Peter wouldn't do that to *you*, Lia.' It's 'Peter wouldn't do that to *Brent*!'"

"If I said Peter wouldn't do that to you, you'd just say, 'How do you know?' I'm trying to be logical here. Logic isn't my strong suit, so cut me some slack.

"Okay, here's another thing. You said she was hanging on his arm. If Peter was conducting an office romance, do you think he'd be engaging in public displays of affection? Sounds more like it's normal to pal around with him and they don't think anything of it."

"I don't know, Bailey . . ."

"Do you even *want* him? You haven't spoken to him for three weeks."

Lia leaned on her elbows and buried her hands in her hair. She stared down at the table.

Bailey took another bite, chewed. Swallowed. Took a sip of tea. She gentled her voice. "This isn't fair to Peter, Lia. You cut him off, now you're upset because he's not banging on the door?"

Lia slowly shook her head from side to side, a futile denial of her situation.

"What *do* you want? You want him to sit around and mope because you blew him off? Tossing a love token into someone's face is a break-up move."

Lia's voice was small. "I'm just so hurt and humiliated that he let me waltz along in LaLa Land like that, Bailey. First he doesn't tell me about Desiree and Luthor, then he doesn't tell me she's been murdered. What else isn't he telling me? How can I trust him? What should I do, Bailey?"

"I don't know what the answer is, but what you're doing? It isn't working."

"Aren't you going to offer to read my tarot cards or see what Uranus is doing to Mars or something? Break out your Ouija board and have a chat with Desiree?"

"You don't believe that stuff. Why should I cast my pearls before swine? Why should Peter, for that matter? How sorry does he have to be, Lia?"

"I don't know. I didn't mean for it to go on so long. I just wanted to sort my thoughts out, and I got wrapped up in the murals I'm doing and working for Scholastic, and the days have just slipped by. It just never seemed to be the right time to call, or when it was the right time, it would slip my mind."

"Uh huh," Bailey said skeptically.

"I'll call him at break tonight. I don't feel like going in, but we're training."

"What else is bothering you, Lia?"

"Dammit, look at the time. I lost an entire day at the retirement center, and now I'm going to be late for work if I don't hustle."

"Lia?" Bailey's eyes were slightly protuberant, making for stellar fish-eyed looks that resulted in speedy confessions.

"I feel rotten about Desiree. I've been having such evil thoughts about her, and now she's dead, and I'm going to be staring at her empty seat all evening. Are you satisfied? Geezelpete, I just remembered. I've got to call Three Sisters about Julia. They'll want her back. Now I really am going to be late." Lia left a ten on the table and rushed out before Bailey could ask more questions.

It had gone so wrong. His long anticipated perfect moment had become a living nightmare.

"No, no, no, no, no!" The Watcher stopped rocking and wiped at his tears, smearing blood on his face. He lifted his head. Desiree's body still sprawled on the floor, a crimson pool on her chest, crimson streaks on her face and neck, red splotches on her blouse, red, red, red. He hadn't been able to revive her. His panting slowed as he gained control over himself. He had to think. What to do? He looked around the room, taking in the scattered bouquet of stargazer lilies, the broken lamp, the upended coffee table, the overturned bookcase spilling chick lit and art books across the floor. Monet meets the Shopaholic.

He'd left fingerprints all over the place on his visits, but maybe he could explain that away. Could they take fingerprints off bodies? They could on CSI, but how likely were the local police to try it? There was one place he had to get rid of his prints. He started to push himself up off the floor but stopped before he left a pair of red handprints to incriminate himself. He curled his hands into fists and pressed his knuckles into the floor, levering himself up. He walked shakily into the kitchen and rinsed his hands, dried them on the towel hanging off a drawer knob. *Have to get the SD card.* The Watcher skirted the carnage in the living room, passed the tiny bathroom and opened the bedroom door. *Quick, quick, before someone calls 911. You've already been here too long. Wait, fingerprints.* He retraced his steps to the bathroom and tore off a length of toilet paper. He used this to handle the clock while he removed the memory card. He thought for a moment. *What the hell, you never know.* He pulled the second memory card out of his pocket, wiped it off and installed it in the clock.

*Something whimpered. Desiree?* The Watcher ran back to the living room, but her eyes still stared blankly at the ceiling, her body continued to cool. The whimper came again, and he remembered Julia. He paused long enough to determine that she was hiding under the bed. He knelt down on the floor and pulled up the dust ruffle. Julia's eye's reflected faintly in the shadows.

"Get over it, dog." He wasn't sure if he was talking to Julia or himself.

94

The Watcher stared at the tiny SD card laying on his desk. He'd been carrying it around like a talisman since he left Desiree's apartment. He didn't know if he could stand to watch the last days of Desiree's life. His goddess, his beautiful goddess, forever out of reach. She still came to him in dreams, but these dreams ran darkly red and he always woke feeling blood on his hands.

Lia's team was headed into the training room when she arrived. She grabbed a seat next to Ted in the back row as Eric distributed handouts.

"You don't look so hot, Lia," Ted whispered, leaning in close to her. "Are you okay?"

Lia shook her head. "Tell you later."

Lia gave up on the training hand-outs when they kept blurring on her. She focussed on listening to Eric and ignoring the sideways looks Ted gave her. She lost her concentration when Eric began to talk about means and averages. *This is making my eye's cross. . . . I'll have to tell Eric. . . . Do I also tell Avery, or do I let Eric do it? . . . One of them could be Foil Man. . . . What would Peter do?*

Her thoughts were interrupted when Eric called for the evening break.

"Ted , you go on ahead. I need to talk to Eric. Snag me a coffee?"

Ted nodded and patted her back. He followed the others out, casting worried glances back at her.

Lia took a deep breath and approached Eric, gripping her tote in front of her for protection. He looked up from his papers, his expression open, questioning.

"What's up, Lia?"

"I went to Desiree's this morning."

"And? Did you find out why she's not coming to work?"

She searched his eyes. His expression became confused, as if she was acting strangely. *I suppose I am.*

"Eric, she was shot Friday night."

"Oh my god." Eyes widening in shock, Eric dropped the papers he'd been scanning. "No wonder she didn't call. Is she going to be okay?"

"No. She's never going to be okay." The misery in her voice made it hard to get the words out. "She's dead."

"Wow. I don't know what to say." He put his hand up to his forehead, stared off into the hall as if the right response would come walking in the door. Then he looked back at her, his eyes full of concern. "Should you be here? I know she wasn't family, but you were friends. I can arrange it so your bonus won't be affected. You qualified for yesterday's question, so you're good to go."

"Thank you, but I'm here now, and we're just training today. I'll be okay."

"Let me know if you change your mind."

"I will, thanks." She gave him a half-smile in appreciation, then went looking for Ted and Terry.

"Wow. She sure saw me coming." Lia ended the call and grabbed a handful of popcorn from Terry's nightly bag.

"Who was that, Lia?" Ted looked up from his paper.

"Susan Herget from Three Sisters. I called her this afternoon to let her know about Desiree. She heads the Beagle rescue where Julia came from. I wanted to make sure they were aware of Julia's situation. It's in their contract that the dog comes back to them if the new owner can't care for it anymore," she explained.

"Let me demonstrate my psychic prowess!" Terry pressed the tips of his fingers to his temple and closed his eyes. "Wait . . . something's coming through . . . I'm seeing a crowd of dogs . . . Julia is outside the gate, barking to get in . . . I see a woman . . . she has a leash, she puts the leash on Julia and leads her away from the gate . . . She's handing the leash to someone . . . Why, why, it's *you*, Lia, she's handing you Julia's leash!" He opened his eyes. "Am I right?"

"Very funny. But yeah, they want me to keep her, just until something opens up."

"Forever, then."

"Are you going to do it?" Ted asked.

"I suppose it's the least I can do. You want a dog, Ted ?"

"You say she's a Beagle?"

"She's very sweet, and small for her breed." Lia tapped the screen on her phone and flipped through the photos, handed the phone to Ted . "Here you go."

"Well, she's just a doll baby, isn't she? Look at those big eyes." He handed the phone back. "I'd have to talk to my wife. She's the boss."

"I'm going to work on you, you know."

"Don't I know it. I'll have my wife on one side, and you on the other."

"A menage a trois? How very European," Terry said, wiggling his eyebrows.

"Ha. Ha," Lia said. "Don't listen to him, Ted . He'll only lead you astray."

"What are you going to do about Desiree, Lia?" Terry asked.

"What do you mean?"

"You said the police were on the wrong track and the case is being handled by incompetents. Are detectival pursuits afoot? If they are, I want in. I barely got my big toe wet before you cracked the last case, and you didn't invite me in on the one before."

"I didn't crack it. I think it cracked me."

"But you discovered the evil-doer before the police did. If their case has gone astray, it's imperative we step in."

"You want to look for Foil Man?"

Ted looked perplexed. "Who's Foil Man? . . . Are you talking about the person who made those little dolls? Do you think he shot Desiree?"

"Foil Man!" Terry exclaimed. "What an ignoble name for a purveyor of mayhem. First we must see the scene of the crime. The obvious opportunity is when we pick up Julia from the neighbor."

Peter sighed when he read the number on his phone. "Hello, Lia."

"Is this a bad time?"

"It's not great." He looked over at the woman seated next to him. *Do you want me to leave?* she mouthed. He frowned, shook his head.

"I won't keep you, then. I was hoping we could get together and talk."

"I don't know . . . ."

"Will you think about it?"

"Lia, I think I need a break."

"Oh. . . . Uh, I also wanted to let you know, Three Sisters wants me to foster Desiree's dog until they figure out what to do with her."

"I see."

"But I don't know how to reach the neighbor who's taking care of her right now."

"Call District Five and ask for Heckle and Jeckle. I'm sure they'll be happy to help you out."

"Uh, Peter?"

"Yes?"

"Are you seeing Cynth?" The words came out forcefully, as if Lia were unsure she could say them unless she threw them out, like hurling a novice parachuter out of a plane.

Peter paused before asking, "How is that your business?" He ended the call, then turned to the woman in question. "Where were we?"

"Wasn't that a bit cruel, Peter?"

"What it was, was necessary."

# Chapter 12

**Wednesday, May 28**

Crime scene tape draped lazily across Desiree's door. One yellow ribbon, unloosed from its mooring, swayed gently in the breeze, brushing Lia's leg as she rang the bell on Geneva Wilson's door. Inside she could hear Julia howling. Lia found it unnerving.

"Watch her carefully," Terry said. "Later you can tell me if you think she has something to hide."

"You think she did it? Why would she kill off a paying tenant?"

"Maybe she had someone who would pay more?"

"For this place? You're dreaming."

They were interrupted by the sound of shoes clomping on stairs. The door swung open.

"Thank Gawd you're here," Geneva said over Julia's lament as she opened the door. "You Lia? Who's your friend?"

"This is Terry. Why is Julia upset?"

"Miss Thang don't think she needs to pee outside. Anyone who pees on my hardwood floor gets locked in the bathroom. I don't care what species they are. If I'd known she wasn't housebroke, I never would have let Desiree keep her. I was getting ready to take her to the SPCA when you called, but you'll do."

Lia pressed her lips together, preventing herself from inquiring exactly how often Geneva bothered to walk Julia. Julia would be out of there soon enough.

"You can have the rest of her food and her dishes, too. You wait here and I'll get her for you." Geneva disappeared and the howling stopped. She returned with Julia on a leash and a brown bag full of kibble. Julia grinned up at Lia and Terry. "It's been real," Geneva told the dog. "I can't say it's been fun, but it's been real." She handed the leash to Lia and the bag to Terry. Terry stooped to the floor and set the bag down. Julia jumped up and licked his nose.

"Awww . . . kiss, kiss," Terry said, ruffling her ears.

"Thank you, Geneva. Julia had some toys. Are they still in Desiree's apartment?" Lia asked.

"I wouldn't know. The police took their sweet time, they only gave me permission to go back in there yesterday. I haven't had time to clear out all that mess. Don't know what I'm going to do with her junk. Her father doesn't want it. He's leaving me to clean it up. Can you believe that? And had the nerve to ask about her deposit! Said it wasn't Desiree's fault her blood is all over the place. Like I got time to fool with that. I work two jobs and I've got to turn that apartment over."

Lia and Terry shared a look. Julia head-butted Terry's hand, which was no longer petting her. He ignored her.

"You know," Terry volunteered, "we could help."

"How so?" Geneva asked, suspicion in her voice.

"Desiree was our friend. We'll take care of it, won't we, Lia."

"You'll haul out her junk and put the trash out Thursday night? And clean up the blood?" Geneva asked.

"Yes, indeed."

"I can't pay you."

"We would not accept it if you tried," Terry said.

"Well, then. Wait here while I get you a key."

101

"Couldn't you have held out for the deposit money?" Lia asked once they allowed Julia to pee and were back in Terry's truck. Julia was crawling over the seats and floorboard, sniffing all the nooks and crannies as if she was hunting a live bomb.

"You smell Jackson and Nappa, don't you, girl?" Terry asked Julia. He looked up at Lia. "This way, we can keep everything. Evidence is more important than money."

"Says the guy who has a pension," Lia groused to Julia, who was now attempting to climb into her lap. Lia lifted her up. "You're just right as rain, aren't you, little girl?" She asked the dog. Julia closed her eyes and sighed.

Julia stuck by Lia like velcro while Honey and Chewy sniffed her, deciphering her scents. Honey gave Lia a perplexed look, as if she knew something was wrong with the newcomer. *Only having her 'mom' killed in front of her. Looks like I'm going to miss another day at the retirement center. Don't know how long clean up will take at Desiree's. This week is shot. Better call Alma and let her know what's up.*

After the dogs completed their ritual of greeting, Lia let them out in the back yard. She sat on the stoop with a cup of chai and watched Julia get acquainted with her surroundings. *It's so easy for dogs. A few sniffs, and you're either friends or you're not. Why can't life be that simple?*

She forgot to watch the dogs while she brooded. Julia popped up, the smudge of dirt on her nose topping a happy grin. Chewy and Honey eyed Lia from a distance, waiting to see how she would react to the obvious transgression.

"I can see you're enjoying your new digs, Julia, pun intended. Let's go see what you got into."

Julia happily led the way, proud to show off her excavation.

Lia deducted a point from the question she was grading and called up the next paper.

"... it looks like we're cleaning out Desiree's apartment," Lia told Ted and Eric as she gave her current paper a barely deserved two points.

"That's very kind of you," Ted said.

"Not at all. Terry just wants an excuse to snoop around. He thinks he's the next Sherlock Holmes. I won't be surprised if he shows up tomorrow with a meerschaum and a deerstalker."

Avery's cologne preceded his appearance. He placed a hand on Eric's shoulder. "Eric told me about Desiree. You have my condolences. Will there be a service?"

Lia blinked. "I don't know. I don't even know who to ask."

"She was such a lovely girl. If you find out, let me know. Perhaps our room could send flowers?"

"What about a donation in her name?" Eric asked. "She have any charities, Lia?"

"She volunteered for Three Sisters Pet Rescue."

"Then that's what we'll do. I'll announce it tomorrow evening. Excellent idea, Eric."

# Chapter 13

**Thursday, May 29**

"I guess Geneva's too busy to take down the crime scene tape," Lia said as she, Terry and Bailey hopped out of Terry's truck.

"The way you described her, she sounded like an entitled control freak. Wish I'd been with you. I'd like to get a look at her aura. Bet it's dark."

"Probably is. Thanks for helping us, Bailey."

"I don't mind taking a break from Cruella. Yesterday she decided she didn't like the location of the fig tree I put in last week. I had to dig it up and move it. Today she'd just want to move something else. She's in that kind of mood."

Bailey held a garbage bag open while Lia stuffed the yellow streamers into it. "I suppose we need a plan," Lia said.

"The garbage truck comes tomorrow morning. I vote we focus on that for today and worry about packing up the rest later," Bailey said.

"A worthy plan," Terry said.

Lia unlocked the door and shoved it in. The three stood at the doorway, gaping. Books, CD's DVDs, dishes, clothing; all were scattered across the floor, topped by poly-fil fluff extruded from eviscerated throw pillows.

Shelves were empty, drawers were open, plants were up-ended.

Terry whistled. "I wasn't expecting detritus from a category three storm."

"Something's wrong," Lia said.

"What is it, Lia?" Bailey asked.

"I could be mistaken, but I don't' think it was like this when the police were here."

"What makes you say that?" Bailey asked.

"Call it a hunch."

Lia pulled out her phone and called District Five.

"Detective Hodgkins."

"Detective Hodgkins, it's Lia Anderson."

"What can I do for you, little lady? Ready to ditch your wimp of a boyfriend yet?"

"I'm at Desiree Willis' apartment. I was going to start cleaning it out, but it looks like it's been ransacked."

"That's what happens when your house gets burgled."

"I think someone was in here after you removed the body."

"What makes you say that?"

Lia surveyed the chaotic sea that was Desiree's belongings. "Well, for one thing, there's no room for a body. I see a broken lamp and an upended table, but drawers, bookcases, everything has been dumped. The landlady said there was blood in the living room, but I can't see it. I can't even figure out where Desiree died."

"I wouldn't worry about it. In that neighborhood, there are sure to be scavengers. Might have even been the landlady."

"What if it's not? What if Desiree's killer was looking for something and they couldn't find it?"

"What movies have you been watching? Think there's a CIA NOC list floating around in there?"

Lia felt foolish. "It just looks angrier than someone who wanted free DVDs and didn't like the selection."

"And what exactly, makes a ransacking angry? "

"I don't know, it just -"

"Tell you what, Anderson, you take pictures of everything, and if we want to look at them, we'll let you know."

Lia tapped the phone off, wishing it was an old-fashioned land line so she could slam it.

"The gendarme were not impressed?" Terry asked.

"Apparently not. I wish I knew what to do. He said to take pictures, but he made it sound like he wouldn't bother looking at them."

"Taking pictures is an excellent idea," Terry said. "I had intended to do so, anyway. It will give me time to commune with the crime scene." He picked his way carefully into the middle of the room and pulled out his phone.

Bailey sat on the porch steps while Lia peered in the windows of Desiree's car. "What do you think will happen with Desiree's car?"

"I don't know," Lia said. "I imagine some bank owns it."

"Too bad. It's cute. I could see you driving it."

"I bet the payments are cute, too. . . . You've got five minutes," Lia yelled to Terry.

"What are you looking for?" Bailey asked.

"Just checking to see if she left anything in here," Lia said. "It looks clean." She joined Bailey on the steps.

"Do you really think the guy who shot Desiree came back?" Bailey asked.

"I don't know what to think. What could Desiree have that someone would want? Desiree's no spy."

"Drugs, maybe?"

"Whatever it is, has to be small. You don't look for a pony in a teapot," Lia said.

"When Terry's done, I want to see if I can pick up any vibes in there."

"Go for it." She stood up. "Ollie, ollie, oxen-free," she called.

"Uno momento," Terry replied.

"We haven't got all day. We're coming in." The two women passed into the gloom of the unlit apartment. "What's taking you so long?"

"I'm trying to figure out the flash on my camera. I need a few more close ups of the gashes in these cushions. It might be possible to determine what was used to cut them at a later date, if the pictures are good enough."

"Gee, Terry, you don't think the shears lying on the floor might be involved, do you?"

"Aha! a clue! We should bag these for fingerprinting."

"They're going into your storage unit. Knock yourself out. Bailey, how long do you need to pick up your vibes?"

"I'm getting a reading now." Bailey pressed her fingers to her temples and picked her way through the debris. "I'm not getting anger, well . . . some, but mostly I'm getting panic, a lot of fear. There's something under that. . . . Grief. . . . It's intense. . . . and there's something obsessive. It's weird, confused. Doesn't feel like a garden variety burglar to me."

"Foil Man's upset because he killed Desiree? There's your clue, Terry. Who wants to hold a garbage bag while I toss junk into it? And who wants to put the books and DVDs back?"

"I'll straighten out the media," Terry volunteered.

"No contemplating her reading habits, Terry. Just shelve them."

"But we could miss something vital."

"Doubt it. If it were important, the killer would have taken it, not tossed it on the floor. Bailey, let's start in the bedroom."

The mess extended into Desiree's bedroom, though the theme of the chaos was more intimate. Underwear was everywhere. Empty dresser drawers were flung at random around the room. The closet door stood open.

Clothes remained on the hangers, barely, and were shoved to either side of the closet as if someone wanted to see if there were any hidey-holes in the back wall.

Bailey pointed at a radio-alarm clock, sitting alone on the bedside table next to an upended mattress stripped of linens. "Do people still use those?" she asked.

"I guess." Lia shrugged. "It's odd, though."

"What is?"

She pointed at the clock. "It's still running. Everything else has been tossed on the floor. Why is the clock still there?"

"You got me."

The tote Desiree always brought with her to Scholastic hung gaping by one strap on the closet doorknob. Lia waded over to it, tossing thongs and lacy underwires up on the bared mattress as she went. "How can one person need so many brassieres?"

Bailey picked up a frilled bit of yellow and orange striped silk and examined it, shaking her head. "The important question is: how can something so small support something so big? This stuff must have cost a mint."

"Just because we don't need them doesn't mean nobody else does."

"Just once, I'd like to know what it feels like when your boobs are so big they give you a backache."

"Not me. I'll stick with my tank tops. Bras compress your lymph nodes and give you cancer. Underwires are the worst. I read a study that says so," Lia said.

"That's been debunked."

"If you read the so-called debunking, it consists of people saying 'I'm a real scientist and it isn't true because it hasn't been proven to my satisfaction.' There have been no follow-up studies that actually disproved the original results, just people whining how the study wasn't valid." Lia peered into the canvas bag. "They're gone."

"What's gone?" Bailey asked.

"The foil dolls. All of them. She kept them in a shoe box and brought them to Schholastic every night so she could look at them while she worked. Or maybe she was showing off. I wonder if she carried them with her to A. Vasari, too."

"You think maybe the police took them?"

"Doubt it. I'll call Heckle and Jeckle later and ask, but I bet they don't have them. Guess I'll ask at the jewelry store, too, just to make sure."

"Who else but Foil Man would want them?"

"Exactly. This proves Foil Man was here. Will they listen? Of course not."

"Do you think she had any contact with Foil Man before he killed her?"

"Don't know. Who knows what happened after he posted that YouTube video? For all I know, they were planning their wedding and Desiree was going to ask me to be her Maid of Honor.

"By the way, you can thank Trees for me, for pulling the video down. Shame it went right back up." Lia grabbed some *Vegan Times* magazines and tossed them in Bailey's trash bag on top of a *Cosmo* and several jars of make-up.

"Yeah, he said that might happen, but it was worth a try. Anyway, I was thinking, maybe Desiree kept a journal on her computer and say she wants to access it while she's away from home, so it's in the cloud. Everything's in the cloud these days. Trees says that makes it easy for guys like him—not that he messes with private citizens.

"All you have to do is know someone's email address, and you can scout the different cloud venues for their accounts. Then, all you have to do is figure out their password. If you want, I can ask Trees to poke around. He can hack her email account while he's at it, maybe Foil Man wrote to her."

"You say this like I want to get involved in Desiree's murder. Terry's the one who got us into this mess, and I do mean that literally." She scowled, shoving more garbage into the bag. She tossed yet another underwire brassiere onto the bed. This one had tiny lavender dots scattered across burgundy silk.

"Umm . . . Didn't you just say you were going to make some calls about the dolls?"

"What of it?" Lia asked.

"Don't look now, but I think you're already involved in the investigation." She looked around at the now cleared floor. "Should we throw the underwear into another garbage bag?"

"Not just yet," Lia said. "I don't want to get it mixed up with the trash."

"What are you going to do with it all, anyway?"

"I don't know, but it's too nice to pitch."

"Why don't we save it for the Northside garage sale in August? It always brings out a big crowd. And if we advertise it's from Desiree's estate, we'll be able to charge premium prices for one of those brassieres."

"Ghoulish, but true, Bailey." Lia sat down on the bed and started folding underwear. Bailey tied off the now-full bag and joined her.

"Crime sells," Bailey said. "We could tag those scissors Terry found as a bona fide clue."

"I can see it now: 'scissors used to rip open cushions during ransacking of Willis crime scene.' If we find the dolls, we shouldn't waste them on a garage sale, we should put them up on eBay," Lia said.

"That's getting mercenary. What will you do with the money?"

"Scholastic is collecting money for a donation to Three Sisters in her name. Why don't we do the same with the proceeds from the sale?"

"Anything for the dogs. Merc away." Bailey folded the last thong, if it could be called 'folding,' and handed it to Lia. "That's about it for the bedroom. What—"

"Evidence! We have a clue!" Terry shouted from the kitchen.

Lia rolled her eyes, but got up to join the dogged detective anyway.

"What did you find, Terry?" Bailey asked.

"I missed it when I was taking pictures." He pointed at the window over the kitchen sink. "This pane of glass has been broken. The rogue who despoiled Desiree's belongings must have used this window as his method of entry."

"Why would anyone want to climb in over a sink?" Bailey asked.

"Because the side windows are eight feet from the ground and the front window faces Hamilton Avenue where they could be seen. This way they're on the back porch. What do you want to bet they pulled a chair up under the window?" Lia asked.

"You called it," Terry said, peeking out the back door.

Lia looked down. "Geezelpete. Did they have to smash so many of her dishes? Some of this is Depression milk-glass."

Bailey sighed over the loss. "I'll grab the broom."

"Rough day, Lia?" Eric asked, nodding at her grimy *Day Soldiers* tee shirt.

Lia was still sweaty, and she could feel the dust they'd raised at Desiree's clinging to her skin. She'd had to forgo a shower, with barely time to feed and walk the dogs and make it to work on time. She blamed Bailey's insistence on smudging Desiree's apartment. Bailey said it was necessary to get rid of all the violent vibes before they infected all the stuff in Terry's storage unit.

Lia was not usually self-conscious. Casual dress was accepted at Scholastic, but she preferred to be clean. She didn't mind being dirty at the dog park, where paw prints and slobber were the norm, and there was something satisfying about a good, healthy sweat while performing hard labor. But feeling sweat and grime congeal on her skin in the corporate air conditioning made her self-conscious and itchy. She hoped for Eric's sake that his nose wasn't too sensitive. *Oh, well, it was his idea to seat me here.*

Lia blew out a disheartened breath and shook her head. "Some asshat broke into Desiree's apartment and ran-sacked her stuff. Weird, because it just looked like they were intent on destruction. Her vintage dinner-ware had to be worth something, but they smashed most of it. We hauled out the garbage because the truck comes tomor-row morning. There was a lot more trash than we ex-pected, due to the damage. Thank God we had plenty of garbage bags."

"That's terrible," Ted said. "I don't understand people who enjoy destroying things."

"Here," Eric said, handing her a Nestle's Crunch Bar. "I wasn't going to hand these out until tomorrow, but you look like you could use yours now."

Lia tore the wrapper off one end and bit down. "You're all heart," she garbled over a mouthful of choco-late.

"Just remember that come evaluation time," he said while handing Ted a bar. "But satisfy my curiosity."
"About what?" Lia asked.

"You and Desiree had an epic blow up. Now you're taking care of her things? What's that about?"

Lia shook her head and huffed. "Terry—you know Terry? His team is in Grasshopper—He volunteered us because he thinks we should investigate Desiree's mur-der. He doesn't buy the burglary-gone-wrong scenario, and he thought we could dig up some clues if we could get into her apartment."
"So why are you going along with it?"

"I don't know. Guilty conscience, I guess. I think we would have worked out our differences if we'd had some time. She sent me a text right before it happened, but I ignored it. Best case, she wanted to mend fences. Worst case? It had something to do with why she died, and I blew her off. So I'm paying penance."

"Bummer." He patted her on the shoulder. "It's too bad things happened the way they did. I thought you both were great, and you looked like you had a lot of fun together. You can't help what went down."

"Can I ask you a question, Eric?"

"Sure, why not." He settled into the chair next to hers.

"Why is it that every single man in the room couldn't keep his eyes off Desiree?"

"Seriously?"

"You can't tell me you never noticed."

"It's not that. I just thought it was obvious."

"It had to be more than her stupendous bosom."

"Well, her impressive chestal region was most of it."

"But not all."

"Look, guys are simple. It doesn't take much more than impressive boobs for most of us."

"Uh huh."

"You really don't know?"

"Give, Flynn."

"Look, Desiree was easy. Oh, don't give me that, I'm not talking about her virtue or lack of. I mean, it wasn't a matter of what did Desiree have that you didn't have. It's a matter of what you have that Desiree never would."

"Come again?"

"You've got this Nicole Kidman kinda vibe. I think Desiree wanted to be *you*."

"Excuse me?" Lia's eyebrows shot up.

"Oh don't look at me like that. You've got a touch of Grace Kelly. Classy. A guy looks at you and he knows he's got to man up, and not in the usual ways."

Lia pondered her wardrobe, 80 percent of which consisted of studio clothes that looked like they survived insurrection in Afghanistan. *Classy? I could be arrested for wardrobe abuse.* "What are you talking about?"

"Desiree was pretty, but she didn't have the bone structure to ever be gorgeous. She was intelligent, but she was no brain surgeon. She was approachable."

"I'm nice."

"That only makes it worse. Because you're nice, guys want you to like them. If you were intimidating *and* a bitch, they'd just want to sleep with you to prove they could. Since you're nice, they want you to like them, only they figure you couldn't possibly."

"Why not?" Lia frowned.

"Look, a girl like Desiree, it doesn't take much to impress her. A good line, a shiny trinket, a nice ride, an impressive job—hell, an *interview* for a job with a regular income, and she thinks you're great.

"You don't need all that stuff and you see through it. A guy looks at you and now his nice new Lexus is just a piece of junk. All his shiny bits he's built around himself fall off and all he's left with is himself, and he's nothing."

"Nobody is ever nothing."

"No, but that's the way guys feel. Most guys would rather rely on waving their shiny bits at a girl than say, 'This is me, here I am. Please don't notice my tiny penis.' And then they look at you: independent, making your own way on your own terms, so a guy can't buy you. And you're talented. I saw pictures of that solstice piece you did on the web. How do you impress a woman who turns the sun into art?

"Now you're doing this crap job so you can donate your time to the elderly. You're slumming with us mortals. Intimidating as all *hell*. A guy either has to be really solid with himself, or else he's got to be so deluded by his own bullshit that he *believes* he's all that."

"Well isn't that just *ducky*." She turned back to her monitor and the next test paper. "I just had to ask."

114

Lia couldn't settle into that zen state required to scan test papers and pull out the essential information. She repeatedly drifted and discovered herself staring at the vacant work station two rows ahead, wondering if Eric was right, that the sex goddess of Northside had envied her. That somehow made everything worse. She was older than Desiree. She should have cut her more slack.

Lia stared blankly at the paper in front of her, realizing she couldn't remember the last two she'd scored. She chided herself while backtracking. *Keep your mind on math, Anderson. This is not the time to indulge in guilt. Think about something else, like why couldn't the person who wrote this question have painted the room a lovely orchid instead of khaki? Khaki is a no-risk option that shows zero imagination. I bet the rug is beige.*

Half a dozen test papers later, someone with loopy, feminine writing Xed out "khaki" and wrote "Conch-shell Pink!!!!!" above it, underlining several times with a heavy pencil. Happy to encounter a like-minded soul, Lia gave the girl a perfect score she hadn't earned.

# Chapter 14

**Friday, May 30**

"Something's missing," Lia said, dropping Julia's lead as she scanned Desiree's bedroom. She set down her stack of collapsed boxes on the floor. Bailey dropped a bundle of newspaper and a roll of garbage bags next to it. Julia scampered under the bed.

"Someone came back?"

"They must have. Desiree's clock is gone."

"How odd. How do you think they got in?" Bailey asked.

"Same way they did last time, I bet."

"That's so weird. Why would anyone want a clock radio? You don't suppose Geneva took it, do you?"

"Maybe. You never know. I'm going to look around and see if I notice anything else out of place." Lia checked out back first. Julia tagged along, dragging her lead behind her. When Lia entered the kitchen, Julia shot through the dog door and off the porch to nose eagerly around the yard.

Before they'd left the day before, Terry dragged the chair away from the kitchen window to discourage would-be prowlers. There wasn't anything they could do about the window except lock it, and that was a futile gesture, with the pane by the lock missing.

He'd placed the chair next to its mate on the other end of the porch. It remained by its twin, two green plastic Adirondack chairs purchased at Kroger for $9.99 each at the end of the previous summer. Were they lined up differently? She stared at the porch floor, looking for drag marks or footprints, or something—

"Lia, you need to come see this," Bailey called from the kitchen.

"What is it?" She found Bailey peering in the cabinet next to the sink. Open cabinet doors blocked Lia's view. She came beside Bailey and followed her line of sight.

"Oh." The vandal had passed this shelf by, leaving a row of coffee mugs intact. A little foil doll sat on the bottom of an upended mug of pressed, apricot carnival glass. The little foil woman's legs dangled over the side of the mug, kicking out while she leaned back on her hands as if she didn't have a care in the world. Below, a tiny silver dog jumped against the side of the mug, mouth open, barking for attention.

"I don't know whether to be creeped out or charmed," Bailey said. Do you suppose that's you? The dog looks like Chewy."

"If that's Chewy, where's Honey?"

They shuffled mugs around, finding Honey behind the second mug down, sniffing a flower on the printed shelf paper. Lia removed all the cups on the shelf and discovered a tiny Beagle inside a Florida souvenir mug sporting ironic flamingos. Mini-Julia's head raised as she bayed to get out of her ceramic prison.

"You have to admit, Foil Man has a sense of humor as well as talent. Are you going to tell Peter about this?"

Lia thought back to the embarrassment of their last conversation. "No, I'm not. He's convinced Foil Man is harmless."

"He might feel differently about Foil Man leaving you presents."

"He asked me for time off. I asked him if he was seeing Cynth, and he told me it was none of my business. If I go to him with this story, it will look like I'm so desperate I'll do anything for attention. He'd probably think I made these myself, just to pull him back in."

"You think Peter would suspect you of doing something so juvenile?"

"I *feel* like doing something that juvenile, and if I called him, I'd be so self-conscious about that, I'd sound guilty."

"Call Brent."

"Then it's like I'm making a point of avoiding him. Same thing, different tactic."

"So call Heckle and Jeckle. Why do you call them Heckle and Jeckle, anyway?"

"Heckle and Jeckle are a pair of thuggish magpies from a cartoon in the forties. Wikipedia says they specialize in insults, slapstick violence and rudeness. Brent thought it fit them, especially since their brains have not evolved beyond the post-war years."

"Oh, so these are Neanderthal magpies."

"Exactly."

"It's their case. You should call them."

"You saw how seriously they took me when I reported the break-in yesterday. What am I going to say? Someone stole a cheap clock and left a doll made out of aluminum foil, and by the way, I think it's supposed to be me? If Peter didn't think it was important when it was happening to Desiree, no way they're going to take me seriously."

"Call them anyway."

"What ever for?" Lia frowned as she touched one tiny foot with her finger, watched the doll teeter on the edge of the mug.

"You don't want to be that woman."

"What woman?"

"You know, the woman in the horror movie who watches a news report on a homicidal maniac, then she hears a weird sound coming from her basement and goes to investigate without her shotgun."

"Oh. That woman. I'd rather be her sister, the one who shoots the UPS guy by mistake." Lia pulled her kubotan out of her hip pocket and waved the pink tube, making her keys jangle. "I'm armed. No worries."

"Lot of good that will do against a bloody chainsaw."

"Right now I'm more worried about getting everything packed before Terry gets here with the truck." She looked around. "Have you seen Julia? She was right behind me when you yelled."

"Try the back yard."

"Right." She poked her head out the door. "I don't see her anywhere. Julia! Come here!" No response. "Well damn. Hang on while I find her."

Lia finally rounded the corner of the house and spotted Julia's tail poking out from under a spreading yew. "Aha! gotcha." She bent down to pick up the leash, which was wrapped around the base of the lilac bush a few feet over. The branches of the yew bush wiggled as Julia ignored the tug on her tether. Lia stooped down to look under the bush, pushing the branches aside. "What are you up to, wench?"

Julia's whole body quaked while her front paws kept up their frenzied digging. Lia pulled on the leash, forcing Julia to back up and turn around. She grumbled and moaned, resisting with dug-in paws. Lia eased up on the leash a bit and Julia whipped around, returning to her excavation.

"What's got you in such a tizzy? Is something under there?" Lia leaned in, parting the branches to give her a view of the situation. It was a doggie treasure trove containing two chewed remotes, a Betty Boop nightlight and a mangled tennis ball. "Oh, Julia," she sighed. "What am I

119

going to do with you. Bailey!" she yelled. "Come here a sec."

"What is it? I see you found her."

"Her and the lost treasure of Solomon's mines. Hang onto Julia, will you? I want to see what else is in here." Lia crawled under the bush to drag out Julia's soil-encrusted prizes. The remains of a baseball glove reminded Lia of a mummified human corpse she'd seen on *Bones*. Under the glove she unearthed uppers from a pair a dentures next to a Phillips screwdriver. "Girlfriend has been busy," she said, retreating from the bush with a formerly fuchsia evening shoe sporting a four inch spike heel. "I bet Desiree was livid about this." She upended the shoe, dumping out loose dirt. A necklace with a purple stone fell onto the grass.

Lia reached in again and dragged out an abalone shell choker tangled up in an underwire bra, this one of cream satin despoiled with grass stains and dirt mixed with dog slobber. She extended her arm into the pit one last time and felt around. Her fingers touched something cool and slick. She had an odd expression on her face.

"This is strange."

"What is it?" Bailey asked

"I don't know, but it feels rubbery." Lia pulled out an object shaped like a slender flashlight and held it up for Bailey to see. It was covered with translucent, purple silicone. the tip of one end was bent and rounded. A small silicone dolphin reared its head half-way up one side. Rows of steel beads, or maybe ball bearings, could be seen through the silicone.

"I hope those teethmarks are Julia's," Bailey said.

"I don't want to think about it."

"You could have discovered a safety deposit box key. You could have found Desiree's last will and testament. You could have at least come up with a picture of Tatum Channing with his shirt off. Only you could come out of that bush with a battery powered pacifier."

120

"Ha, ha."

"I've seen those on Groupon for 25 bucks. I've always wondered how they work."

"I'm sure the batteries will be dead."

"You never know. Give it a shot."

Lia looked at the array of buttons near the base of the vibrator. "This looks like Mission Control. How do you know it won't blow up the house next door if I push the wrong button?"

"Give it to me," Bailey said. She studied the control panel and tapped one tiny button. The vibrator began to hum.

"Nothing's happening. It's broken."

Bailey touched the dolphin's nose with the tip of one slender finger.

"I don't know, Flipper's getting a good buzz on." She tapped another button, this one with a "12" on it. The humming grew louder. She tapped the "12" again, and this time the dolphin's nose vibrated so furiously, it blurred. More taps, and the vibration went through a series of syncopated rhythms.

"Geezelpete!" Lia said.

Bailey pressed an arrow near the base and the steel beads rotated around the inner shaft while the bent tip gyrated. Absurdly, it reminded Lia of her mother's habit of twirling one index finger while saying "Whoopie ding!"

Bailey pressed another button. The beads and tip reversed direction.

"Amazing. If this thing had flashing lights, I'd put it on top of my Christmas tree."

"It's May, Bailey."

"I can wait six months. Do you suppose this was Desiree's?"

Lia shrugged. "Who's to say. The dentures aren't. Not the baseball glove, either. But I doubt it. She had plenty of action without it. I bet it was Geneva's."

"That explains why she was so mean to Julia. Maybe the glove was hers, too. Maybe she needed it in case this thing heated up and tried to take off. What are we going to do with it?"

Lia shuddered. "Toss it back in the hole?"

"You don't want to keep it?"

"Bailey, you don't know where that's been!"

"True." Bailey knelt down and shoved the gaudy vibrator back under the bush. "Good bye, Flipper, it was nice to know you," she said, burying the sad device with dead leaves and mulch.

Bailey stood up and brushed the dirt off her hands. "Poor Flipper. He needs a headstone."

"Oh, for Christ's sake!"

"Hey, Dourson," Hodgkins settled his bulk on the edge of Peter's desk, reaching for the last slice of the goat cheese pizza Peter and Brent shared for lunch.

"Get your own," Peter said, barely glancing away from the report he was writing.

Hodgkins retracted his hand. Sneered. "Stupid yuppie pizza. Why don't you ever get pepperoni, like normal people? By the by, your girlfriend called. Second time. I think she's lonely for a real man. I think I should help her out. What do you think, Jarvis?"

"I think we should both help her out. That was pitiful, that story she cooked up about an *intruder* leaving a little doll made out of aluminum foil at the Willis crime scene. How does someone make a doll out of foil? Sounds screwy to me."

"I told her after the way she took on the Willis chick in that YouTube video, she shouldn't worry about some wimp who plays with dolls. Don't you agree, Dourson?" Hodgkins asked.

"Lia? With a couple of mugs like ya'll?" Brent laid his lazy magnolia on thick to emphasize his contempt. He snagged the lonely piece of pizza. "Dream on, and toss in Jessica Alba and Scarlett Johansson while you're at it, make it a quintet. Sorry, forgot you don't know that word. Make it a *party*. And Hodgkins? Back up a ways, will you, before I'm forced to hide a bottle of mouthwash in your desk.

"I wouldn't make any untoward moves on Lia," Brent continued. "You might end up on the floor, playing dolls with the wimp. She spent a few weeks with my girl, Cynth."

"Way I heard it, she's Dourson's girl, not yours. Come on Jarvis. We have *real* police work to do."

"Is too my girl," Brent muttered as the duo retreated, watching them with one eye. His other eye took note of the color returning to Peter's knuckles as he unclenched the fist he held underneath his desk.

"You know the only reason I forgive you for accepting that assignment with Cynth is because the resident thugs were next in line for it. I hope you remember to tell her what a great catch I am during your tete-a-tetes."

"You want to be caught?" Peter asked, mildly.

"No, but you have absolutely no basis for extolling my sexual prowess, so let's just stick with my status as a highly desirable companion for the right woman."

"For all you know, I'm extolling my own sexual prowess."

"A former Eagle Scout like yourself would never do that to a partner, never mind Lia."

Peter grimaced. "She threw my opal at me. I think that means I'm a free agent."

"Brother, don't tell me you weren't about to pick up a charge for assaulting an officer a few minutes ago. And it wasn't over a slice of cold pizza."

"You don't have to fight my battles."

"I wasn't standing up for you. I was protecting Hodgkins' not-so-pretty face. We've got too much ugly around here as it is. You think there's anything to this doll thing?"

Peter shrugged. "It's not surprising that Foil Man left a final tribute for Desiree. That wouldn't have anything to do with Lia, and it doesn't mean he had anything to do with Desiree's murder. Everything still points to burglary gone wrong, committed by an inexperienced doer."

"You really *ought* to talk to her."

"No, I really *ought* not. And you really *ought* to mind your own business."

# Chapter 15

"If Jeffrey Deaver were here, he'd say the dolls were an elaborate distraction disguising the coldly rational actions of a domestic terrorist or a scheming corporate hack," Terry opined while scratching behind Napa's ears. As Napa was standing on the picnic table where they gathered, he leaned over and faced her, eye-to-eye. She licked his nose. "Aw . . . kiss, kiss. Of course, he is the Master of Obfuscation. Probably covering up your typical, ill-conceived, liberal commie plot."

"What would a corporate hack or a domestic terrorist want with Desiree?"

"Perhaps Desiree isn't the target. Maybe her murder was meant to scare Geneva. Has she had any offers on her property lately?" Terry asked.

"If that's the case, what do the dolls have to do with it? I don't think Desiree even told Geneva about the dolls. And if they're meant as window dressing, why did he steal them back?" Bailey asked

"Do you suppose there's something about them that he didn't want anyone else to know? Something hidden inside, maybe?" Lia asked.

"There's still the doll of Lia. I wonder if there's anything inside that one," Bailey said.

Lia stopped making smoochy noises at Julia and looked up. "You want me to deconstruct myself?"

"That's not a bad idea," Bailey said. Figure out how it's made. It might tell you something about him."

"You mean, like if he's using platinum wire for an armature, and there's only 3 places in the western hemisphere that sell it? I know, maybe Foil Man used Desiree's dolls to smuggle bugs into the Scholastic scoring center. It's a plot by a group of failing high school students to get their hands on the scoring rubrics," Lia said.

Terry picked up her train of thought "—and he had to keep giving her new dolls because the batteries on the bugs only lasted for a couple days. Maybe Desiree was in on the plot and that's why she was never creeped out by his love offerings. "

Lia shrugged. "Makes as much sense as anything."

"We're all forgetting something," Bailey announced.

"What's that?" Lia asked.

"We have a witness."

"What are you talking about? There was no witness," Terry said.

Bailey made a flourish with one graceful hand. "Julia." She said this as if it were obvious.

"What kind of help is that?" Lia asked. "Are we going to walk her around until she decides to bite someone?"

"I know, we can put together a line up and let her sniff the participants," Terry said. "When she decides to pee on someone's shoes, we'll know we have our man."

"Mock me all you want. I'm calling Louella Zuckerman."

"The animal psychic?" Lia asked. "What do you think she can do?"

"Animal communicator. She's not psychic. She'll tell us what Julia remembers."

"Hog wash," Terry pronounced.

"How would you know? Have you ever seen her work?"

"I don't need to. It's pure New Age nonsense."

"Luella's different," Lia said. "She's been document-ed. I don't know how she does it. Hundreds of people have vouched for her abilities. I don't know if it will help, but it can't hurt. Doesn't she book up way in advance, Bailey?"

"Months. But she might squeeze us in since Julia is traumatized."

Lia looked down under the table, Julia's safe place. Julia looked up at her, then returned to scanning the park for peril.

"She has been acting anxious. If nothing else, maybe she can help us with that," Lia said.

"Mumbo jumbo," Terry said. "I say we go to the fu-neral and see who shows up."

"How cliche," Bailey said. "Do you know anything about a service for Desiree, Lia? I think we should go, be-cause it's the right thing to do. Not to spy."

"We can do both," Terry said. "That's what makes man a superior animal, having the ability to address two different aims at the same time. Unlike the unfortunate birds."

"What unfortunate birds?" Bailey asked.

"Why the pair who were killed with the single stone, of course."

"We won't be able to kill anything if there is no funer-al," Lia said. "Avery asked me to let him know when it was. I checked online, but I couldn't find a notice."

"I wonder how you could find out?" Bailey asked.

"First we have to know who has possession of the body," Lia said. "I've met the assistant coroner. I can make a call when I get home."

"On a Saturday?" Bailey asked.

"Death is no respecter of weekends," Terry intoned.

"Tell you what, Terry. You go hunt in the woods for the tree Foil Man climbed to shoot that video, and I'll go call Amanda Jeffers. Find us some clues."

Terry brightened and pointed his index finger up in the air. "A worthy task for my ratiocinative abilities. Where's my camera?"

⚘

"This is Doctor Jeffers," the voice on the phone said.

"Amanda, it's Lia Anderson. Peter's friend."

"For real? You two are still friends?"

"Ouch. What have you heard?" Lia kept her casual tone despite the sudden hole in her stomach.

"Now don't be expecting me to repeat gossip." Amanda's scolding made the corner of Lia's mouth quirk up despite wondering what the assistant coroner knew.

"Umm, you'll only have to say it once?"

"That line is so tired, I'm going to buy it a bottle of Geritol."

Desperation crept into Lia's voice. "Please Amanda? I swear I won't say who told me."

"I don't want to be getting into the middle of anything. Both of you are liable to wind up shooting me instead of each other. Not this girl. Uh-uh. No way. But it's so lovely to talk to you. What ever made you think to call me? We gonna do that lunch we always talk about?"

Lia sighed at the forced cheerfulness in Amanda's voice.

"I'd love that," Lia said, giving up. "Let's set it up. But first, I was hoping you could give me some information."

"Uh, huh," Amanda's voice was skeptical.

"Oh! Not about Peter, about Desiree Willis."

"You mean that poor child who was shot a week ago? You knew her, didn't you?"

"How did you know that?"

"Something Heckle and Jeckle said while they were here for the autopsy."

"Do I even want to know?"

"No, probably not."

128

"Tell me anyway. I promise, if I decide to shoot anyone, it won't be you."

"I just heard some snickering. I think it was 'I wonder if Dourson ever did both of them at the same time.' No names, but I just this minute put it together."

Lia's jaw dropped. She said nothing.

"That wasn't all of it. I guess I'll give you the rest, but don't you come after me if you don't like it. Heckle said that first bit, then Jeckle says, 'too bad she's dead. The way Cynth is hanging on him, he could've had himself a real party.' Do you know anyone named Cynth?"

"Oh, God, Amanda," Lia said.

"Look, now, don't you regard anything those two creeps say. I'm sure if I hadn't been watching, one of them would have felt that poor girl up. Nobody listens to them. Forget I said it. What can I help you with?"

Lia stammered, trying to remember why she called. "I've been looking online for information about a funeral for Desiree and I can't find any. I was hoping you could tell me where the body went so I could call the funeral home."

"You can't find anything about a funeral because that body is still sitting here. Her father, and I do use that term very loosely, refuses to have anything to do with it. Fine by me. No girl deserves to be spit on by her father when she's dead."

"He *spit* on her?"

"Right in the face. Identification is supposed to be done by video, has been ever since that creep, Thomas Condon, photographed corpses without permission and tried to call it art. Well, Mr. Willis complains that he can't see her properly on the screen because of his cataracts, and says he needs to see the body. So I let him in back and he walks up to her and leans over and spits. He was chewing tobacco, too. Looks me right in the eye and says he'd been waiting years for that very moment, and it's the only reason he agreed to come in. I told him to get out before I had him arrested for desecrating a corpse. He sneers at me and says, 'Thou shalt not suffer a witch to live.' Sprayed me good while he said it. I had to change my scrubs."

"I'm speechless."

"You obviously aren't since you just said that, but I understand the feeling."

"What happens to her now?"

"If I can't find someone to take her off my hands, the county will dispose of her. We're supposed to be hunting up her friends, but we've been swamped lately."

"So anyone could just come in and take her?"

"It's not as easy as that. They'd have to be vetted first. We have to document all attempts to locate the proper person, and then there's a waiting period. It takes weeks. It would be better if she'd appointed someone her designated agent, then there wouldn't be any question about their right to the body, but I can't imagine that happening, her being so young. Still, she should have had one with the father she had."

"Designated agent? How does that work?"

"If you're concerned about who will wind up making your funeral arrangements, you assign someone, and you fill out a designated agent form."

"Wouldn't someone know if they'd been assigned?"

"That would be the polite thing to do, but not necessarily. Desiree's signature needs to be notarized with two witnesses. She might have left it in her belongings, if she had one. Fat chance finding it. I understand the landlord dumped all her things."

"I think I can help you with that," Lia said.

"For real?"

Julia followed Lia back and forth as she gathered her tools. The Beagle was exhibiting signs of separation anxiety, not wanting to let Lia out of her sight. It was bothersome, nearly tripping over the dog everywhere she went, but she could understand Julia's fears. "Can't send you to therapy. Maybe a session with Louella is the next best thing."

Lia sat at her drawing table and Julia curled under her chair. The table was equipped with a thin bamboo skewer, a dental probe she'd used during a bronze casting class and a pair of tweezers. Next to these lay her camera. The Lia doll sat on a clean sheet of butcher paper under a faux-vintage magnifying glass on a stand. She'd bought the magnifier because it looked cool, never dreaming she'd have a use for it.

She started by taking photographs of the doll from all angles, using the macro setting on her camera. It seemed such a shame to destroy it, but it was better to know if there was something malevolent tucked inside. At least she could preserve it through pictures.

She gently pushed the torso and legs down, so that the little woman lay spread-eagled under the lens. It made her some how uneasy, as if she were about to skewer herself on a pin like a butterfly. The arms, legs and body were twisted, she suspected to help the foil hold it's shape.

Delicately, she untwisted the appendages and the torso. These lengthened as the material uncoiled. Where she found an edge of folded in on itself, she slid her dental probe underneath to loosen it.

The head appeared to be rolled rather than coiled. She marveled at the light touch Foil Man must have used, to maintain an unblemished silver sheen on the face, without any ugly crimping. She used the tip of the bamboo skewer to tease the ball apart.

The head slowly unrolled, unfurled, unfolded until she was left with nothing except a single strip of foil which extended from the body. She went back to the arms and legs and continued there. Each revealed itself to be nothing more than foil, cleverly twisted. Lia-doll now lay like a mutant starfish under the magnifier. If she held any secrets, they lay in her heart. Lia continued to tease the foil apart, swapping the skewer for the probe when she encountered tightly crimped bits. The tip of her probe hit something solid between the layers. A few more tugs revealed a tiny red heart. She caught a whiff of cinnamon.

Lia sat back, stunned. She hadn't expected to find anything. Still, a candy heart was pretty innocuous. She peered closer. Something marred the surface of the candy. It looked scratched. She angled the magnifier, bringing the red candy into focus. "831" was scratched into the face of the heart. She tipped it over. "ICU" was etched into the back. ICU. Well either that meant intensive care unit and was some kind of threat, or it meant she was being watched. Which was another kind of threat. What could 831 refer to?

She opened up her laptop and searched the Urban Dictionary. "Monterey Bay area code." No, that couldn't be it. "831 Eight letters, three words, one meaning. I love you." Could Peter have left this? No, she decided. Peter didn't have the skill and he wouldn't have been so tasteless, considering her concerns.

She double checked ICU to see if there were any additional meanings. "IcU" meant "I'm cool. You?" She wondered if ICU meant the Foil Man wanted to give her intensive care. Whatever, with the engraving, the little doll and her canine escort had morphed from charming to creepy.

Lia leaned over. Julia lifted her head up off her paws, meeting Lia's gaze with solemn bug-eyes. "You be sure to bark if anyone comes near, okay? I don't need any creeps sneaking in here. Biting's okay, too, especially if it's someone you recognize. Deal?"

Julia tilted her head, blinked, and lay back down, sighing as if there were no light left in the world. Chewy bounced up, his paws on Lia's thigh, giving her an intent look that typically meant, "What am I, chopped liver?"

Lia set down her bamboo skewer and ruffled his ears with her hands. Holding his face, she bent over and gave him a kiss on the nose. Not much for kisses, he jerked his head away and sneezed, then play-snapped at her hands. "You're still my little man. You know that, don't you?" Satisfied that all was still well with his world despite the clingy interloper's morose outlook, he returned to napping on his bed in the living room.

Cinnamon hearts . . . she'd seen some recently, maybe, but where? She didn't even walk down the candy aisle when she went grocery shopping. Most of the candy she'd run into lately was at Scholastic. Could one of her co-workers be Foil Man? She tried to visualize the various candy caches around Maple room. While she liked chocolate, she didn't go in for other sweets, so she hadn't paid much attention. She'd have to keep her eyes out on Monday when she went back.

The Watcher grunted at the stationary dot on his GPS program. Lia hadn't gone anywhere since she'd returned from the park. He could not think of a pretext for getting a spy cam into her apartment, or a cam that he could sneak in that she wouldn't notice.

He wondered what she would think if she found out he'd pulled the tracking device off Desiree's car and installed it on Lia's Volvo. This time he was not satisfied with casually sticking it under a wheel well. He'd crawled under the car and attached it to the undercarriage behind the gas tank, where it wouldn't be seen unless the car was up on a rack.

It might not occur to Lia that he had followed Desiree and was now following her. If it did, he did not want her to find The Watcher's little helper.

He turned back to the sheet of foil laying on his desk, smooth, shiny, pristine, and stroked it delicately, lover-like, with one finger. *I wonder what you will become. -*

# Chapter 16

## Sunday, June 1

"I don't know why we've never been in here before," Bailey said to Lia as she pushed open the door to the dim bar.

"Maybe because you get up at 4 a.m. and I rarely drink? Good thing The Comet is open for brunch on Sunday."

They stood in line at the end of the bar and considered the options on the chalkboard menu. "Eggs Benedict? Quiche?" Bailey said. "I was expecting a breakfast burrito."

"I guess they class up on Sundays," Lia said.

A man with black hipster glasses and well tended gray hair past his shoulders wrote down their order. He tore off the top copy and handed it to Lia. "Take this to the kitchen. They'll hand you a marker for your table." He got their coffees. "Cream and sugar in the next room, in front."

Lia and Bailey were almost through with their meal and discussing the merits of sharing a flan When Lia looked up to see Dave approaching, bar towel in hand.

"Hey, welcome back," he said. "How's your quesadilla?"

"Terrific. I wish you were open for lunch all the time. Dave, this is Bailey. We're hoping you might help us with something."

"Shoot. Never know till you ask."

"I talked to the coroner's office yesterday. They said Desiree's father refused to take her body, and it's just sitting in the morgue."

Dave shook his head. "Desiree said her father frequently told her she was going to hell. He sounded like a total head case."

"I'm looking for someone close to her to step up and take possession of the body."

"Why don't you do it?"

Lia stammered. "I really didn't know her that well. I wouldn't know what she wanted or who was important to her. I'm traveling blind here."

"So how does this work? Can anyone just walk in and claim her body?"

"I guess you could if you made a good enough case to the coroner that you were her nearest and dearest. It's a long process, though, and it would take weeks.

"The person I talked to at the morgue said there was a slim chance Desiree had a designated agent form." Understanding by Dave's expression that he was as clueless about this as she had been, she went on to explain. ". . . so tomorrow I'm going through her papers to see if I can find one. But I thought I'd stop in here and ask about her friends, in case I come up empty."

"I'm glad you stopped in. I'll put the word out and see if we can't dig up the right person to take charge. I'd be glad to help you search. I'm off tomorrow."

"That would be a godsend. No one else is available, and this needs to be resolved."

"Once we find this person, did you have any idea how her funeral would be paid for?"

"I hadn't gotten that far yet. Truthfully, I hoped to find Desiree's BFF and end my involvement there."

"Desiree wasn't exactly a BFF kinda gal. But don't worry, we'll think of something."

Lia and Bailey left the bar an hour later.

"You know," Bailey mused, "you wouldn't think ginger-ale would go with eggs, but it does."

Lia stopped on the side walk. "Okay, what's wrong with him."

"What are you talking about?" Bailey asked.

"An attractive, single man sat at our table for half an hour and you haven't said anything about him."

"You mean the guy carrying a torch for Miss Double D, A.K.A. Dead Desiree?"

"Yeah, that one. Don't you want to soothe his wounded heart?"

"Oh, I figured you could have him."

"Me? Why would I want him?"

"I figure you need a distraction since Peter's decided to take a vacation. Anyway, he didn't know I was there."

"That's not true."

"Which part? That you need a distraction, that Peter's on vacation, or that Dave Cunningham only had eyes for you? You may not have been paying attention, but I was."

# Chapter 17

**Monday, June 2**

Dave was leaning on his car by Terry's storage unit when Lia pulled up. Lia opened the lock and lifted the door. The garage-sized unit was packed with furniture and stacks of boxes that towered over their heads.

"All this was Desiree's?"

Lia laughed at his astonished look. "Only a small corner is hers. Most of it belongs to the guy who owns this unit. We need to go through that pile of boxes over on the right."

The indicated boxes were penned in by an upended sofa and stacked dining room chairs. They worked in tandem to move the furniture out of the unit, opening up space to spread the boxes out.

"If I'd known I was getting back in these boxes so soon, I would not have let Terry talk me into blocking them in like that," Lia said between grunts as they tipped the monstrous sofa over and carried it out. They plopped down on the sofa, never minding the seat cushions were still on top of an old depression era armoire.

"I could use something cold to drink right about now," Dave said as he wiped sweat off his forehead with his sleeve.

"They have a Coke machine at the office. What's your poison? My treat."

"Coke or Pepsi. I prefer Coke. Unless they have Red Bull."

"Coming up." Lia drove to the other side of the storage facility, got a can of Coke and chose an ice tea for herself. When she got back, she saw that Dave had pulled the first stack of boxes down and was now placing them outside the unit.

"I went though this batch. Mostly dishes and books. Looks like it was packed in a hurry. Shame the boxes aren't marked."

"We didn't have much time. If we'd left it up to the landlady, it would all have gone out on the curb."

"I'm glad you were able to save it then." He popped the tab on his soda can and took a long pull. The way he tilted his head back, the way his throat contracted as he drank, it reminded her of Peter and had her fingers itching to reach out and stroke the long line from his chin to his clavicle. She shoved the thought away, annoyed by the wistful impulse.

He wiped off his mouth. "Tell you what. I'll pull the boxes down and you go through them. Then we can shove them out of the way so we don't confuse ourselves."

"Sounds like a plan."

Lia sat on her heels as she opened the third box, finding a mess of papers on top of a half-dozen Beanie Babies. She recalled gathering the pile up off the floor and shoving it in a box, counter to Terry's insistence that he didn't have room in his storage unit for garbage. "We don't have time to figure out what's garbage and what's not. We can always throw it out later if it's not important. This is Desiree's life, what's left of it, anyway."

She pawed through unopened junk mail, advertising circulars, some bills. Digging a little deeper, she unearthed a copy of the insurance policy for Desiree's car. Under that lay a plain, white envelope she didn't remember. The flap was tucked instead of sealed. She opened it, withdrawing the thin stack of paper. The pads of her fingers rubbed against the bumps of a notary seal.

Lia had figured this afternoon to be a necessary exercise in futility. Stunned by her unlikely find, she unfolded the paper and scanned it. Dave turned away from the pile of boxes to read over her shoulder.

As she scanned the paper, her excitement grew: *I, Desiree Willis, an adult being of sound mind, willfully and voluntarily appoint my representative, named below, to have the right of disposition, as defined in section 2108.70 of the Revised Code, for my body upon my death. All decisions . . . .*

"I don't believe this! I can't believe we found it." She continue reading, her eyes racing back and forth. Then they fell on a name and stopped. Lia sighed and shook her head, poked her tongue in her cheek.

"What's the problem?" Dave asked.

"Do you really expect me to believe this?"

"Believe what? That Desiree would want a responsible, business-owning friend to care for her after she died?"

"Let me guess. The notary is your cousin, Vinnie. The witnesses owe you money and you traced Desiree's signature off of a cancelled paycheck. You stuffed it in that box while I was getting your coke. Fast work, Cunningham."

"You wound me."

"Yeah, I see the blood."

"Think they'll buy it?"

"If I don't tell Amanda that you helped me find it. I'm sure she'll be so delighted to have official paperwork taking this off her hands, that she won't check to see if the ink is actually dry."

"I'll owe you one."

"You're asking me to lie to a friend about a felony, and it could get her in trouble."

"The coroner is your *friend*?" His eyebrows shot up. "Assistant coroner."

"I'll owe you two, then."

"Help me up. My legs are stiff." She extended the hand that wasn't holding the felonious document. He pulled her up and she limped over to the sofa, picked up the now-warm half-can of tea. Dave plopped down beside her. He watched her while she considered.

"Dave, what's your investment in this? Why did you go to all this trouble?"

He shrugged, looking down at his hands draped between his knees. He gave her a wry look. "I always had a soft spot for Desiree."

"You and everyone else," Lia grumbled.

"Oh, I think everyone else had a hard-spot, if you don't mind me saying. She was a good kid, trying to find her way. She would have found it, too, if she hadn't been shot."

"Were you in love with her?"

His head drooped. "I figured once she grew out of her taste for pretty bad boys, she might realize I'd always been there for her. It'll never happen now."

"I'm so sorry."

"I'd like to do her justice. She had friends at the bar. Last night I started a collection to pay for a cremation. We can have a memorial service. You decided what you want to do with all that?" He nodded towards Desiree's now-scattered belongings.

"We were thinking of selling it at the Northside garage sale in August and donating the money to Three Sisters Rescue. That's where she got Julia. Why? Do you have something in mind?"

"I'm sure she didn't have a will, though I guess we'll need to go through all this to make sure. I imagine her friends would like a chance to have something of hers. We can have a silent auction at the bar during the memorial, give the proceeds to charity. We'd raise more money that way than at a garage sale."

Lia blinked. "Well," she said. "I guess that's worth lying for."

"I was only trying to give you plausible deniability."

"You couldn't have put someone else's name on there?"

"Let another man have the body of the love of my life I'll never have? I don't think so."

Lia tucked the document in the glove box of her Volvo. They resumed combing the boxes, now looking for a will. Ninety minutes and a couple of overly sloppy Big Bufords from Ralley's later, they completed the job of unearthing every piece of paper and relegating it to the status of Not-Desiree's-Will.

Lia looked around at the foraged boxes strewn across the concrete like shipwrecked flotsam. "Oh, goody. Now we get to put it all back. Let's sit down for a few. I'd like to let my sweat dry so I can layer fresh new sweat over the old when we start up again."

"Shall we label the boxes as we put them back?"

"What's the point? We didn't pack her things in any particular order, just grabbed what was closest and jammed it in a box. I guess we'll get to organize it when we get it back out for the auction. You really going to have a silent auction, with all her undies in it?"

Dave twisted his mouth."I don't know about that. I'm sure there are people who would buy them, but I'd feel funny about it. So what do we do with them?"

"I'll ask Bailey. She'll know."

Lia stopped by Avery's desk on the way to her work station that evening. The transparent sides of a pyrex mixing bowl (courtesy of his wife, she imagined) revealed a kaleidoscope of sugar: Dum Dums, Smarties, miniature Tootsie Rolls, saltwater taffy, and little cellophane packets of cinnamon candies. She dug her hand in and pulled one out. Red Hots. Not hearts. Darn.

"Lia, I'm so glad you stopped by," Avery said, dropping a stack of files on his desk and taking his chair. "Is there any word about Desiree's funeral?"

"There isn't a date yet. It's probably going to be a simple memorial service after a private cremation. By the way, thank you for taking up that collection. Three Sisters really appreciates the donation."

"Of course, of course. This may only be seasonal work, but you're still family to us. Such a beautiful girl. Such a shame." He sighed, then opened the top file. Avery spotted the little bag of candies in her hand. "You like cinnamon candy? I thought Ted was the only one around here besides me who did. He's been gradually making his way through my store of them."

"Cinnamon is a brain booster," Lia said lamely.

Avery looked up and gave her an assessing look. He stretched lips in an oily smile.

"I was not aware. Maybe we should hand it out to everyone."

Lia swept both sides of the aisle with her eyes as she made her way back to her team, scoping out the bowls and tupperware containers of candy. She spotted the usual sweet potpourri, but no more Red Hots. *I could be going about this the wrong way. Maybe I should sniff everyone's breath at break time to see who smells like cinnamon.*
So that kept Avery and Ted on her list. Perhaps she would leave the little packet out by her monitor and see if he commented on them.

# Chapter 18

**Tuesday, June 3**

"I feel like Dr. Watson in drag," Bailey said as she and Lia crossed Telford on the way to A. Vasari, "tailing along with you while you snoop. You really think the old guy had anything to do with it?"

"Peter said in police work, it's more important to be thorough than smart. Which explains how Heckle and Jeckle keep their jobs. It's important not to have preconceived notions about who is or isn't likely to commit a crime. He also said most people will commit a crime or even kill someone, under the right circumstances. The motivation just has to be powerful enough to overcome their self-imposed limits. That's why you try to learn as much as you can about everyone and everything in a victim's life."

"What about her father? He sounds like a real gem with his 'thou shalt not suffer a witch to live' BS."

"I feel safe in saying he didn't do it."

"Why not? He sounds like he's crazy enough to murder someone."

"He probably is. But he spit on her."

"So? That just makes him crazier."

"He said he'd been waiting years to spit on her dead body. If he'd killed her, he would have done it then, and he would not have done it in front of the coroner because it might give him away. And if he did spit on her both times, from what she said, he's not smart enough to come up with something as subtle as saying he'd been waiting to do it."

"Don't you think you should talk to him anyway? He might know things that could help."

"He's not likely to tell them to a woman. That's why Terry is going."

"Makes sense."

"We're just waiting until we have info about the memorial service, and Terry's going to pretend that we don't know her dad hated her and refused to take the body. All we know is Desiree wanted Dave to take care of it."

"Smart thinking."

Lia opened the door to Desiree's former place of employment. "Bailey, what does this remind you of?"

Bailey wrinkled her brow as she considered the barrister cases glowing in the dim recesses of the store. "The snake house at the zoo?"

"That's what I thought."

"Ups the creep factor, even if it does show off the jewelry. Maybe he did do it."

Alfonso Vasari attended a customer at the back of his store when jangling bells on the door alerted him to Lia and Bailey's arrival. He peered at them, frowning, then appeared to remember Lia. "You again? You ever find that no-good girl?"

A Clifton matron took her bag and passed Lia and Bailey on her way out of the store, giving them a bland, practiced smile.

Alfonso eyed Lia as she approached. "You don't look too good."

"Mr. Vasari, I'm sorry to tell you, Desiree was murdered 11 days ago."

"Murdered? Little Desi?" His face paled and he sat down hard on the stool behind the counter. "Who did this?"

"The police don't know. They suspect she came home and walked in on a burglar."

"A burglar. . . . Poor Desi." He shook his head mournfully. "Such a world that a pretty girl gets killed for being in her own home."

Lia felt pity for the old man, who now undoubtably felt guilty for his ill thoughts about Desiree. "They're having a memorial service for her at The Comet. Would you like me to let you know when I get the details?"

"You're a good girl, to think of me. You do that. Is there anything I can do?"

"I was hoping for some information. Desiree kept several little dolls made of aluminum foil, but they weren't in her apartment. We were wondering if she left them here."

"Those little dolls? I saw her little dolls, but I don't think she left them here. Lonzo!" he yelled into the back. "Come out here." He turned back to the women. "Lonzo does her job now. If they're here, he would see them."

A tall twenty-something man with dark, tousled hair that was a shade too scruffy to be sexy came out of the workroom. "What is it, Pop?" He eyed Lia and Bailey under heavy lids. *I bet he thinks he's irresistible.*

"Little Desi. She had those tiny dolls made out of foil. Are they around?"

"Dolls?" his lip curled. "No dolls. What do you want with that trash."

"I don't think it's trash to Desi's friends. Did you throw them out?"

"No, Pop, honest. You need anything else? I got work to do."

"Not right now. We'll talk later." Vasari Jr. ducked into the back as Vasari Sr. turned back to the women. "I'm sorry we couldn't help." He squinted at Lia, beetling his brows. "Your amethyst pendant. It's very nice."

"This?" Lia touched the stone laying against her chest. "It's unusual, isn't it? It was Desiree's."

"She give that to you?"

"I found it when I was clearing out her apartment. Do you know anything about it?"

"It's old. Worth a few dollars, not much more. A hundred years ago, amethyst was precious. Not now."

"I was hoping it was valuable. We're having a silent auction of some of Desiree's things at the memorial, so people who knew her could have a memento and to raise money for charity. We're selling it then." She stroked the stone, wishing she could keep it.

"I would like a memento of Desi. You sell me the necklace? It would be nice to remember her by. I'll give you fifty dollars for your charity."

"Come to the auction. You might find something else you like even better. I'll let you know as soon as the date is set."

"You do that. I'll be there."

"What a nice old man," Bailey said as the door to A. Vasari shut behind them. "He really cared about her. I thought you said he was a grouch."

"He sure was last time I was here. Shame her own father doesn't care about her like that."

"So why didn't you give him the pendant?"

"He's a jeweler. What would he do with it besides give it to a woman who never met Desiree, or reset it and sell it? I want to be sure the person who buys it values it for its connection to Desiree. "Plus," she added as she stroked the purple stone, "I like it."

"You think people will love us this much when we're dead?"

"Who knows, Bailey. I hope so."

# Chapter 19

**Wednesday, June 4**

Honey whined and strained towards Lia's apartment as she juggled leashes and keys. Chewy jumped up, scrabbling his claws against the wood while Julia wrapped herself around Lia's legs.

"Brats. Hooligans. I'll feed you if you just let me open the door. Sit, Chewy."

Lia reassured herself that her Schnauzer hadn't damaged the door, then untangled Julia's leash from around her legs so Julia wouldn't pull her off her feet in the rush to get inside.

"What's wrong with you today?" she scolded.

Once the door was unlocked, Julia nosed it open then bolted. The leash tore out of Lia's hand as Julia raced for the bedroom. Before Lia could unclip Honey and Chewy, Julia trotted back, dragging a freshly laundered tank top. She dropped the tank on the floor and rolled over, squirming her back on it.

"Julia!" Lia admonished. "Where did you get that?" She took possession of the top and stalked into the bedroom to toss it in the hamper.

Chaos greeted her. The contents of her dresser were in a pile on the floor, and all the drawers hung open. The mattress and bedding had been dragged halfway off the box-springs. Her jewelry box was upended on her dresser.

She retreated from the wreckage and went into her bathroom. Toiletries lay in the sink, the cabinet shelves empty. Back in the living room she was confronted by the heap of cotton batting, entrails from eviscerated throw pillows. Her lovely collection of hand-made throw pillows: quilted, embroidered, painted, sequined. Accumulated over years. Gifts from far-away loved ones and fellow artists. Her emotional history, gutted.

Lia stumbled into the kitchen and dropped onto the nearest chair, stupefied. Glassy eyes struggled to take in the open cupboard doors, the contents of her drawers dumped in the sink. The only sounds were the distressed whines of her dogs as they gathered around, sniffing her as if her distress had its own, unfamiliar odor. She collapsed, wrapping her arms around Honey for support, taking comfort in the Golden's silky fur as Honey nosed her face, licking her wet cheeks to reassure her.

Officer Hinkle responded to her 911 call. Lia was thankful to see Cal Hinkle, an earnest young officer who was barely out of rookie status. Lia liked that he was polite and respectful. Peter said Cal barely scraped through the academy. Despite his deficiencies, nobody wanted the job more than Cal, and nobody worked harder.

More importantly, he was not Heckle or Jeckle, whose questionable competence as police officers, she was convinced, was based on their ability to think like the thugs they pursued.

Lia spotted honest concern on his pudgy, freckled face as he stood on her porch and immediately felt better. She attempted a half-smile as she opened the door. It came out as a grimace, then fell with a thud, like free weights on the last rep of a long workout.

"Hi, Lia, sorry we're meeting again this way," he said. He removed his cap as he entered her apartment, which made his hair stick up. He ran a hand through it, increasing its untidiness. Lia thought of hay and forced herself to curb the urge to smooth it down. If it had been anyone but

Hinkle, she would have said something. Hinkle was too easily embarrassed.

"Can you tell me what happened?" he asked, drawing her attention back to her current situation.

"I just got back from the dog park and found it like this." She walked him through the shambles her apartment had become.

"How long were you gone?"

Lia added up the time in her head. "About ninety minutes. It's like he knew exactly when to do it. Any other time, the dogs would be here."

"You think the dogs would go after a burglar?"

"I don't know. I've never been burgled before."

Hinkle rubbed his chin. "Maybe he tried before and couldn't get in because the dogs wouldn't let him. Then he'd know to wait until you were gone. I bet he's been watching you. He made good use of a very narrow window of opportunity."

Lia stared, having not considered this. "I guess I've been stupid."

"What's missing?" Hinkle asked tactfully, changing the subject.

"I don't know if anything is missing. I won't know until I put everything back."

He examined the doors. "No sign of forced entry. Anyone else have a key?"

"Only Peter."

"Right. Is he on his way?" Lia examined his face, but saw no sign that he was in on the gossip at District Five.

"I haven't called him yet."

Hinkle nodded but didn't comment. The gesture was weighty, serious. "Have you checked your windows?"

Lia frowned. "I didn't think to check." She led Hinkle on another tour of her apartment, this time examining the windows. The tour ended in her studio. She lifted the bamboo blind hanging over the window next to her easel. The window gaped wide, reminding Lia of Munch's "The

149

Scream." Or maybe it was MacCauly Culkin in *Home Alone*. Whatever. She briefly imagined herself letting loose with histrionics that she would never allow herself, pounding on the floor and screaming obscenities until her throat was sore.

"Oh," She said.

"You normally lock this window?"

Lia said "no" in a tiny voice. "I leave this window open for the air circulation when I'm painting. I didn't think it was a problem because it's over eight feet off the ground."

Hinkle peered out the window, eyed the bent and broken branches in the ancient lilac bush just outside. "Looks like your visitor used your bush to boost himself up. You might want to trim that back."

"Oh," she said again.

"I'm going to look around your yard, knock on a few doors, see if anyone saw anything. When you figure out what's missing, call me at this number and I'll add it to the report." He handed her his card. "You don't want to be alone with this mess. Is anyone on their way to help you?"

"I hadn't thought that far ahead, but I have someone I can call."

She watched him checking the outside of her house. *He really is a nice guy. Shame the other cops give him such a hard time.*

Bailey arrived twenty minutes later. She breezed in the door and made a quick circuit of the apartment. When she reached the bedroom, she stopped dead, staring at the mayhem. She shook her head. "I thought we were friends. I can't believe you threw a party and didn't invite me."

Lia flopped down on the exposed box springs and groaned.

# Chapter 20

The tiny woman reclined on her side, her head propped on one hand as she leafed through a book. Long hair swept around her neck to pour forward over one lowered shoulder, forming a curtain that partially hid her face. The book had individual pages and was pierced and bound with thread. Her long hair was accompanied by a slender build, like that of the librarian looming over the silver doll behind the counter where it lay.

Kathy Bach's eyes glowed. "Delightful, isn't it? It always gives me pleasure to look at her. Is this the kind of thing you were referring to?"

The break-in spurred Lia to search for Foil Man. She didn't know if he was responsible, but action distracted her and made her feel in control. She started at the library where he'd uploaded the video onto YouTube, hoping for a lead of some kind; a name, a memory, something. When she approached the head librarian at Westwood she hadn't been expecting to encounter another of Foil Man's creations.

"It's lovely. The posture is so expressive. Where did you get it?" She worked to suppress the frisson of uneasy excitement that materialized when Kathy produced the little figure. *Keep it light. Keep it friendly.*

"A patron gave it to me, a bit over a year ago."

"Do you remember who it was?" Lia asked.

"Of course. That was Ernest. He was one of our oddities."

"What do you mean?"

"I had the sense that he had been homeless at one time. He always wore several layers of clothes, even in the summer. He rode a bike that had been painted like a kind of folk art sculpture, and it had a big wire basket on it. He was always carrying around bundles of Heaven knows what.

"You said you were from Northside. I imagine you see a lot of that sort of thing down there. Westwood is very conservative by comparison. He stood out, but he was always clean and very polite and never bothered anyone."

Lia's anticipation grew. She could feel her heart beating.

"Do you know where I could find him?"

The woman shook her head. "He got sick about a year ago, then he stopped coming in. Sue," she called to the sturdy woman at the other checkout terminal, "do you remember Ernie's last name?"

Sue, a large woman with a pale Dutch-boy haircut, tapped her teeth with a pencil. "It was something German, I think. Muller, that was it."

Margie began pressing keys on her computer. "We're not supposed to give out patron information, but since it's about his little foil people, I'm sure he'd want you to know. . . . Here we go." She handed Lia a piece of paper. "It's on Lischer Ave. Go out the front to Epworth and turn right. It's two blocks down."

"Thank you so much."

"Just don't tell anyone. You either, Sue."

Sue pursed her lips and sternly said, "I know noh-zing," in her best Sergeant Shultz. Lia thought Sue looked like Shultz as well, including the pale hint of a mustache.

The cozy Craftsman-style house featured immaculately groomed iris beds and a neatly edged walkway leading to the deep front porch. The house exuded warmth and care, and she approved of the dark teal paint. The door-bell announced her with a Westminster chime, a pair of high-pitched Yorkies harmonizing on the other side of the beveled glass side-lights while they skidded around on wood floors polished to a high sheen. The woman who answered the door reminded Lia of a young Shirley McLaine, with a wispy red pixie cut and an open expression.

"Shhhh, Rocky, Bullwinkle, we have company. Hush! What can I do for you?"

"I'm looking for Ernie Muller. I'm told he lives here?"

"No, I'm afraid not. We've been here since last September. I don't know of an Ernie in this neighborhood. Are you sure you have the right address?" Her voice was friendly, tentative.

"This is the address he had on record. Perhaps he lived here before you?"

"I wouldn't know. The woman we bought the house from was not living here, and it was vacant when we looked at it. You might try Mrs. Glassner next door, she's been in the neighborhood forever." She indicated the red brick on her right. "I'm sure you'll find her in, she hardly ever goes out."

Lia thanked the woman and made her way to the other house. The septuagenarian who answered the door looked frail, but her eyes were as bright as Alma's. The involuntary comparison had her feeling guilty for all the time she was taking from the convalescent center. She mentally vowed to do better.

"Mrs. Glassner? My name is Lia Anderson. I'm looking for information about Ernie Muller. Your neighbor thought you might be able to help me."

"Ernie? My goodness, come in." She opened the door wide. "Ernie's been gone since last summer. Come, sit down. Would you like something to drink?"

Lia followed her into the kitchen. "A glass of water would be very nice."

153

Mrs. Glassner poured Lia's water and the two women sat. The plate Mrs. Glassner pushed at her was piled with pale cookies dusted with confectioner's sugar. "You have to have some of these so I don't eat them all. I love to bake, but treats are so bad for me."

Lia took a bite of cookie, tart lemon dancing across her tongue. "These are wonderful. What did you mean about Ernie being gone? Did he move, or has he passed away?"

"Oh, he passed. Emphysema," she confided. "He was only sixty-four, but he'd lived outside too long before his sister talked him into staying next door. That war," she shook her head. "It was no good for anyone, and some never recovered. Ernie was one of those. PTSD. Lived outside, homeless, for years, as if he didn't have any family to care about him. Beth finally convinced him to come back home after his mother died. He grew up in that house, so it was familiar to him."

She nodded out the wide kitchen window into the back yard. A bike that could only be Ernie's was parked on the grass, petunias spilling from the panniers and front basket. "My granddaughter, Liz, she loves the craziest things. When Ernie didn't come home from that last trip to the VA hospital, she asked Beth if she could have the bike to make a planter. She always liked Ernie."

"I don't understand. If he was so sick, how did he manage that house?"

"Oh, that wasn't him, that was Watcher."

"Watcher?"

"Creepy name, isn't it. And he looked it, too. Creepy, I mean. I never knew what his real name was and I don't know why Ernie called him that. Maybe because he looked after Ernie when they were on the street. When Ernie came inside, he wanted Watcher to come with him. Beth wasn't too keen on it, but her son checked with the Homeless Association. They said he was okay, so Beth gave in.

"Looked a fright, all those dreadlocks and that beard, but he was always making the loveliest little dolls out of bits of foil and giving them away. Liz has a dozen of them—I never left her alone with him, you understand, though he never was anything but polite. Ernie said Watcher used to trade the dolls for food and such when they were on the street."

"Do you have any of them?"

"The dolls? Liz might have one or two in her room, the one she uses when she stays here. That's up on the second floor. I don't do steps so well anymore. If you like, you can go look. Second door on your right."

The little room was sunny, with a white, wrought-iron daybed topped with a menagerie of pastel animals: unicorns, bears, a floppy-eared dog. She found The Watcher's Lilliputian offerings on top of a French Provincial dresser. These were meant to appeal to a young girl. A deer grazing, a clown, a pair of ballet dancers in a pas de deux.

Photographs loomed behind the small figures. Three generations of women: Liz, at various ages from three to sixteen or eighteen; Mrs. Glassner, and the woman Lia presumed linked them, Liz's mother. Lia was thoughtful as she returned to the kitchen.

"Lovely things, aren't they?" Mrs. Glassner asked.

"Very. Were you ever afraid of him? Was he ever inappropriate with your Granddaughter?"

"Afraid? Of Watcher? Oh, no. Ernie was the one that could be strange if he didn't take his medication. Turned out to be a godsend, having someone to look after Ernie. He made sure Ernie took his pills and ate and had clean clothes. Beth didn't like the idea of that young man living off Ernie's disability, but Watcher took good care of him."

Lia frowned. She was having a hard time seeing the young man who took care of a dying, mentally-ill veteran as Desiree's deranged stalker. Perhaps losing Ernie affected him in some way.

"Do you remember what he looked like?"

"Taller than me, but that's everybody. As I said, those dreadlocks and a beard that hung down on his chest. Couldn't see much of his face, all that hair."

"Mrs. Glassner, what happened to Watcher?"

"I honestly couldn't say. Beth put the house up for sale right after Ernie died. She might know."

Mrs. Glassner wouldn't let her leave without a packet of lemon cookies and an invitation to drop by any time. Lia resolved to invite her to the reception for her murals when they were finished. Who knew? The woman might make some new friends at the center.

Beth Harding answered the phone on the second ring. It took her exactly seventy seconds to tell Lia that Watcher vanished when Ernie died, she did not know where he was and had no desire to find out.

# Chapter 21

**Friday, June 6**

"I don't know why I didn't think of this before," Lia told Terry as they walked down 12th Street. "I led a public service project to paint their facade a few years ago. Seven high schools collaborated. You'll see in a minute."

"If you've been here before, why do you need me along?"

"The clientele is unpredictable. You never know what you'll walk in on."

"Ah, I am your armed escort."

"Forget armed. Escort is plenty. I'm less likely to be hassled if I have someone with me. Whatever happens, do *not* pull your gun."

They could see the colorful facade a block away. The storefront windows had been replaced with painted plywood panels featuring helping hands, military dog-tags, food, home, a woman bursting through barb-wire, and other symbols of security and empowerment. "These were all created by high school students. I coordinated with each school and led brainstorming sessions."

"It's quite . . . cacophonous, don't you think?"

"The director liked the idea of being impossible to ignore."

"A noble effort ably achieved."

As they neared the door, Lia could hear yelling from inside.

"Egad. Should we proceed?" Terry asked, hesitating in front of the door.

"I don't want to stand out here on the street. They're used to this. Come on. Just remember what I said, and let them handle it."

"I hope you have one hand on your kubotan."

Lia pushed the door open.

". . . I am an American, a citizen of the U. S. of freaking A. You got no right to throw me out of here!" The man was tall, gangly and odiferous. He curled his long body over the high counter into the face of a round, bald man sporting a well-trimmed, white goatee. Lia remembered his name was Steve. She didn't understand how the man could stay calm while spittle flew in his face.

"Sure I do. You can't be in here when you're yelling like that. You know the rules." The bald man had a voice that was high and gravelly. Lia marveled at the way he kept his composure.

"My right to say what I want is constitutionally protected! You can't do this to me. I got rights." He stabbed the counter with a knobby finger graced with a ragged, grimy nail.

Terry stepped up to the counter. "Sir, free speech as protected by the Constitution only applies to public places. This is a private non-profit, and therefore exempt. You, my friend, have no rights here."

"You got that right!" the gangly man yelled.

"Who the hell are you?" Steve asked Terry, raising his voice for the first time. "You're not helping, Buddy." He turned back to his abuser. "Leave now, Leon, or I *will* call 911." Steve had been joined by a co-worker who stood arms crossed, impassively eyeing Leon.

"Go ahead and call them, you can't make me go. You, neither, Gloria," he hissed at the woman.

Steve picked up the phone and tapped out three digits. He rolled his eyes and began talking quietly into the phone. Leon stuck a hand in his pocket. He tensed and began to vibrate. Lia held her breath, wondering if he was going to pull a knife. She put her hand in her own pocket and gripped her kubotan, her thumb rubbing against the safety on the mace like a worry stone.

Leon continued screaming as Terry took a step back. Lia noticed his hand casually moving into a position that would make it easy for him to pull his gun. Lia caught his eye and shook her head vigorously. Terry ignored her and kept his hand in position, his eyes glued to Leon. He reminded Lia of a dog who has just spotted a cat and was tensed in anticipation of a chase.

"I don't have to stand for this! You'll see! You think you're gonna take care of me? I'm gonna take care of this situation right now!"

Leon whipped his hand out of his pocket. He was gripping something. Lia could not see what it was. He jammed the offensive index finger into the palm of his hand, into the mysterious object. Lia was confused when he put the object up to his mouth.

"911? My rights are being vi-o-la-ted. I am being illegally evicted from the Homeless Association. I need you to send someone to take care of this a-hole at the desk. You send them right now!" He ended his call and glared at Steve. "We'll just see what's what." He turned to face the back of a little woman with apparent obsessive compulsive disorder who had been straightening the cheap stacking chairs lining the lobby and was now aligning the lid and tap on the coffee urn. "I got rights!" he screamed at her. "This is a public place! Just because I'm homeless, they gonna toss me out. It's unconstitutional!" The little woman blinked, ducking her head and fumbling as she attempted to line up the wrinkled paper napkins with hands that were now shaking.

The young junkie nodding out in the corner whined, "Cut it out man, you're killing my high."

A police siren gave a brief whoop. Steve nodded to Gloria and went outside, returning immediately with a pair of officers. Leon interrupted his tirade to address the new arrivals. "You tell him he can't throw me out of here," he demanded, pointing at Steve. "You tell him this is a public place and I got rights! You got to help me! I'm an American citizen! I pay your salary!"

"Leon," the taller of the two officers addressed him, "let's go outside and discuss this situation privately. Will you do that for me?"

Leon grumbled but went. Steve sighed and shook his head as his shoulders relaxed.
"Busy morning, Steve?"
"Lia! You know the floor show was just for you."

"I feel so special. This is my friend, Terry Dunn. Terry, Steve Reams. What's going to happen to Leon?"

"He didn't threaten anyone, so I asked them not to put him in jail if they could help it. If they can, they'll just encourage him to move along. I imagine he'll be back tomorrow. What brings you downtown?"

"We're looking for a homeless man."

"How many do you want? We're running a special this week."

"Cute. I'm hoping you can give me some information."

"Let's take a walk. Gloria, I'm going on break." Steve grabbed a dapper straw hat from behind the counter and clapped it on his head. "My sister," he explained. "She's concerned that I'll get skin cancer if I let the sun beat down on my head, now that there's no hair left to protect it.

Steve led them down an alley next to the building. "Let's head over to Coffee Emporium. We can talk there."

160

They cut through the alley to Central Parkway and the former-machine-shop-turned-hipster-nexus. Once seated with drinks, Steve got back to business.

"I'm not supposed to talk about clients, and especially not in front of other clients. They can be so paranoid."

"Oops, sorry."

"You have the patience of Job, friend," Terry said. "How do you manage it?"

Steve shrugged. "I had one foot off the curb at one time. It could be me babbling into my Wild Irish Rose. So what do you need this guy for?"

"Someone's been leaving little foil dolls for a friend of mine," Lia said, leaving out the part where Desiree was deceased and Lia thought Foil Man killed her. "We're trying to figure out who it was. I tracked the dolls to a guy named Ernie who was homeless and hung with a guy—"

"Oh, you mean Watcher. Skinny guy, dreadlocks, beard down to here." He indicated the middle of his chest.

"Watcher?"

"Sure, takes scraps of aluminum foil and twists them into little sculptures. We used to keep a roll of foil on hand for him. This was after you did the facade. He was amazing to watch. Haven't seen him for quite a while. We still have a few of his sculptures around the office. Did you see the one behind the counter?"

"I only had eyes for Leon. What can you tell me about Watcher? We're not sure what to think about the dolls, whether he was stable or not."

"Well," he scratched his chin. "There's basically three types of homeless that I see. First are your mentally ill, the folks who would be in mental institutions if Ronnie hadn't defunded those in the 80's. Mostly, they're too low-functioning to do much more than stumble through one day to the next, but there aren't adequate housing options for them. They usually don't have the capacity to cause any trouble that requires planning. It's just when they get agitated that you have to worry.

"Next you have your addicts and alcoholics, and all they think about is their next high. Watcher got high sometimes, but he was young and and he still had a few brain cells. For being homeless, he could be responsible, especially after he decided it was his job to take care of Ernie. I think it gave him a sense of purpose. I always thought Watcher was behind door number three."

"Which is?"

"One paycheck away from the disaster and something happens. It occurs more often than you think, these days. These folks are focused on finding their way back off the street. I think he lost his job and his girlfriend tossed him out. If I remember, he was living in his car. He was obsessed about being dumped, otherwise I think he might have bounced back."

"Do you think Watcher is stable?"

"Relatively speaking, yeah. He was a little twisted, but he knew which shoe went on which foot, and what time of day it was. He and Ernie'd recycle cans and Watcher would sell his little dolls. Since he was always clean, some of the guys would have him go into stores for them. Never said much. Haven't seen him since Ernie died."

"How does a homeless person stay clean?" Terry asked.

"Mary Magdalene House has a bath house the homeless can use once a day, as long as they obey the rules and don't get tossed out. Leon, of course, has been banned for life. I never figured out where Watcher washed his clothes. I never had any problems with him."

"You said 'relatively.' What's relative about his stability?"

"Well," Steve scratched his chin again. "He could be a little spooky. He just . . . watched everything and didn't say a word most of the time. It was kinda creepy."

"Only *kinda*?" Lia asked.

"A voyeur, then," Terry said. "How would we go about finding him now?"

Steve looked up at the ceiling while he considered this question. "He didn't exactly leave a forwarding address. Tell you what. I think he used to get mail sometimes. Can't get food stamps without a physical address," he explained. "And he would have given them his real name. Would that help?"

"That would be great."

"I'll ask around and check our files this afternoon, but I can't promise anything. We get mail for close to two thousand people. It's been so long, his name might not be on the list anymore. Even if it is, I might not recognize it if I see it."

Terry parked his truck across the street from the cheerless brick cracker-box in Price Hill. The house was fronted by an anemic scruff of grass, reminding Lia of an unfortunate grunge musician's beard. She was sure rust was the only thing keeping an ancient Chevy station wagon atop the array of cinder blocks in the driveway. She imagined the next strong wind blowing defunct car parts all over the neighborhood. Sympathy bloomed for Desiree. If the place repelled her from the outside, what would it have been like, growing up in that house?

"Our target is this abominable abode?" Terry asked, mirroring her thoughts.

"This is the address I got from Amanda. Doesn't look like much, does it?"

"You sure you won't join me? I don't know how long I'll be."

"From everything Desiree and Amanda said about Josiah Willis, he's not likely to open up around a woman. He might be able to relate to you since you're wearing camouflage," Lia said, referring to Terry's concealed carry vest. "Just keep your vocabulary in check. Remember, he's a heavy-duty bible thumper."

"Surely the man who sired the comely Desiree is not a total ignoramus, but I shall essay to make my verbiage intelligible." He pulled out his cell phone and tapped a couple buttons. Lia looked at him quizzically as her phone rang.

"Keep the line open so you don't miss anything." He winked as he climbed out of the truck.

Lia rolled her eyes and slumped down in the passenger seat of Terry's truck, holding the phone in her lap and lifting her chin so she could see out the driver's side window while remaining concealed. She heard Terry knocking on the door through her phone and pressed it against her ear.

A black slit appeared above Terry's head as the door opened. Terry remained in front of the door, blocking her view of the occupant.

"Josiah Willis?" Terry asked.

"Who wants to know?" The voice was thin and contentious.

"My name is Terry Dunn. I want to express my condolences for your loss, sir, and let you know that there will be a memorial service for Desiree at The Comet next Monday . . . ."

"You friends with Desiree?" the unseen man interrupted.

Lia could see Terry duck his head in modesty. "I'd like to think—" Lia heard a rachetting that sounded like the pump stroke on a shot gun.

Terry jumped back. "What the . . . that's . . . ."

"The only daughter I recognize is named Remington. Now get out of here, you filthy Satan-worshipping liberal hippie!"

Terry backed away a few feet until the door slammed shut, then jogged briskly to the truck. He leapt in, cranked the motor and tore down the street, saying nothing. Lia noticed his face was red. She waited until they were safely around the corner and driving at a safe speed before she spoke.

"Blood pressure up?"

"I was not anticipating a brush with death. That is not the usual response to a condolence call. The man was clearly mistaken in his estimation of my motives."

"Obviously," Lia agreed, keeping her voice suitably serious. "I take it the camo didn't impress him. What was it he called you? I couldn't quite hear," she lied.

Terry muttered something indecipherable.

"I did discover one thing," he said finally.

"In the two seconds you were at the door? What was that."

"The man is no stranger to firearms."

# Chapter 22

**Monday, June 9**

Lia tapped on the doorjamb to Dave's cubbyhole office. Dave looked up from the time sheets he was totaling and raised an eyebrow at the stack of index cards in her hand.

"I just wanted to ask you about the bid cards for the silent auction. Should I put them out now, or wait until after the service?"

"Put them out now. No one will be going down to the basement until the auction starts."

Lia toyed with the top card. "I hate to see the necklace go."

"The purple crystal? You should keep it."

"Really?"

"Sure. Without you, Desiree would still be in cold storage and Three Sisters wouldn't have a sizable donation coming in. She'd want you to have it. We can spare one item from the auction."

"Thanks, Dave. I'll treasure it. And thanks for letting me bring Julia." Julia, lying by Dave's feet, wore a big pink bow around her neck and a tee shirt that said "I'm an Orphan, Adopt Me," on the back. She looked up when Lia said her name and thumped her tail on the floor. "And you, Missy," Lia said to the pup, "best behavior. No running off with cell phones or car keys."

Bailey was first to arrive for the invitation-only event. "I thought you might need a hand."

"I think we're okay until it's time for the food to come out, and I believe the cooks have that handled. Dave has the coffee all ready to start perking once the service begins. Maybe you could look at the auction tables and tell me what you think?"

They descended to the basement, set aglow with tiny, multi-colored Christmas lights vining around the ceiling pipes like an invasion of kudzu.

"It's . . . a basement." Bailey commented, looking around at the concrete walls.

"Yep. They have bands down here sometimes. Has more of that underground club feel, don't you think? Help me rearrange this table," Lia said, crossing to the other side of the room. "Dave said I should keep the amethyst. That would be alright, wouldn't it?"

"I don't see why not. We're bringing in plenty of cash on eBay with Desiree's collection of lingerie."

"You can't be serious." Lia stared at Bailey, horrified. "Tell me you didn't."

"Did. Posted links on the YouTube video, and we're getting bids in the hundreds. The brassiere she was wearing in the video is now at $1,837 and the auction isn't over until tomorrow night.

Lia shook her head. "Shame she didn't live longer. She could have been the next William Hung. It will buy a lot of kibble, anyway. There's something I don't understand."

Bailey tilted her head, waiting for Lia's question.

"You're a feminist. Why are you auctioning off her intimate apparel? Isn't that a violation of sorts?"

"I didn't know her as well as you did, but from every thing I've seen, she got a kick out of being noticed. Taking pride in her sexuality was a way for her to make a feminist statement. She would see this as becoming a minor sex-goddess, and be pleased that the devotion of her followers will do so much good for homeless dogs. . . . I know, not how you or I might see it, but that was Desiree. She enjoyed being an object of desire."

"You're doing this to *honor* her?" Lia blinked with disbelief.

"There isn't anyone lining up to spend two K on my grannie panties. Yours, either. Bids already total more than five grand. Someone must like her."

Lia didn't know what to say. She turned back to the now pathetic array of vintage and kitsch housewares, CDs, books and costume jewelry and stroked a finger across the purple stone. "I think I'll wear this. Will you find something else to go here while I put this on?"

By 7:00 pm, the back room was packed with mourners. As requested by Dave in the invitation, they were all wearing bright, happy colors to honor Desiree's pseudo-pagan inclinations. Paul Ravenscraft, ordained minister, massage therapist and drummer in a world rhythms band, stood resplendent in a painted silk robe, waiting for the crowd to settle. He tapped the standing mic and nodded to Dave when the PA system issued a loud *THOK, THOK.*

Dave left his post to lock the front door for the duration of the service. He had the key in the lock when a slight, dour man knocked on the door. He wore a black suit that was older than Dave. The fit of the suit was terrible, the jacket bagging in a way that suggested he was wearing several colostomy bags.

"I'm sorry," Dave said, "this is a private event."

Paul's voice came over the PA. "As we gather here today to honor the life of Desiree Willis, a beautiful young woman whose adventurous spirit and loving generosity touched all who knew her . . ."

"Can't a loving father grieve his daughter?" The man's eyes were bloodshot and his thin hair greasy and wild. Could it be possible that Desiree's father regretted his treatment of her? Josiah Willis shoved the door open and pushed past Dave. He stopped at the entrance to the back room, taking in the brightly colored crowd. Dave locked the door and joined him, determined to keep him close.

"... we take joy and comfort in the thought that she will be returned to the body of the Goddess, becoming one with the earth. Her breath continues to be shared with the earth's atmosphere and with all things that live and all things that die...."

Under Paul's sonorous pagan ode, Dave heard a metallic click. A ring of cold steel pressed against his neck. "That's some grief you've got there," he said.

Josiah hissed, "Keep quiet and do what you're told."

Lia noticed the derelict wearing a baggy suit and Jesus sandals standing by Dave. *How Odd.* Next to her, she felt Terry stiffen.

"Oh, shit," Terry muttered. She elbowed him.

"... Her blood returns to the streams, the rivers, the oceans and the clouds that float over us all. Her thoughts return again to that great Sky of Mind from which all thoughts arise and return. And that flame which is of Spirit again burns in yet another form. So, in a very real sense, this is not so much a good-bye as a farewell until we meet again, and again, and yet again—"

"Blasphemers!" Josiah screamed. He kept one gun on Dave and shot a second into the ceiling. *That's why his suit was bagging. How many more guns does he have?* Everyone stared at the little man standing behind Dave in the doorway.

"Hands in the air!" He shot again, this time putting a hole in the vintage photo-booth in the back corner. "That's right, I'm armed. Don't do anything funny. I've got another gun on this guy, and I'm packing four more. I'm Josiah Willis and that's my daughter you're talking about, so you're all going to listen to what *I* have to say. You, Red." he waved his gun at Bailey, who was sitting with

Lia, Terry and Jose in the back. "You're going to grab that trash can and collect everyone's phones, right after you take this guy's keys. Anyone who tries to call 911 is going to get shot. Get a move on, girlie."

"What do I do?" Bailey whispered to Lia.

"No talking!" Josiah Willis fired another shot, this time over Bailey's head.

"Humor him!" Lia hissed between her teeth. "Buy time."

Bailey picked up the wastebasket set under the coffee urn in the back of the room. She took the keys Dave still held in his hand.

"Cell phone, too," Josiah snarled. Dave dropped it in the plastic bin. One by one, Josiah allowed people to briefly lower their hands to give their cell phones to Bailey. There was a certain amount of noise as people scooted their chairs around to allow her by. Terry used the noise for cover.

"Jose," he whispered, "I'm packing. How about you?"

"Got my taser," Jose hissed out of the corner of his mouth. "If I manage to get behind him and zap him, you think that will make him squeeze the trigger, or will he freeze before that happens?"

"It's a distance, but I think I can pull off a head shot from here," Terry said. "Or I can just shoot through Dave to hit him. Better lose Dave now than after that maniac manages to shoot half of us. It's simple math."

"Stop it," Lia hissed. "If the gun is pressed to Dave's head, he'll get tased, too, and the gun will go off when they hit the floor. You'll get Dave killed. As for you," she whispered to Terry, "you pull your gun and I'll mace you before you can get a shot off. We have to wait until Dave isn't at risk."

"Who's talking?" Josiah fired again, this time taking out one of the beer bottles displayed on a high shelf that ran around the room. Glass rained down, but mourners were too scared to move. Lia noticed a thin trail of blood forming on the cheek of one woman where she was hit by a glass shard.

Bailey completed her rounds and deposited the phones at the front of the room.

"You!" Josiah waved his gun at Paul. "False preacher! Sit down over there." Josiah marched Dave over to the mic stand, keeping the gun to Dave's head. "This is better." His voice boomed through the PA system. "You may rest your hands on your heads. Keep them where I can see them. I should have exterminated this nest of Satan's vipers when Desiree first told me she was working here. . ."

Mark Hoebbel pressed his sinewy body against the hall wall by the rest rooms, listening. He didn't like to use the men's room at The Comet. The toilet stall was accessed by a swinging, louvered half-door, like in a 19th century Western saloon. The gap between the floor and the bottom of the door was 30", at least, and if someone opened the men's room door while you were using it, there was a good chance you would flash the ladies passing by on the way to their bathroom. The only protection it afforded was hiding his face, so no one would know whose ass they were seeing. His friends thought his modesty ironic, since his normal attire included jeans belted below his hips.

Despite being in extreme discomfort, he'd waited until he was sure everyone was in the back room and the service was about to start, then he'd slipped out to use the toilet. Now he was the only person in the building not under the control of Desiree's deranged father.

Mark was a good guy, but no way was he going up against a half dozen guns. He slipped out the rear exit to the deck, ran down the steps and cut around the side of the building. Once he felt safe, he leaned against a brick wall and pulled out his phone. Panting, he explained the situation to the 911 operator, then hung up without giving his name. His mom lived up the street. He'd hang on the porch and listen for the sirens from there. *This is gonna be sick. Gotta call the guys, they can't miss this ... oh, yeah, they're still inside. . . . Wonder if Mom has any brew?*

✿

". . . New Age Devil worshippers poisoned her heart against God, against her own father. You taught her the ways of sin. You sent her home with witch marks upon her skin. Well, *'Thou shalt not suffer a witch to live!'"*

Lia gasped. *Did Desiree's father just confess to killing her?*

". . . contaminated the pure and innocent fruit of my loins. This shall be your last day. But I am merciful. You have led lives of sin against God, but you have one chance to be redeemed before you meet your Maker. You may come up here, one by one to renounce your sinful ways and take Jesus Christ as your own personal savior. You who are saved, I will take you first to lessen your suffering.

"You, Red. Will you be saved?" Josiah's kind invitation sent chills down Lia's back.

Lia elbowed Bailey. "Say yes! Buy time!" she hissed.

Bailey walked up to the front of the room.

"Stop right there!" Josiah commanded when she was six feet away from him. "Kneel!"

Bailey obeyed.

"Repent your sins!"

"I repent," Bailey croaked, fear strangling her voice.

"Louder! Let the Lord and all his angels in Heaven hear you!"

"I REPENT!" Bailey yelled.

"Do you Take Jesus Christ as your Lord and personal savior?"

"YES!" She yelled.

Lia heard faint sirens that suddenly stopped. She prayed that somehow, they were on their way to The Comet and had turned off their sirens for the final blocks. Josiah Willis seemed unaware of the approaching rescue.

172

When called, Lia went up to ask forgiveness for her sins, reciting the Lord's prayer in her most convincing "terrified hostage" voice to buy time. When she turned around, she noticed a faint aura of hope and relief over the crowd of hostages.

Josiah was elated. He had walked into the Devil's den alone and was saving souls. So far no one had refused his offer of Salvation. Some were offering prayers, even. Surely God saw his works in Heaven and he would be blessed. The light seemed to sparkle and flash colors around him.

"Josiah Willis!" the sound boomed around him. He gasped in wonder. God was calling *him!*
"Yes Lord! What will you have of your most devoted soldier?"

Through the windows behind him, a dozen police cars with flashing red and blue lights could be seen arrayed across Hamilton Avenue.

"Put your guns down and come outside."

This time he recognized the crackling of a bull horn. "Blasphemers!" he screamed in frustration. The mic squealed. "I will not be deterred from my holy path! You shall not interfere with the work of the Lord! The time of Judgement has come! Only the righteous shall be saved! You!" he roared at the next man in line. "Will you be saved, or shall I send you to Perdition *now*?" He aimed a gun at the man's head.

The man's voice quavered. "I'll repent. Give me a chance to repent."

Mollified, Josiah resumed welcoming the soon to be dead into His flock. In an eerie counterpoint to the bizarre revival, the lights continued to flash and a SWAT team could be seen assembling.

The phone behind the bar rang. Lia was sure it was a hostage negotiator attempting to make contact.

"Josiah Willis! Pick up the phone!" The bull horn boomed.

"Ignore it!" Josiah yelled. The phone continued to ring.

"You!" He waved his gun at another mourner. The woman came up and dropped meekly to her knees. She began reciting the Lord's Prayer. Josiah Willis kept one eye on her and another on the dozens of hands tiring on top of the sea of heads in front of him. Soon he would have saved everyone in the room. He had to work out his next move.

How to control the crowd so as to deliver them all from the earthly plane before someone succeeded in stopping him? He hadn't been expecting such a large crowd, or to face a police presence. How many cops were there? If he turned around to look out the window, he'd lose control of the Devil worshippers.

Julia had gone to sleep under Lia's table when Paul started his sermon. At the first gunshot, the terrified dog crawled behind Lia's legs to press herself against the back of her ankles. Now she crawled out from her sanctuary and padded towards the front of the room.

Lia was horrorstruck. The woman on her knees in the front of the room kept praying. Josiah glared over the top of the crowd as he continued in his mission of salvation, defiant against the barking of the the bull horn. Julia persevered in her solo trek forward, keeping under Willis' radar. Lia's heart thudded wildly as more people became aware of the dog's passage. Josiah droned on.

Driven by a dim memory of the loud man, the bad man, the man who hated and yelled, Julia continued toward her objective. She emerged from under the front table, padding across the open expanse of linoleum towards the trio at the front of the room. She sniffed at the kneeling woman, who flinched in surprise. She stopped in front of Josiah and looked up, searching the face of the man who hurt her mistress. Josiah ranted on, oblivious.

Julia did the unthinkable. She turned towards the crowd and slitted her eyes in contempt. Then she squatted and peed on Josiah's foot.

Josiah jerked involuntarily as hot urine poured over his foot. Dave, aware that the gun was no longer drilling into his skull, ducked and rammed his shoulder into Josiah's solar plexus. The two men tumbled to the floor and the guns went off. One shot went into the ceiling. The other tore through the plate glass window.

The SWAT team responded, launching three flash-bangs through the shattered window before they blew the front door open.

Lia watched Julia wobble her way back to their booth as Josiah Willis was led out of the room, hands cuffed and an officer on each side. "Poor pup," she said, or at least thought she said since she couldn't hear herself. She picked the traumatized dog up and cuddled her in her lap, stroking the soft head gently. Exhausted from all the excitement, Julia went to sleep.

The disoriented group sat at their tables, blinking and waiting for their hearing to return while medics treated minor injuries caused by the flash-bangs and detectives attempted—without success—to take names and statements from people who could not hear them and could not read lips.

"Well, dang," Jose yelled, bracing his hands on the table and shaking his head in an attempt to restore his hearing, "I was all set to stun him into submission once Dave took him down."

"We should get to watch him twitching and incontinent on the ground after that," Terry yelled back. "Now they're going to put him in a nice comfortable cell where he gets three meals a day and medical care."

Lia shook her head and rolled her eyes. Heckle and Jeckle were approaching her booth, followed by Dave Cunningham.

"Dammit, I already had him when you came busting in," Dave shouted, "Why'd you break down the front door? The back door was open!"

"Guess we didn't get the memo," Heckle said, trying to shake him off. "Talk to my captain if you have a complaint. He stopped beside Lia, sneering as he looked down at her. "Should've known you'd be in the middle of this."

"Dave's right. You could have saved the firepower. We had it handled without your help. Is Peter here? I'd like to give my statement to him, if that's all right."

"Dourson and his pretty sidekick had better things to do. You'll have to make do with us," Heckle smirked.

Lia felt like she'd been shot in the gut. Surely they meant Brent, not Cynth.

"So far, no one knows how the perp knew about this little soiree. You got any ideas how the whack-job found out about it?" Jeckle said.

"That was me," Terry volunteered. "I invited him."

"Why did you do an idiot thing like that?" Heckle demanded.

"We believed it was too soon to rule him out. I wanted to scrutinize the man. Inviting him to the service seemed the best pretext for talking to him."

Heckle and Jeckle looked at each other. "Rule him out for what?" Jeckle asked.

"Desiree's murder, of course."

"You were investigating the murder of Desiree Willis?" Jeckle asked softly.

"Of course," Terry said.

Lia kicked Terry violently in the shin. He shot her a look.

"Why of course?" Heckle asked.

"Well," Terry shrugged. "the incompetent boobs assigned to the case dropped the ball. We had to do something."

"Terry," Lia gritted out. "Meet Detectives Hodgkins and Jarvis. They have Desiree's case."

"I see," Terry said. "I hope you appreciate that I was right."

"What makes you say that?" Jeckle said.

"'*Thou shall not suffer a witch to live,*'" Terry quoted. "He said it. It's as good as a confession, don't you think?"

"Where's the evidence that Desiree Willis was a witch?" Jarvis sneered.

"There isn't any," Terry said. "But he thought so. He was convinced her friends at The Comet turned her into one. If you watch the tape, you'll see."

"There's a movie of this shindig?" Heckle asked, eyebrows raised.

Lia nodded to the video camera mounted near the ceiling for recording musical acts. "Dave was recording Paul's service. He intended to put up a memorial page for Desiree and wanted this to be a part of it. It's probably still running."

Jeckle left to secure the video file. Heckle stuck a finger in Terry's face. "We oughta haul you in for interfering with a police investigation, Bub."

"Now, see here, I—"

"Can't leave it to the professionals, can you? What else have you been doing, besides inciting riots?" Heckle sneered at Lia.

"Nothing, really," Lia lied.

"Why do I doubt that? Keep it up, and we will haul you in and charge you, and your *boyfriend* won't be able to help you."

Lia stuck her tongue out at him as soon as his back turned.

A fiddle danced a riff from "Orange Blossom Special." Ed Cunningham of The Comet Bluegrass All Stars walked up to the mic. "Folks, Cincinnati's Finest have asked us to remove ourselves from the scene of the crime so they can collect evidence. We think everyone needs a little cheering up after facing our collective mortality. We're relocating in the basement, where the silent auction to benefit Three Sisters Pet Rescue is kicking off.

"We all knew and loved Desiree, and now you can serve her favorite cause while obtaining a personal memento of this fabulous lady. We'll be playing for your entertainment. Dave's providing free beverages and nachos for all survivors. Follow me downstairs and celebrate your continued existence on this earthly plane. Remember, be you Pagan, Christian, Atheist or Beer-itarian , we welcome *all* at The Comet."

Ed resumed playing as he led the crowd downstairs. It appeared that everyone was staying. Lia figured that like her, nobody wanted to face an empty apartment after such an intense experience.

Everyone wanted to pet Julia and feed her treats. Al made his way through the crowd and gave Julia the obligatory pat.

"Al, I'm glad you stayed. Desiree thought of you like a father, you know."

Al scoffed. "That girl, she needed a better father than the one God gave her. A lovely girl who deserved better."

"Crazy, huh?" Eric set down a plate of loaded nachos and pulled up a chair at the end of the table. Julia lifted her head from Lia's lap and gave him a grin. He let her sniff his hand, then stroked her head. "Cute dog. How are you holding up?"

"I'm holding." She introduced him to her friends.

Avery and Ed joined them and the group scooted their chairs around to make room for the newcomers.

"I must say," Avery said, "this is the most memorable memorial I've ever attended."

"Very sad," Ted said. "Desiree was such a sweet girl. I'd bid on some of the Beanie Babies for my wife, but she wouldn't like having something that reminded me of a pretty girl." He looked longingly at the table. "I could get a coffee mug for my own use. Maybe I won't tell her where I got it."

It was late when Lia finally pulled up in front of her home, satisfied with the evening's outcome despite Josiah's appearance. "If nothing else, no one who was at that service will ever forget your mama," she told Julia, who curled up in the back seat. "But I'm glad to be home. I bet you're one tired puppy. Did you like any of the people you met?"

Julia started barking and jumping at the car window.

"Cool your jets, Julia, I'll have you out in a minute." Lia was opening the door to the back seat when someone grabbed her by the hair and the tip of a knife pressed under her jaw. *Shit.*

"Do exactly what I say, or I'll cut your throat," the man behind her snarled.

"O-okay," she quavered, thumbing the safety off the plunger on her kubotan. She shut her eyes tightly as she swung the tactical keychain up over her shoulder, spraying mace in her assailant's face. *God bless Peter and his drills.*

The man screamed, dropping the knife as he clawed at his eyes. Holding her breath and eyes shut, she felt her way around the car, out of the cloud of pepper spray. She let Julia out of the other side of the car and dragged the pugnacious animal inside, locking the door behind them as Honey and Chewy crowded around, sniffing and barking in agitation. "I appreciate you wanting to protect me, Julia, but your timing is all wrong."

Julia, continued to bark nastily and bounce against the door. Honey and Chewy joined her, the three scrabbling to get out while Lia peered through the window, looking for her assailant. Lia whipped out her phone and started to hit Peter's number on her speed-dial, then changed her mind.

"911, what's your emergency?" Lia could barely hear the operator over the barking of the dogs.

"I was just attacked outside my apartment. I maced him and got away, but I'm afraid he's still out there."

"An officer has been dispatched. Please stay on the line. Were you injured?" She continued to talk to Lia, verifying that she was unhurt and all doors and windows were locked. Lia responded distractedly, wondering what Peter was up to and wishing he was there. She leaned against the doorjamb and began to cry. She watched through the front window as a police car drew up. The officer got out and shone a flashlight up and down the sidewalk, then went around the side of the house. He had the erect carriage of a military man and his long-legged stride was full of confidence.

After he made his circuit, the patrolman came up to the front door. In response to Lia's request, he showed her his ID. She opened the door to Officer Brainard and invited him in, introducing him to the dogs to ease their agitation.

While Officer Brainard couldn't be described as chiseled or lantern-jawed, there was something heroic about him. His deep chest attested to regular weightlifting. Lia suspected you could bounce a quarter off the biceps straining his shirtsleeves. Lia didn't normally go for muscular guys, but after the day she'd had, Officer Brainard's presence gave her a sense of security, like an Incredible Hulk teddy bear.

"Sorry, I'm feeling really paranoid right now. I was held hostage at The Comet earlier this evening, and now this."

"You've had some night. He seems to be gone now. You've got a cut on your neck. Where's your kitchen? Let's clean that off before I take your statement."

Lia rubbed her neck where she could still feel the point of the knife. Her fingers came away smeared with red. She blinked. "Uh, it's back here." She led him to the rear of her apartment, the three dogs trailing behind. Kitchen meant biscuits.

"Let me see that in the light," Brainard said, tilting her chin up and examining her neck. Lia felt a jolt at the touch of his fingers on her skin. His warmth penetrated, the dry warmth from his hands and the moist warmth of his breath on her cheek. She inhaled his earthy, natural scent, spiked with a bit of perspiration from his jog around the house.

Lia was acutely reminded that she hadn't had sex in more than a month as her body started humming. It continued humming as Brainard wet a paper towel and dabbed at the drying blood on her neck.

"It's not deep," he said, giving her shoulder a rub with a hand the size of a skillet. "It should heal without a scar. I wouldn't bother bandaging it. Put a little peroxide on it after I leave."

He gave her hair a sniff. "You picked up some overspray. It'll linger in your clothes and hair. Best thing to get rid of the oils is Dawn dish detergent. Be sure you rinse several times and don't touch your eyes, or you'll regret it."

"Thanks. I'll uh . . . just get myself a glass of water. Can I get you something, too?"

"I'm fine." He followed her back to the living room and sat on a Mission style chair when Lia took her place on the matching couch. Lia's dogs crowded around her, nosing her free hand to remind her of the treats she'd forgotten to give them. *Distracted much?* She jumped up. "I'll be back in a minute."

She recounted her story from her perch on the sofa while feeding biscuits to the dogs, keeping her head down so he wouldn't notice her flushing face. "As you can see, it's not much."

"Fast thinking on your part. You never saw the guy?"

"No. I hoped the pepper spray would slow him up long enough for me to see him leaving after I locked myself in, but it didn't. Maybe he stayed down on the other side of the parked cars until he got his bearings."

"Did any cars pass by while you were waiting for me?"

Lia thought back. "Two. I didn't pay much attention to them."

"He might have been picked up by an accomplice."

Lia mentally smacked her forehead. "I guess I'd better turn in my Nancy Drew merit badge. It didn't occur to me that he might not be alone."

"I know you didn't see him. Did you have any impressions of him?"

"Just his voice. It was low and mean. He was hissing at me, so it wasn't his normal voice."

"Did you get an impression of size or age?"

Lia closed her eyes and compared her impressions tonight with her many experiences being fake-mugged by Peter. "Bigger than me, but not much. He didn't sound old."

"Any reason to think this might be connected with the shooter at The Comet?"

"I don't think so. I never met Josiah Willis before tonight, and I'm sure he was acting alone. If he'd had friends, they would have helped him at the bar, wouldn't they?"

"Probably. Any chance your attacker followed you here?"

Lia thought about the twisted shortcut she took home and shook her head. "I came the back way, down Innes. I think I would have noticed if someone was behind me."

"So either it was random, or they were waiting for you. Is there anyone you can think of who might have done this? An old boyfriend, perhaps?"

*Peter? Could Peter have possibly pulled this as another drill? He* couldn't *be so cruel, could he?*

"No one I can name, but someone's been leaving me little dolls, and they broke in recently."

"Dolls? You think someone who is leaving you dolls wants to hurt you?"

"Desiree Willis was receiving little dolls made out of aluminum foil, and then she was murdered. After she died, I got dolls that looked like me and my dogs. So, maybe."

"Have you filed a report about this?"

"I told Hodgkins and Jarvis about the dolls because they're in charge of Desiree's case. I don't think they took me seriously. I filed a report about the break-in. There really isn't much you can do about this, is there?"

Brainard sighed and set his clipboard down. He leaned forward, elbows on thighs like oak tree trunks.

"We'll step up patrols on this street for the next few days. Other than that, the reports go to establishing patterns that may help us figure out what's going on. I wish I could be more encouraging. How did someone manage to break in with three dogs here?"

"We were at the park. We go every morning."

"So someone knows your habits. That's something to think about. How did he get in?"

"I left a window open."

He nodded, said nothing.

"You might want to swap your locks out for double deadbolts that key-lock on both sides. Nu-Set has a jimmy-proof lock that isn't expensive."

"Peter's been after me to upgrade my locks for ages. Guess I need to do that."

"Peter?"

"A friend."

He stood up to leave. "Do you have someone you can call to stay with you tonight?

*'Dourson and his pretty sidekick had better things to do.'* She shoved the thought away. "No, but I have my dogs. I'll be all right."

"I'm on patrol all night. Here's my cell number. If you hear anything, anything at all, you call me."

"This isn't usual, is it?"

"No, but if you call in a prowler to 911, it might get ranked as low priority and get lost on the bottom of the pile. I want to make sure someone shows up right away if this creep comes back."

"You think he might return? Maybe I will call a friend."

"Good thinking. I'll flag Hodgkins and Jarvis on this report, but you may not hear from them for a few days. I imagine they'll be busy with Willis for the next little while." He tipped his hat on the way out, then stopped half-way down the walk. "You know, if you need a hand upgrading those locks, give me a call."

"If I were a ninety year-old cat lady, would you make the same offer?"

"Yes, but I wouldn't enjoy it nearly as much."

Lia shook her head and locked the door.

"You left out the most important thing," Bailey said after Lia explained her reason for the late-night invite.

"What's that?"

"Brainard. Was he cute?"

Lia shook her head. "Only you, Bailey. Pick up a half-gallon of ice cream on the way over, will you? I want chocolate while we research burglarproof deadbolts on the Internet. No, wait. Make that Denali Extreme Fudge Moose Tracks."

# Chapter 23

**Tuesday, June 10**

"Tell us, Dourson," Heckle said as he sat on the edge of Peter's desk, toying with a paperweight, one Lia made for him while experimenting with polished concrete and broken glass. Jeckle lurked behind him, grinning. "Why is your girlfriend calling Brainard when things go bump in the night? You scared of the dark now?"

"What are you talking about?" Peter was reviewing transcripts of interviews, desperately hoping for a lead to jump out and bite him on the nose.

"You know Brainard," Heckle said, "the jarhead who posed for that Marine beefcake calendar before he signed on here. He answered her 911 call last night. Bad move, Dourson. Hard to compete with a big, strong guy like Brainard, even if he is a little on the dim side. Now every time you make love to that sweet piece of yours, she'll be thinking about him instead of you."

"Damn shame about her getting mugged, especially after being involved in that hostage situation yesterday," Jeckle said.

"*What?* Lia got mugged? What hostage situation?"

"Awww, didn't she tell you?" Heckle affected an expression of sincere commiseration. "Yessir, your girl had a busy day yesterday while you were doing whatever it is you do. What is it that you do, Dourson? . . . Well, wish we could stay to chat, but we've got a religious nut to terrorize."

Jeckle winked as, their work done, the pair sauntered off towards the interview rooms, Heckle whistling the tag-line from Jackson Browne's "Rosie."

"Breathe, brother," Brent said. "Shooting a fellow officer looks so bad on the record."

Peter stared after the pair and imagined unloading a clip in their backs. "What am I going to do, Brent?" he groaned.

"First, you're going to review the reports about The Comet and Lia's mugging. Next, you're going to ignore anything those idiots said about the ironically named Brainard. He's not her type and you know it. Then you are going to *end* this Mexican standoff you've got going with Lia and call her like any decent person would do, to see how she's holding up."

# Chapter 24

**Wednesday June 11**

"Goodness, Lia, look who's here," Bailey said, eyeing the parking lot from her perch on their picnic table.

"Huh?" Lia looked up from the to do list she was making on her Kindle Fire. Peter exited his ancient Ford Explorer carrying a cup of coffee, a Pepsi and a white paper bag she suspected held at least one chocolate covered Bavarian cream doughnut. Viola tagged along after him.

"He comes bearing gifts. Are you going to go meet him, or are you going to make him walk all the way back here and beg to talk to you in private?"

"I honestly don't know what I'm going to do." She thought about the number lying beside her phone at home, feeling guilty. She'd walked by it countless times since Monday night and each time she felt echoes of the raw, animal pull she'd experienced with Brainard. *You don't even know him*, she reminded herself. *You don't even like him. All he is, is muscles. Stop thinking like a guy!*

Viola reached her long before Peter made the trek across the four acre enclosure. The dog wiggled and jumped up on the table, making urgent little "uh, uh, uh" noises while she covered Lia's face with her rapidly flicking tongue. Julia, her territory transgressed upon, jumped up on the table and snarled at Viola. Viola interrupted her reunion with Lia to snap at the new girl. Lia jumped off the table and pulled a water gun from its make-shift holster on her belt and began spraying both dogs. The dogs stopped their confrontation. Julia sulked, retreating underneath the table to nurse a tennis ball. Viola, her face dripping, looked affronted and betrayed. "Sorry, girlfriend. Dog fights aren't allowed."

"What's your excuse for spraying me?" Bailey asked. "I wasn't biting anyone. And where did the gun come from?"

"Sorry. Collateral damage. I just got the water pistol. Too many scraps up here lately." Lia eyed the wet table with disgust. "I didn't expect to be using it on anyone I knew. I guess a change of venue is in order. Damn it, I like this table. It's got the best shade."

Peter walked up, escorted by Honey, who eyed the doughnut bag like it was the holy grail, and Chewy, who hopped along on his hind legs, a desperate bid for attention.

"Backstabbers," Lia muttered.

"Unconditional love is a good thing, Lia," Bailey said.

"I'd wave my white handkerchief, but my hands are full," Peter said as he arrived.

"You got a handkerchief on you?" Lia asked.

"Always."

She took the coffee. "Hand it over."

Bemused, he pulled the handkerchief from his pocket. Lia took it and sopped up the water on the table. She handed the wet and grimy cloth back to Peter, then resumed her seat. "Thank you." She smiled. "What brings you here?"

Peter looked at the ruined cloth and sighed. He handed it to Chewy, who shook it in Julia's face, then took off at a run. Julia abandoned her tennis ball to chase after him, starting a game of tug-of-war.

"I brought a bribe," Peter said.

"So I see," said Lia.

"Where's my bribe?" Bailey said.

"If you get lost, you can have the entire bag of dough-nuts," Peter offered.

"No way is Bailey getting my doughnuts," Lia said, snatching the bag away. She looked inside. "Bailey, I'll give you two chocolate iced, glazed doughnuts from Bonomini Bakery if you stay here."

"Those are mine," Peter said. "I'll bring you a brownie from Whole Foods tomorrow if you find another table."

"Make it a chocolate mousse cup, and it's a deal."

"Done."

Bailey hopped down off the table. "Come, Kita, let's find a place where they don't spray you."

"Traitor!" Lia called.

"Sticks and stones," Bailey retorted as she headed for Jose and Terry's table, Kita sauntering after her.

Peter climbed onto the table and sat a few feet away from Lia. He looked off at nothing. "You know you hate glazed doughnuts," he said as he twisted the top off his Pepsi. "And you can't give them to the dogs because they're chocolate."

She handed the glazed doughnuts over, then pulled out the expected Bavarian cream treat and took a bite. "What brings you, Dourson?"

"A couple of little birdies told me about Monday. I wanted to see how you were holding up."

"Would these birdies be a pair of thuggish magpies?"

"They would."

"As you can see, I'm fine."

Peter eyed the red line under her chin and privately disagreed. "I don't know where to begin. I've been an ass."

"True enough." Lia concentrated on her pastry, licked a dollop of custard that threatened to fall into her lap.

"Why didn't you call me? You know I would have been there."

Lia sighed. "I thought about it."

"And?"

"Heckle and Jeckle said you were with your pretty sidekick, and I didn't think they were talking about Brent."

Peter swore, vehemently.

"Peter, that's not the only reason. I'm confused enough about us without tossing two near-death experiences into the mix. It would have been too easy to lean on you and let everything go back the way it was because I was needy."

"Are you going to lean on Brainard, instead?"

Lia barked a laugh. "Is *that* what this is about? Officer Hunky?" She rolled her eyes. "*Men*. You don't want me until someone else comes sniffing around. I'm not a tree you can pee on."

"It's not like that."

She gave him a look.

"Okay, it's a little like that. But mostly not. When I heard about Monday, I realized it had gone too far. Between you sorting things out and me sorting things out, we were slipping away from each other, and I wasn't there when you needed me. I hate myself for that. I can't blame Brainard if he hit on you. . . . Did he hit on you?"

"I'll never tell."

"I deserve that. I want us to fix this."

"What are you suggesting?"

"I don't know. I thought we could start by you telling me about Monday."

"I could use some help installing my new, jimmy-proof locks. Bailey was going to give me a hand, but she's pretty busy these days."

"I can do that."

"Peter, I need to take this slow."

"Tell you what. I'll pick up a pizza and my tools after work, and you can fill me in on what's going on while I take a whack at it."

Peter pressed his lips together, willing himself to remain calm while he listened to Lia's story. Heckle and Jeckle had left out some important facts, like not telling him the foil doll resembled Lia. He focussed his attention on dismantling the kitchen door lock so he could avoid looking at her.

He reminded himself that Lia felt like she was handling things well. She *had* run off the mugger. She *had* remained calm for too many desperate minutes while Willis held The Comet hostage. And if he hadn't come by, likely she and Bailey would have done a credible job of installing new locks. He stared at the disjoined pieces, wanting to take her in his arms and hold her so tight that nothing could hurt her.

"This is going to take care of the door, but what about your windows? Isn't that how he got in before?"

"Bailey inspired me to follow a low-tech Peruvian custom."

"Oh?"

"She showed me a picture from a trip she took. They embed large glass shards and plant cacti in a layer of concrete on the tops of walls so no one can get over them. I've got permission to do that to the sills. That way, someone can break the glass, but they still can't climb in."

"Huh. Interesting idea. Your landlord gave you permission to do it?"

"He did. It appealed to Rudy's misanthropic tendencies. I promised him it was reversible."

"And is it?"

"I'll make it so it is. What's happening with Josiah Willis? Did he kill Desiree? That's what Terry thinks."

"We don't know. He's crazy enough to have shot her and he has no alibi, but there was nothing about the crime scene that suggested religious fanaticism, and we can't place him there. The powers that be hope we'll uncover more as we pursue the other charges."

Lia's doorbell chimed.

Puzzled, she returned to the front of her apartment to see Brainard's earnest, all-American face outside her door. It brightened as she undid the chain and leaned out.

"Officer Brainard, what can I do for you?" She gave him a quizzical look.

"Ms. Anderson, I just wanted to stop by and make sure everything was okay. Say, you got a new lock. I see you went with the Nu-Set. Nice."

"That's very considerate of you. As you can see, I'm fine, and the apartment is now jimmy-proof."

"That's good to know. I was just on my way in to the station, and wanted you to know I'm still keeping up those extra patrols. You still got my number?"

"Yes, it's right by the phone."

"Be sure to call me if anything happens." He glanced over Lia's shoulder. "Hey, I know you. You're a detective. Dourson, isn't it?"

"That's right." Peter stood behind Lia and did his best to loom, taking advantage of the three inches he had on Brainard.

Brainard smiled, showing perfect teeth. With forty pounds of muscle on Peter, he was not in the least intimidated. "Ms. Anderson said a friend was after her to upgrade her security. That must be you."

"It must be." Peter smiled back despite gritted teeth and felt something vaguely feral surging in his veins. He swore he heard Lia whisper "Down, boy," out of the corner of her mouth.

"Well, I'll be on my way."

"Thanks for stopping by. I really appreciate the extra patrols," Lia said. She watched as Brainard strode down the walk and hopped onto a motorcycle the size of a Buick and roared off. She could feel Peter vibrating behind her.

"Thanks for stopping by?" he asked.

"What was I supposed to say?"

"He wants you to call him."

"I figured that out. Are we going to argue about this? Because I haven't encouraged him, and I don't intend to."

"You thanked him for stopping by," Peter pointed out.

"That was just manners. And I *do* appreciate extra patrols. Only an idiot wouldn't. I wouldn't worry about him."

"Don't worry about Mr. July from the Marine Corps beefcake calendar for 2011?"

"Mr. July? Really? I didn't know the Marine Corps had a beefcake calendar." Lia turned her head to stifle a grin.

"I didn't either, until Heckle and Jeckle enlightened me," he grumbled.

"Relax, Peter. If there were anything to worry about, he'd be the one manhandling my back door right now instead of you. I will admit I got a bit hot and sweaty when he was here the other night, but that was just a visceral reaction. It didn't mean anything."

"What do you mean, it didn't mean anything?"

"What? Your autonomic nervous system can kick in when you see an attractive woman, but mine can't? Besides, if I were looking for a new boyfriend, I'd go for Dave before the Incredible Hulk."

"Dave?" His eyebrows shot up.

"He owns The Comet. Nice guy."

Peter was silent as he packed his tools up and hooked Viola to her leash.

"Dumbass. The only reason I noticed Dave is because he reminds me of you."

"Oh."

"Peter, I don't know how I feel about us right now, but it's not because I'm hankering after a new boyfriend. Ignore Brainard. That's what I intend to do."

"Okay then."

She gave him a hug. He looked questioningly into her eyes. She placed her index finger on his chin and turned his face to the side, kissed him on the cheek. "We'll talk soon. Thanks for installing the locks."

"You'll call me if anything happens?"

"Cross my heart."

# Chapter 25

**Thursday, June 12**

Lia gave each dog a rawhide chew, then returned to the kitchen and her lentil sprout experiment. Bailey and Louella Zimmerman were coming over and she needed to finish up in the kitchen and pick up the living room. Five minutes later, Honey and Chewy cornered her by the sink. They stared at her, rawhide chews nowhere in sight. Honey gave two sharp barks to ensure she had Lia's attention. Lia washed her hands and followed them back into the living room.

Lia searched the floor. No chews. "You can't have eaten them so fast. What happened? And where's Julia?" Honey barked again and Lia followed the two dogs to the bedroom. Honey and Chewy stopped at the bedroom door, panting and looking at Lia expectantly.

Lia looked in the door. Nothing was out of order. She walked around to the other side of the bed. Nothing there. The closet door was cracked. She pulled the door open and gasped when a stack of winter scarves fell out on top of her. "Is this your idea of a joke?" She asked the dogs. They cocked their heads as if they were trying, but could not understand, what she was saying. *Riiiggghhhttt.*

Julia was not in the closet. Lia gave up the search, picked up the scarves and hats and sat down on the bed to refold them. She heard a low, grinding mutter of some kind. She froze, trying to figure out where the sound was coming from, her mind scrambling to decipher its meaning. *Is Foil Man here? But where? How did he get in?* She looked around the room for hiding places, then realized that she was sitting on top the only place he could be.

She stood up and the rumbling noise stopped. She sat down and it started again. She abandoned the scarves, got down on her knees at the side of the bed and lifted the dust ruffle. The hoarse, gravelly noise began again, louder. It sounded like an engine full of rocks having an asthma attack, like Darth Vader in his death throes, and it came from under the dust ruffle.

Lia dropped the ruffle and the sounds of a thousand mutters emerging from the pits of Hell stopped. She lowered her head, ear to the floor, and pulled up the ruffle again. This time the sound rose and fell as it rumbled, as if someone was trying to crank the rock engine, revive Darth Vader, and open the Hell gate.

She lifted the ruffle all the way. Red-rimmed eyes glared out of the darkness. Julia snarled. Wild, vicious, a demon undergoing exorcism. A dragon protecting hoarded gold from encroaching hobbits. Lia counted 8 mangled strips of rawhide scattered in Julia's inky hidey-hole.

She stood up and dusted off her hands, relief warring with irritation.

"This is going to stop."

Swiffer in hand, she tucked the dust ruffle under the mattress, and ran the floor sweeper under the bed. Julia barked in protest as Lia dragged out the dusty bits of leather.

The rawhide chews must have been the source of Julia's unearthly power. Once the last chew was retrieved, she popped out from under the bed, confronting Lia with wide, affronted eyes. She lunged at her lost treasures. Lia grabbed Julia's collar and marched her out of the room, shutting the door on all three dogs. One of them, Julia, she thought, scratched at the door and whined.

"This is unacceptable, Julia. If you can't share, we just won't have any." Lia swept the treats into a pile and wrapped them in a ratty scarf she'd made for her first (and only) knitting project. She held the package high as she opened the door, out of reach of jumping dogs.

Julia lay on the floor, alone. Honey and Chewy had apparently realized the excitement was over, or else they decided to abandon Julia to her fate now that they ratted her out.

Julia lifted her head. The big eyes were bereft. Lia thought she saw a glimmer of tears forming. That was silly. Dogs don't cry. *Well, maybe Julia does.*

Louella Zuckerman was a petite woman with blushing cream skin and wispy, pale, angel hair, wreathing her head in disordered waves. Her draped tunic in washes of pastel hues added to the ethereal look. Something about her reminded Lia of roses, cream-colored roses with blushing edges.

Louella stood in the doorway, and her hair became a halo as she was backlit by the sun. The sunlight fell away when she followed Bailey into Lia's apartment. The effect disappeared, but not the whisper of unearthly presence.

Louella knelt on the floor, then sat as the dogs crowded around her. Honey licked her face and Chewy head-bumped her hand for pets. Julia crawled into her lap. Kita sniffed her hair, a drool streamer dangling precariously near Louella's lovely silk top.

"I've never done this before," Lia said. "How does it work?"

"I need to be in physical contact with the animals, one at a time, and I let them talk to me. I'll repeat what they say, as best I can. They show me images, so it doesn't always translate well. Is Julia the baby doll in my lap?"

"How did you know?"

198

"I'm picking up some anxiety off her. We need to start here at your apartment, where Julia feels comfortable. We might be able to get everything you need without going back to her home. That would be best, less traumatic for her. I've never communicated with an animal who witnessed murder, so I don't know quite what to expect. Let me say hello to everyone else first." Her voice was sparkling dew, innocent and friendly as childhood. She cooed over the dogs, petting them.

"They can't wait to talk to you," Bailey said. "They already know you understand them. Is it okay if we record this?"

"Certainly, if it will help."

Bailey turned on the recording app on her phone and set it on the coffee table, near the pile of dogs and woman.

Louella handed Julia over to Lia, then turned her attention to Kita. Kita sat proudly, the tenacious streamer dangling off her chin.

"Such a regal head," Louella said, rubbing Kita behind the ears. She closed her eyes for a moment in concentration as she stroked Kita's back.

"I like this place," she said.

Lia blinked and started to say something. Bailey put a hand out, signaling her to remain silent.

"I don't live here, but I come here lots. Happy dog and little dog are my friends. Sad dog is scared. Sad dog is new. This is a nice place. I like it here.

"I like it here, too," she told Kita. She gave the hound a final pat. Honey nosed under Louella's arm.

Again, Louella focused, one hand stroking honey's shoulder. Honey sat on her haunches and grinned, tongue lolling.

"This is my house. I've been here a long time. I was a little dog when I came here. Pesty dog has been here a little long time. Pesty dog is my friend. Big dog is my friend. Big dog visits, big dog doesn't stay. Dark dog isn't here. Dark dog stays sometimes. Dark dog does bad things sometimes. I never do bad things. I'm a good dog. Sad dog has been here a little. Sad dog misses her mom.

"Yes, Honey, you are a very good dog." Louella gave Honey's ears a ruffle and focused her attention on Chewy, scratching under his chin. She ran her fingers through his overgrown coat.

"Someone doesn't like the groomers," she said.

"You can tell that?" Lia asked.

Louella closed her eyes. "I'm seeing him yap and yap at the clippers. He's a wiggler. He won't stay still for her."

"I always knew he was afraid of the groomers. I over-tip because he behaves so badly."

"Not afraid so much. . . . He doesn't want a hair cut. He likes being casual," Louella said. "Oh, now he wants to talk.

"I'm Mom's good little man," she said. "I can sit and wait my turn." Chewy demonstrated this by plopping his haunches onto the floor. "I like the park. Sad dog is park friend. We played before. Now Sad Dog stays. I hope Sad dog doesn't stay long. Sad dog wants all the mom pets. *I* want the mom pets. She's *my* mom."

The look on Chewy's face was so indignant, Lia burst out laughing. Then she blinked, as tears threatened. She wasn't sure what to call what she was experiencing, how to explain what it felt like to be able to understand what her dogs were thinking and feeling this way. She only knew that her chest felt full and she wanted to hug her dogs to her and not let them go.

Louella continued. "Sad dog scared when she came. Sad dog not scared now. I take care of sad dog."

Julia was curled in Lia's lap. Lia patted the sofa cushion next to her. "Come here, little man, I can pet you both." Chewy looked at Louella for a minute, decided they were done talking, and bounced over and onto the couch.

Louella called to Julia and held her arms out. Julia abandoned Lia, returning to Louella's lap. "What big, beautiful eyes she has." Louella stroked her head and long ears and continued stroking as she began communing with the dog.

"I like you. You're a nice lady. This is a nice place. Here are nice dogs. Before was a bad place, a small place. Dark woman wouldn't let me out. I cried and cried. I had to pee. I didn't want to pee in the small place. Dark woman yelled and yelled. I cried for Mom. Mom didn't come." Lia wanted to cry, realizing how Julia must have felt while she was locked in that bathroom.

"Okay, I'm going to ask her some questions. You won't be able to hear me, just what she says. We'll see how she does. I'll stop if she gets too upset." She resumed petting Julia and they spent a long moment communing silently.

"I miss my mom. Little dog's mom is nice, I like her. I want *my* mom. . . . Mom was down. I went to sniff mom. My paws got sticky. . . . Big man, angry, mess, I hid . . . big noise, hurt ears, mom fell. . . . Mom still. . . . Shiny furry man there. Shiny, furry man sad. Shiny, furry man has sticky paws. Shiny, furry man plays with me sometimes, not then, not when he was sad. . . . Alone. Mom won't move. Dark woman came. Dark woman yelled at us. Mom was still, didn't move. . . . Dark woman put me in small, bad place. Pretty dog mom got me—" Louella broke off her narrative. "Julia's telling me she's very happy you took her away—we went to find mom, mom wasn't there. Where's mom?"

Lia was stunned. Louella gave Julia a big hug and rocked her like a baby.

"Wow," was all Bailey said.

"Did that make sense to you?" Louella asked. She continued to baby Julia, who was now huddled in her lap and not inclined to leave.

"Some of it did," Lia said.

"Do you understand what she meant about a 'big noise' and 'sticky'?"

"I can guess," Bailey said. "Her mom was shot, that would be a big noise. And she bled on the floor, so Julia's paws were sticky if she tried to get her up. If shiny furry man touched the body, he would have gotten sticky, too. Why does she call him shiny, furry man?"

Louella stroked Julia again "I don't understand about the shiny, it's not clear. But he's been there before, and I would say he has a lot of hair. Dogs think of hair as fur."

"Shiny for foil? He was in her apartment? He knew Desiree?" Lia asked, eyebrows raised.

Louella asked Julia. "Mom gone. . . . Did Desiree have a dog walker, someone who would come by to take care of the dog when she was working?"

"Not that we know of."

"This man was never there when Desiree was there. Julia is clear on that."

"So. . ." Bailey put the pieces together. "Either Desiree had a dog sitter or else her stalker was in her apartment when she was gone and made friends with Julia so Julia wouldn't raise cain. Can you ask her how many times he came?"

"We're both exhausted. We were lucky to get this much from her. Their sense of time and numbers is vague, we wouldn't be likely to get a solid answer, even if we were both fresh. Her memory is likely to fade, as well. This is probably as good as it gets. Will you share the recording with the police?"

"If we tell them the dog saw a big shiny, furry man, they'll fall down laughing. It's not really enough for them to go on."

"Are you going to keep her?"

"Only until Three Sisters finds a foster home for her."

"She's anxious. The less change she has to deal with, the better. It would be best if she went from here to a permanent home, and if she had time to adjust to her new owners before she went to them. She knows Honey and

Chewy, and she feels safer here than if she were some-where else. Who is the dark woman?"

"That was Desiree's landlady. I don't think she likes dogs."

"Julia doesn't think she likes them, either, do you, Julia?"

Julia gave her a sorrowful look.

"Feel free to call me when it's time to transfer her. I might be able to ease her anxiety."

"Thanks, Louella."

The bowl was glazed with a cheery cobalt blue, intended to distract Bailey from the flat, grayish legumes with curly white tails that filled it.

"This is your idea of post-seance eats? At least the dogs got liver."

"Where's your sense of culinary adventure?"

"I tossed it in the garbage with the last smoothie you tried to feed me."

"Bailey, you're a disgrace to vegans everywhere."

Bailey sighed and dipped her hand cautiously into the proffered bowl of freshly washed lentil sprouts and popped a few in her mouth.

"What do you think?" Lia asked while Bailey crunched.

Bailey made a face. "Tastes like cardboard."

"But they're so healthy!" Lia insisted.

"They still taste like cardboard."

"They're dirt cheap and easy to grow."

"Okay, they taste like dirty cardboard."

"Living food, Bailey. And they're alkalizing out the wazoo."

Bailey dumped the rest of the sprouts back in the bowl and dusted off her hands. "Exactly what is it about 'tastes like cardboard' that you don't get?"

"Okay, okay. There's got to be a way to make them palatable." Lia tapped her lower lip with her index finger, thinking.

"I find I can disguise almost anything in spaghetti sauce, especially if I use a lot of garlic."

Lia just looked at her.

"Why don't you settle for a pot of mujadara? That's easy enough to make."

"Enzymes, Bailey. You cook them and you kill enzymes. You know that." Lia scowled.

"A marinade, maybe?" Bailey suggested, conciliatory.

"Takes too long. I want something I can whip up. Miso maybe? It's savory, so it should go with the taste."

"If you can call it taste. That might be too ambitious."

Lia pulled out her blender and her single cup coffee maker from their place at the back of the counter. "I know! A miso lentil smoothie." She poured a cup of cold water into her one-cup coffee maker to heat it up, then pulled the miso out of the fridge. While the water heated, she rinsed a cup of sprouts and dumped them in the blender. She added a heaping tablespoon of red miso, returned the tub to the fridge and emerged with a bag of washed, chopped kale. "I put this in my blueberry smoothies all the time. It should be fine with the lentils."

"I don't know, Lia. You sure you want to make so much? What if it tastes bad?"

"Have a little faith. There isn't a smoothie alive that I can't swallow." She dumped a large handful of greens on top of the sprouts. Now the hot water was ready. She poured it on top of everything, closed the lid and turned the blender on. Sixty seconds later, Lia turned it off and popped the lid.

They peered in at the lumpy green mess.

"This reminds me of something," Bailey said. "I can't think of what it is, though."

Lia filled a glass with her concoction. "Want some?"

"You first."

"Bottoms up." She tilted the glass and took a drink. Eyes wide, Lia thumped the glass down on the counter then leaned over and spat into the sink. She grabbed a clean glass, filled it with water and rinsed her mouth several times. Finally she set the glass back down and leaned back against the counter. All while Bailey doubled over with laughter.

"That was the single most revolting thing I've ever tasted," Lia admitted. She dumped her invention back in the blender and hauled it into the bathroom, Bailey following.

"Must you watch?"

"I'm so starved for entertainment."

Lia dumped the green mush into the toilet and flushed.

"Linda Blair," Bailey said.

"Huh?"

"You looked just like Linda Blair spewing out vomit in *The Exorcist*. That's what that stuff reminded me of. You know, after her head spins around backward? Watching you spit it out reminded me."

"So glad I could be of service. Still starved for entertainment?"

"Maybe. Got any DVDs with good beefcake?"

"That depends. Are you going to tell Peter about this?"

"Hmmm."

"Bailey, promise me you'll never tell Peter I spit out one of my smoothies."

"I dunno." She held one hand out, palm up. "Beefcake," she said, looking at her hand as if she expected a tiny stud muffin to appear there. ". . . humiliating you in a way that you will never live down." She held out her other hand. She hummed while she joggled her upturned palms, mimicking a scale while she weighed her options. "This is a really tough decision."

"Bailey, you tell Peter and I'll never talk to you again."

Bailey pursed her lips, nodded her head thoughtfully, considering.

"Bailey!"

"I'm thinking, I'm thinking."

"I'll download season one of *The Doll House*."

"Well . . . I don't know . . . ."

"Okay, okay. If you'll go pick it up, I'll order Dewey's."

~

"What's this obsession you have with lentil recipes?" Bailey asked around a mouthful of spinach, garlic and goat cheese pizza.

"I'm trying to up my raw food quotient. I ate lentils all winter because they're the only alkaline bean and I'm trying to keep my PH balanced. There has to be a way to eat them raw. I refuse to turn my back on all those lovely enzymes."

"What about just munching them? I don't like eating cardboard, but that's just me."

"I tried that while I was running errands the other day. I was so proud of myself for eating a whole cup of lentil sprouts. Then my car drove itself to UDF and when I came to, I was at the register with a couple of custard filled, chocolate-iced Bismarcks. It was totally counter productive."

"Sure, but you got to eat chocolate."

"There is that."

Lia pulled out her phone on break at Scholastic that night to check her messages, hoping Peter called. She had one message on voicemail. It was Steve from the Homeless Alliance. She almost hung up her phone out of disappointment. "Lia, It's Steve Reams. I kept asking around, and I finally talked to someone who remembered your mystery guy's real name. It's Eric Flynn. Hope this helps. Let me know if you need anything else."

Lia's ears rang and her breathing became shallow. *Eric?* Nice Eric, who she picked out for Desiree? *Eric is a stalker . . . a killer?* She looked at the clock. Seven minutes, and she had to be back at her workstation. Next to Eric. She felt nauseated, as if she might throw up. *What am I going to do about this? How am I going to make it through the next two hours? Act normal. Just act normal, and after you get off work you can tell Peter. He doesn't know you know and he can't hurt you while you're at work.*

Lia avoided looking at Eric as she made her way to her chair. She kept her eyes on her monitor and tried to concentrate on her work. Good thing employee chatter was discouraged. Her mind extrapolated possibilities. *Eric killed Desiree. Eric made me a doll. Is Eric going to kill me?* She would have given anything to leave right that moment, but she didn't want to call attention to herself.

She had to reread many papers several times to get her focus. Twice Eric showed her scoring mistakes she'd made. She kept her eyes down while her heart pounded and nodded in response to Eric's concerns, promising to try harder.

The clock moved so slowly it would have lost a race with continental drift.

Finally Eric announced that it was time to finish scoring the current paper and shut down.

Lia grabbed her bag and scooted her chair back, preparing to make a quick exit. Eric put a hand on her arm to stop her.

"Lia, can you stick around? I need to talk to you."

"I, uh, someone's waiting on me," she lied.

"Five minutes?"

"Uh . . ." She did rapid mental calculations. Five minutes, and people would still be in the building, even if they weren't in this room. There would still be cars in the parking lot. She could hold it together for five minutes, sure she could.

Her insides froze as Eric collected folders and her teammates gathered their belongings and joined the evening exodus.

Finally, the room was empty. Eric sat back down.

"What did you need, Eric?" she asked, anxious to get away.

"You've been off your game the entire second half of shift. Are you okay?"

"I'm fine, really." *Except for my heart pounding in my ears.*

"Something's bothering you, I can tell. What happened over break?"

"Look, it's personal. I promise I'll do better tomorrow. I've got to go." She stood up, fingering the kubotan in her sweater pocket anxiously.

"I really have to go." Her voice turned into a squeak. Appalled, she lunged for freedom.

He grabbed her arm, "Lia, you're freaking out. What is this?"

"Let me go, Eric," she exploded. "Don't ever touch me. I know what you are. I know what you did to Desiree." Shocked, he dropped her arm. She backed away, keeping her eyes on him.

"Now wait a minute. . . ." he began, coming towards her.

"Stay back!" She pulled her hand out of her pocket and before she thought about it, she depressed the plunger on her kubotan, hitting Eric in the chest with pepper spray. He howled with pain and surprise.

She turned and ran, not stopping until she'd crossed the parking lot and arrived, panting and sobbing at her old Volvo. Only to see a little foil doll perched on her driver-side mirror.

Lia gave a strangled cry of frustration and struck the doll. It bounced off the next car and passed through the headlights of a car pinned in the nightly logjam. It landed on the asphalt where another departing employee stepped on it.

She looked back as she fumbled with the Volvo's lock, her hand shaking so hard she dropped her keys twice. *If this were the Terminator, he'd pop up in front of me right now, looking like Terry and calling my dog by the wrong name. . . .* A security guard was standing in the doorway, scanning the nightly traffic jam. *Yep, that's Eric, he's killed the guard and morphed into a replica of him so I won't realize he's following me. I've got to stop this. I'll go into hysterics and I won't know if it's because I'm laughing or freaking out.*

There were too many cars. No way would Eric be able to pick her out. Heart pounding, she eased her car into the melee. The stop and go traffic increased her distress as she attempted to avoid rear-ending the car in front of her while struggling to absorb her confrontation with Eric. The nightly exodus snaked around the building at a snails pace until, finally, she pulled out on the boulevard. She gunned her car, squealing her tires as she tore down the road. She slammed on the brakes when she saw the lights of the first gas station, over a mile from Scholastic.

Lia sat in her car with her phone in her hand and waited for her heart to stop pounding. *Breathe. Remember what Asia taught you.* When she thought she could speak again, she speed dialed Peter.

"Hey, I wasn't expecting to hear from you tonight. What's the occasion?"

"Peter," she quavered. "I know who killed Desiree, and he knows I know."

❧

Peter tapped his foot impatiently as he sat on Lia's porch, waiting for her to get home. Four dogs watched through the living room window, paws propped on the sill, heads in a row, whining to get out.

Lia had refused his offer to come get her, saying she'd feel better if she kept moving. He'd promised to wait for her. *That creep knows where she lives.* There wasn't much chance that Eric could beat her home, not since she'd

maced him and he'd be busy filing an incident report, if not a police report. *No. He won't go to the police. Too much explaining.*
Really, she was at greater risk of having an accident than she was of being accosted. He'd made her promise to drive carefully.

Headlights broke the night from the far end of the block, growing as they drew near. Lia's black sedan pulled into the only available parking space, two doors beyond her two-family. Peter breathed a sigh of relief as she got out of the car.

A dark van pulled out of a driveway a half-block away. It slowed as it drew abreast with Lia. Before Peter could react, the back doors flew open. Someone wearing a visored motorcycle helmet tossed a pillowcase over Lia's head and dragged her in. Her screams were cut out as the van's lights switched off. Her abductors peeled out leaving Peter standing in the middle of the street, hoping for a plate number.

The light over the license plate was out.

Peter raced towards his car, beyond the spot where Lia had been taken. Something pink caught his eye and his step faltered. He coughed as he entered the residual cloud of pepper spray, his eyes lured by the rosy gleam on the pavement. The kubotan, his birthday present to Lia, lay on the pavement. The bulk of the shot must have hit the visor of her attacker's helmet. That's why it hadn't incapacitated him.

*It'll just have to lay there.*

Peter jumped into his Explorer, whipped it around and squealed his tires in pursuit. Kirby Road was two blocks away. He had to get there before the van disappeared. He pulled up to the stop sign, in front of the decommissioned Kirby Elementary School, looking both ways. No vehicles in sight.

He slammed the wheel with his fist. Eenie, meanie, miney. . . . Left was better traveled and well lit, leading to the Northside business district. In that direction, it was a straight shot to the stoplight several blocks away at Chase Avenue, and not a van in sight. *Their lights were off. Maybe I just don't see them.*

To the right the road darkened and curved, leading into the backroads. He went right, grabbing up the mic on his radio to call it in, Lia's screams echoing inside his head.

Lia tensed when the lights of a car caught her eye to the left. The van pulled past her, then stopped. She screamed as a sack of some sort came down over her head, but still managed to get off a shot of mace from her kubotan keychain. The pepper spray filled the air and she started coughing as rough hands dragged her back, into the cargo bay of the van.

*Where's Peter? Why didn't the pepper spray work?* She kicked, twisted and squirmed while her abductor held her arms against her side, his fingers digging into her biceps.

"Jesus," her abductor coughed. "Open the windows, will you, this stuff is killing me."

"The windows are down. Fumes are coming off your helmet. Put your helmet in the garbage bag, like I told you, asshole," Abductor Number 2 said.

"How'm I supposed to do that?" Abductor Number 1 spat out, coughing. "I gotta hold her, don't I?"

"Oh, for Chrissake." The van veered suddenly, drove up a short incline, whipped around and screeched to a stop, rocking on bad shocks. Seconds went by. Lia felt a gun pressed into her shoulder.

She stilled.

"That's right, bitch. You be good now while my friend ties you up or I'm going to shoot your shoulder. You don't need your shoulder for what we want." He coughed. "Get rid of that damn helmet and tie her up. And hurry."

The worst of the fumes dissipated, then rough hands pulled her wrists together behind her back and wrapped duct tape around them.

"Tape that pillowcase around her neck. I don't want her seeing us."

*They don't want me to know who they are. They must not plan to kill me.* She prayed they didn't change their mind.

The coarse hands gathered the pillowcase around her neck. Fingers groped the chain of Desiree's necklace and pulled it out of Lia's shirt. "Nice," Abductor Number 1 said, tugging on the pendant.

"Hurry up. We've got company."

Cherie Jackson traced one glittery nail across the well-muscled thigh of Officer Brainard, who was sitting in his patrol car behind Kirby Road School with his pants down around his ankles. She was satisfied when she heard his sharp intake of breath. "Jesus, you're killing me," he gasped. "Put me out of my misery."

"Sugar, you're spoiling all my fun. Don't be in such a hurry."

"Your fun is about to spoil itsel—" Brainard's head jerked up at the sound of screeching tires. Annoyed that someone else was using his favorite break spot, he looked out the windshield and wondered why the headlights on the midnight blue van were off.

"Wait here. I need to check this out." It had been easier to take his pants down than it was to pull them back up. The van sat, motionless. He zipped up his pants with difficulty and left the car door open after he exited, not wanting to alert his target until he was ready. Flashlight in his left hand, he unsnapped his holster with his right. He reached for his weapon when the memory of his unfortunate encounter with that jackass at the bank and the ensuing ass scalding halted his hand.

When he was 15 feet away, he switched on the flashlight, illuminating the van. There was no one in the driver's seat. He circled around towards the windshield so he could shine his light inside the back of the van.

A man in a ski mask popped up and fired three shots out the driver's side window. Brainard was raising his gun when the fourth shot hit him in the chest.

Cherie screamed as the van peeled out. When it got to the edge of the parking lot, the back door flew open and a body tumbled to the asphalt.

Peter heard the call for officer down at Kirby School and cursed himself. *That's why the van disappeared so quickly. It pulled onto Innes and hid behind the school, and like an idiot, I drove right past them. I thought they'd be hightailing it. Makes no sense.*

He followed an ambulance onto the lot. As he drove up the incline to the school parking lot, he spied a white blur on the pavement. It shifted, and he saw that it was attached to a body. Lia's body.

He forgot about his fellow officer, jumping out of the Explorer as a line of patrol cars blew past him towards an unidentified woman kneeling over the body he assumed was The downed officer.

"Hold on, Babe. I've got you. I've got you. Everything's going to be okay." He prayed he was right as he felt her arms and legs for broken bones, then pulled out a pocket knife and began sawing through the duct tape binding her wrists.

"Peter?" Her voice was weak and muffled by the pillow case.

"I'm here. Are you okay?"

"I hurt."

"Where, Babe? Tell me where?"

"All over."

"I'm sorry, Babe. I've got to give you a redneck wax. It's going to hurt, but the sting will go away."

"What are you talking ab—"

He ripped the duct tape off, taking all attached body hair with it. She screamed.

"It's like a Brazilian, but cheaper," Peter explained.

Her wrists freed, she felt around for his arm and began hitting him.

"Ow! Hold on, you want me to get this pillowcase off, don't you?" She lowered her fists so he could reach her neck.

Sirens blasting, more patrol cars pulled up. He waved them on to the back of the lot.

An EMT approached. "Your man is stable. We're taking him in," he said to Peter. "How are you feeling, Miss? Up for a ride to the hospital?"

"Can't you look at me here? I think it's just road rash and some bruises."

"The young lady with Brainard said you were tossed out of a van. Did you hit your head? You might have a concussion."

He checked her vitals, peered into her eyes.

"I'll look after her," Peter said.

The EMT wasn't happy, but he gave them both instructions for the next couple days.

Brent joined them, stooping to keep the knees of his pants off the pavement. "Well, now, Lia, aren't you a sore sight for my eyes? Anything I can give you a hand with?"

Lia twitched one corner of her mouth in a ghost of a smile.

A line of patrol cars filed out of the parking lot, presumably to search for the van. One remained behind to secure the area for the crime scene techs.

"What's happening?" Peter asked Brent.

"Well, now, let's see. Brainard was on break, apparently having a chat with Miss Cherie, whose claim that she is 21 is entirely suspect, despite her possession of an official replica of an Ohio State ID Card. Incidentally, they were chatting with his radio off, which would be why he didn't hear the BOLO ."

"A chat?" Peter raised his eyebrows.

"Actually, I think it was more of a 'chat.'" Brent hooked two fingers of each hand to frame the quote. "But I digress. Miss Cherie says the van pulled in and Brainard thought it was strange and decided to investigate, though I think he wanted to chase it off so it wouldn't disturb his tete-a-tete with the young lady. When he approached the vehicle, the driver fired several times, hitting Brainard once in the chest. Then he drove off, discarding our lovely Lia on the way out."

"How's Officer Brainard?" Lia asked.

"Lost some blood. Doesn't seem to have hit any organs, but they won't know for sure until they get him on the table. Good thing he's unconscious. Come morning, he's going to have some 'splainin' to do."

"Why is that?" Lia asked. "He got shot saving me."

"That was just dumb luck, emphasis on dumb. If he'd had his radio on, he'd have known about the van, and he'd have called for back-up before he approached. And if he'd been wearing his Kevlar vest, he would be bruised but not bleeding. Then there's the questionable presence of Miss Cherie, who is well known to the constabulary for her entrepreneurial activities and her official replica state ID."

Lia's mouth made a big 'O.' "Why do I think this doesn't bother you?"

"Well, now, it's just so nice to know that God still looks after drunks and idiots. I'm so very happy he didn't die, because I'd hate like hell to give a hero's send-off to an officer who bungled himself to death."

"I think you're afraid he'll take your title as the department pretty-boy."

"No one, Miss Lia, not even Officer Brain-dead," he reached out and flicked her on the nose, "is taking away my title as department pretty-boy, if I have to ream his colon with my Manolo Blahnik knock-offs. Let's get you home before the vultures—I mean press—show up. Can you walk?"

Brent and Peter helped her stand. She took a few steps and pronounced herself fit.

"I know why I'm going home with Lia, but why are you coming?" Peter asked Brent.

"Because I am the detective in charge and I need statements from both of you."

"You go detect something. I'll get Lia's statement."

"You, sir, are a witness. Besides, the powers that be wanted someone working this case who doesn't have carnal knowledge of the victim. You should thank me. Captain Roller wanted to give it to Heckle and Jeckle, but I suggested that since they were too busy with Desiree's murder to respond to Miss Anderson's reports that she was being targeted for unknown nefarious purposes, that maybe someone else should take it, if he wanted the victim to cooperate."

A jazzy tune played from Brent's pocket. He pulled out his phone. "Talk to me. . . .You don't say. So soon? . . . Good work. I'll be right there." He ended the call. "Change of plans. Your van has just been discovered up the road by that little church on Kirby. Turns out, it's stolen. I'm going to meet the crime scene investigators there. Looks like poor Hinkle is stuck on scene here until they've got another crew available to search this location."

Suddenly tired, Lia leaned against Peter and let him fold her into his arms. She sank into him, felt his body heat, shut her eyes and wished everything would just go away.

"You okay, Babe?"

"Babe is a pig," she muttered into his shirt.

"Yep, you'll live. Let's get you home." He helped her into his Explorer. Was she really only a block from home?

Peter would mother her. He would insist on staying the night and watching over her. She was too hurt to care about the ramifications. Right now she needed him and she was glad he was there.

While the dogs huddled around Lia, Peter dug out her ancient brick of epsom salts and ran a bath, scenting it with her lavender oil. He led her to the candlelit bathroom like a small child, then left, insisting that she soak at least fifteen minutes.

She slid down in the tub so the hot water covered her shoulders, leeching the panic out of her bones. She lay there and cried, silent, hot tears streaming down her face, dripping into the water, mingling with her bath while she shook.

A warmth enveloped Lia's head, Peter's hand stroking her hair as he sat on the edge of the tub. She scooted up so she could lean her head against his thigh.

"I'd like to put you straight to bed, but we've got to get as much of the pepper oil off you as we can. You've got overspray in your hair."

Obediently, she unclipped her hair and dunked it in the bath. Peter lathered it up with Dawn dish detergent and massaged her scalp. She dunked her head again in the bathwater, then Peter had her stand up while the tub drained. He lathered her all over, his touch soothing and gentle, while she stood, helpless and limp as a rag doll.

He turned on the shower so she could rinse, and she stood with her face turned to the pelting water, the sting driving everything else out of her mind. Despite his innocent intent, the touch of Peter's hands roused a tiny flame deep inside her as he sluiced soap off her body. She concentrated on this bit of life, on the trail of sensation his warm hands left as he ran them over her limbs. She fanned it until it was a hot, insistent glow, like a propane torch.

Peter turned off the shower and guided her out of the tub. She stood on the bathmat while he toweled her hair and wrapped her in a second towel. Then he sat on the toilet and drew her into his arms.

Lia curled up in his lap, seeking his warmth. She slipped a button on his shirt open so she could rub her cheek against his chest. The heat of his skin against hers wasn't enough. With animal instinct, she continued unbuttoning his shirt as she let the towel drop, and pressed her flesh against him.

Peter took her shoulders and pushed her a few, necessary inches away. He lifted her chin and looked into her aching eyes.

"I'm trying to do the decent thing here, Babe, and you're making it impossible."

Lia held his gaze as he searched her face.

"I don't want you to be decent. I want to feel alive. I want to forget. Make me forget, Peter." She took his hand and drew it to her breast. His hand responded, unconsciously stroking the drying skin with the scattered drops of remaining water, absently thumbing her nipple, sending hot frissons through Lia's body that exploded in little thrills at her core. Lia pressed her other breast into his chest, rubbing, and sinking her fingers into his hair.

"Won't you hate me in the morning?" he asked.

"Forget tomorrow." She kissed his chest. "Forget the rest of it." She nuzzled the notch at the base of his neck. "I don't want to think right now." She pressed her mouth against his neck, kissing wetly, then gently sucking the skin. She worked her way up to his ear lobe and nipped. "I've never wanted you so much, Peter," she breathed into his ear.

Weeks without her persuaded Peter's body to join forces with Lia and gang up on his brain. He surrendered to the onslaught of sensation draining the blood from his head. Peter stood up with difficultly, Lia in his arms, and carried her into the bedroom, kicking the door shut in the muzzles of four affronted dogs.

He placed her on the bed and lay down beside her. She reached for the button on his jeans.

"Uh uh." He ran a hand down her cheek, turning her face to him. "We're doing this my way." He ripped off his shirt, gathered her in his arms and rolled on top of her naked body, his head buried in the crook of her neck, seeping himself in her. Finally he snapped. His body quaked as he shook in anguish at the night's events.

"Oh, God, Babe, I thought I'd lost you," his voice was raw as he choked the words out.

His vulnerability and need pulled Lia out of herself, the first blush of a new awareness dawning in her. "Shhh," she soothed. "I'm right here."

# Chapter 26

**Friday, June 13**

The beep of an incoming text woke Peter after three hours sleep. He sat up in Lia's bed and looked at the message.

"OMW 2 Lia's. R U There?"

He tapped out a reply. "Yes. Don't ring bell. Text when U arrive."

He laid the phone back on the table and turned to look at Lia's face, softly lit by the overcast morning slipping through the curtains. Her chest rose and fell evenly and her face was relaxed, absent the distress of the night before. He resisted the urge to stroke her face, kiss her awake.

Last night had been tender as an open wound, an aching, animal kaleidoscope of need and sensation, speaking body to body what they would not say out loud, exorcising their fear with an exquisite blend of howling need and blind animal response. A marriage of fear-driven hormones with love, heightened by their recent sexual desert. They'd drunk deeply at this oasis, which would, like a mirage, like a dream, disappear as soon as Lia woke up. He sat in the gray light and watched her breathe, wishing.

. . .

Brent arrived with bagels and cream cheese. "Dough-nuts," he explained, helping himself to a cup of freshly brewed coffee "seem frivolous under the circumstances."

Lia smelled coffee before she opened her eyes. Gradually, she registered the murmuring of the men in her kitchen. She drew back the covers and rolled onto her side, nearly colliding with the row of dog muzzles lined up on the edge of the bed. Eight eyes stared at her. Julia whimpered for attention and Chewy danced around on his hind legs.

"I know, I abandoned you. Sorry, pups. Ow!" The pain in her back was unexpected. She looked down at her arms, saw the bruises purpling there, the scrape of asphalt scabbing her belly, and ached all over. Four dogs sniffed at her. She took a moment to pet them.

And remembered.

Someone kidnapped her when she got out of her car, someone who knew she carried pepper-spray. She didn't know who or why.

The memory of her abduction was overtaken by other memories, tender memories of Peter taking care of her, soothing her, and when she did not want to be soothed, scalding memories of Peter taking her out of herself in a sea of surrender and sensation that was as terrifying as it was glorious.

She picked Peter's torn shirt up off the floor and rubbed it against her face, inhaling the scent of him. She thought about putting it on, then discarded the idea in favor of her oldest, rattiest, most comforting robe. Moving cautiously, she went to join Peter and Brent with her furry honor guard trailing after her.

"There's our girl," Brent said, pulling out a chair at the kitchen table. "Let me get you a cup of coffee. I brought bagels with lox and cream cheese because you need to keep up your strength. Are you ready for one, or would you like to wait a bit?"

Lia accepted a steaming souvenir mug gratefully and wrapped her hands around it, pressing it against her chest with her eyes closed, concentrating on the heat seeping into her skin. Honey pressed to her side. She responded by reaching a hand down and running it through the silky fur.

Though her eyes were closed, she knew Peter's eyes were on her. They would be thoughtful and maybe a little sad. She couldn't think about that right now. She wondered, instead, where he'd dug up the tee shirt he was wearing.

Finally, she raised her head, took a sip. She did not look at Peter. "What did you find out?" she asked Brent.

"Nothing so far. We got fingerprints, but we need to get exemplars from the family who owns the van. If the perps wore gloves, it's a waste of time. Are you ready to talk about it?"

"Any news on Officer Brainard?"

"He's busy charming nurses and reporters at Good Samaritan. He'll be on medical leave while he heals. They're giving him a public commendation for foiling an abduction. Of course, that will come with a private ass-whipping. What I wouldn't give to be a fly on the wall for that."

Peter slid a toasted blueberry bagel smeared with cream cheese in front of her. She smiled at him, picked it up and took a nibble, decided that she could handle food, took another bite. "Okay, I'm ready."

Brent set up his recorder, noted the date time and participants while Lia tore bits off her bagel and handed them out under the table. She distracted herself by guessing which muzzle nosed each treat out of her hand. Lia recounted her story between bites of bagel and sips of coffee.

"What I don't understand," Brent said, "is why they dumped you. They had you, and before they could accomplish their purpose, whatever it was, they had to pull

222

over to secure you and neutralize the fumes from the helmet. Then Brainard interferes. But they take care of Brainard, and considering they had to expect pursuit, wouldn't a hostage be handy?"

"Could one of those men have been Eric?" Peter asked Lia.

"I don't think so. I was thinking maybe he had friends, but if that's it, he set them on me while he was still washing pepper-spray out of his eyes. It would take longer than that to steal a car."

"Truth," Brent said.

Lia put her hand over her mouth. "Oh my God," she moaned.

"What is it, Lia?" Peter asked.

"What if Eric didn't kill Desiree? What if he's guilty of nothing more than leaving her little dolls? I pepper-sprayed an innocent man. No wonder he acted like I was nuts."

"He was spying on you and posted that video on YouTube," Peter pointed out. "That's worth at least one squirt of pepper-juice."

"Maybe several," Brent said. "It's not the act of a sane man. And if it wasn't him, who was it? It's too coincidental that he and some other dude would fixate on Desiree and then you at the same time."

"There has to be a connection," Peter said.

"Thanks for the bagels," Lia said, leaning on her door.

Brent winked at her. "You'll be okay with the tall guy looking after you. Call me if you think of anything else, whether you think it's important or not." He bent down to pet Honey and Viola, flicked a dog hair off his slacks and waved to Peter over Lia's shoulder.

She shut the door and turned around. "Are you looking after me?"

"If you'll let me."

Lia's knee jerk response was to say she wanted to be alone. How could she process any of the previous night's events with Peter around?

Peter read her thoughts. "Let's put it away for a while. Just pretend I'm your body guard, nothing more."

"You sure?"

"I want to keep you around long enough for us to figure things out, so, yeah."

"Goddess, what happened to you?" Bailey eyed Lia's ever-darkening collection of bruises as Lia and Peter accompanied their horde through the dog park corral. "I swear, we can't leave you alone for a minute! When did this happen?"

"I was getting out of my car. Peter was waiting on the porch for me, and they grabbed me right in front of him."

"Who? Who did this?"

"We don't know," Lia said.

Lia limped over to their usual table and climbed up. Bailey joined her, along with Kita, who circled on the table top next to Bailey.

"What's that smell?" Bailey asked.

Lia sniffed her own shoulder. "I used my mace twice last night. I guess it lingers, even if it doesn't hit you directly. Sorry about that. Looks like my bath didn't take care of it. I've been told it can stick around for a few days."

Peter lured the dogs away with a pair of tennis balls and sent them racing to the other end of the park, allowing Lia some time with her friends. Terry and Jose strolled up, Jackson bounding around them, playing tag with Napa, while Sophie ambled behind, bearing her usual woeful expression.

"What's the word, what's the—Holy crap! What bus did you run into?" Terry asked.

Lia filled them in on the previous night's events.

"Let me get this straight," Jose said. "Someone goes to all the trouble to kidnap you, then they let you go two blocks away and they didn't even steal your wallet?"

"That's troubling," Terry said. "If they did not accomplish their purpose, they may be back."

"And Foil Man was disabled. What if he didn't break into your house, either? What if the break-in had nothing to do with him?" Bailey said.

"I still vote for Willis," Terry said. "He's obviously off his rocker."

"And Foil Man isn't?" Bailey challenged.

"Have we got enough fruitcake, or should I go dig one out of the bottom of my freezer?" Jose asked.

"Just what we need," Lia muttered. "Yeah, Jose, it will give me something to toss at the asshole next time my pepper spray doesn't work."

"We need to write everything down in one place," Terry said. "There's so much confusion, even my superior brain can't make sense of it. We need to establish a time-line."

"I'm sure Brent is doing that, Terry," Lia said.

"A little redundancy never hurt anything," Terry said.

"You just want to play detective," Bailey said.

"'Tis true, 'tis true. We shall see who solves the mystery first. I vote we reconvene at Lia's this afternoon."

Lia mourned another day lost on her convalescent center project. She didn't think she could paint right now anyway, and putting all the events down might help eliminate the morass of confusion that was her brain.

"I'll call Alma. Again."

"What about your job? You can't work the day after you get abducted." Bailey pointed out.

"I don't know if I even have a job left, after I maced Eric."

"Assume you do until you know for sure. Why don't you call in sick and see what they say."

Honey chased Viola to Lia's table, both dogs jumped up and slathered her face with kisses. She put an arm around each. "Hello, baby," she said to Honey. She turned to Viola, "Hello, Schizo-pup."

"Insulting my dog, Anderson?" Peter said, dropping down on the bench. Julia snagged the tennis ball he was carrying and crawled under the table. Chewy head-butted Peter's now-vacant hand. He patted the Schnauzer distractedly.

"If the paw fits . . . ," Lia said.

"Have you figured out whodunnit yet?"

"How would you know what we were talking about?"

"I suppose you were talking about ice fishing? Monster truck rallies? I know, the location of Miley Cyrus's latest piercing. No, wait, that's old news. How about a Kardashian sex change?"

Lia sighed. "Terry wants us to create a time line. I told him Brent was probably already doing that."

Peter shrugged. "Not a bad idea. You might come up with something that Brent misses."

Lia arrived home to a blinking message light. "Lia, It's Eric. I'm sorry I frightened you last night. I think there's been a misunderstanding. I didn't report our incident, and I'd like to meet you outside of work to clear things up. I saw on the news about your abduction. I took the liberty of telling the office that you were taking a day or two off to recover and you'd call in when you were ready to come back. Please call me."

"What do you think?" she asked Peter.

"I think he's afraid you're going to tell Scholastic why you maced him and get him fired for sexual harassment."

"Should I meet with him?"

"I wish you wouldn't. If you do, make it public. Maybe have Terry tag along and keep an eye on things from a short distance. Or I'll do it if I can. But you're almost finished with Alma's project. Do you really need the job anymore?" Peter stopped himself before he reminded her that he wasn't crazy about her working nights anyway.

"I'll have to check my finances," Lia said, crinkling her brow.

Peter kept his mouth shut here, too.

"Thank you for staying with me last night."

"I'd do anything for you, do you know that?"

"I know." She smiled a little, but her eyes remained sad. "It's going to take time, and there are things to talk about."

"Crime keeps getting in the way."

"It has a way of doing that." She rose up on her tiptoes and kissed him on the cheek. "Go fire up those cold cases. Call me tonight?"

"I'll do that." Peter knew better than to say it, but there was no way he was letting her go unprotected until this matter was settled.

"Say hello to Cynth," Lia said sweetly as Peter and Viola walked out the door. She was quite satisfied when he missed a step on the stoop.

Bailey and Terry arrived together. Bailey brought vegetarian burritos for everyone.

"I figured you wouldn't be up for cooking," Bailey said.

"I might die if I don't get my daily requirement of animal protein," Terry groused.

"Buck up, carnivore, it's got cheese," Bailey said.

"That's sissy protein."

"Thank you, Bailey." Lia unwrapped the burrito, topped it with hot sauce. "There are plenty of squirrels in the back yard, Terry."

Terry looked out the back window, where two chittering squirrels chased each other around a tree trunk. "Bah. Greasy stuff and not enough meat to be worth the effort of killing it. I brought my laptop. I figured two computers would be better than one."

"I brought mine," Bailey said.

"How should we proceed," Lia asked over a mouthful of black beans, avocado and brown rice.

"I think we need a calendar program, like the online Zoho calendar." Terry suggested. "That way, we can color code events according to who was involved. Meanwhile, I can set up a Google doc that we can all work on, where we can list our suspects and what we know about them."

"How far back should we go?" Lia asked.

"How about when you started your job at Scholastic?" Bailey asked. "Everything started happening after that."

"When did Foil Man make his first appearance?" Terry asked.

Lia thought back. "It was before I started working at Scholastic."

"What about when Desiree started working at Scholastic? Was it before then?" Bailey asked.

Lia frowned. "She worked a small project a few weeks before I started. When I met her, she'd only received two of the dolls, so maybe not. But if Eric is Foil Man, then Foil Man had nothing to do with my kidnapping. There was no time for him to beat me home from Scholastic."

"We only think he's Foil Man. He said there was a misunderstanding, didn't he? Maybe there was a mistake. Did he ever act like he lusted after Desiree?" Bailey asked.

"Well, no. . . ."

"Then we leave Foil Man in the equation," Terry said.

It took them an hour to hammer out the calendar of events.

"One thing is clear," Terry said.

"What's that?" Lia asked.

"Nothing of a criminous nature happened to you until Desiree died. While we can't assume anything, it looks like whatever went on with Desiree transferred to you at that time."

"Now, why would that be?" Lia asked.

"You were a known associate, one of very few females she spent time with."

"We stopped hanging out three weeks before then."

"But there *is* that YouTube video. Perhaps I should examine it tonight for clues," Terry said, twisting his mustache and wiggling his eyebrows.

Lia punched him on the arm.

Bailey said, "Perhaps we need to treat Foil Man as different from Desiree's killer. What do you think?"

"Maybe so. And list all the men who knew us both."

"There is a small chance you don't know the men who kidnapped you," Terry said, "if it turns out this is all about Desiree."

"Maybe list three perps. Foil Man, Desiree's killer and my abductors. We can merge them later if it makes sense. We honestly don't know that the person who killed Desiree abducted me."

"Who do we start with?" Bailey asked, pulling out her phone and opening an app for taking notes.

"We need a list of all the men who were around Desiree," Lia said.

"Three hundred scorers at Scholastic, about half male . . .," Terry mused.

"Get serious," Lia said. "Alphonso and Dave knew her best."

Bailey tapped their names into the app. "Who else?"

"Ted talked to her a lot at work," Lia said. "I was always catching Avery staring at her—that's our room supervisor."

"Oh, so he'd have access to her personnel file," Bailey said. "He'd know where she lived."

"Eric could have gotten the same information from the forms she handed in."

"Alphonso, Dave, Ted, Avery, Eric," Bailey read off. "Anyone else?"

"There were two painters at the house next door, they seemed to know a lot about her," Lia said. "Though they claimed they were drinking margaritas when she was shot."

"They offered you an alibi?" Terry asked. "Sounds suspicious."

Lia rolled her eyes. "No, they just mentioned it. Though we don't know when Desiree was shot, so that could be bogus."

"What about other men she knew from the bar?" Bailey asked.

"Who says it has to be a man? Maybe we're looking for a spurned woman."

"We don't know of any spurned women, so we can table that idea," Lia said. "And Heckle and Jeckle checked out all her known boyfriends. For now, let's assume they were clean."

"Wouldn't Dave have been at the bar when she was shot?" Bailey asked.

"He was a block away," Terry said. "He could have slipped out."

"Where did the extra guy come in?" Bailey asked.

"Dave would be able to scare up any number of young guys to help him," Lia said.

"How about Avery and Eric? Those depths are untapped." Terry said.

"Ugh," Lia said, "Let's leave them that way. Bailey, you've been writing all this down, what do you think?"

"The painters are the obvious choice if you're looking for two healthy younger guys, but I'm really curious about Ted. What do you know about him?"

"Not much. He's married," Lia said.

"Correction," Terry said. "He told us he was married. Not the same."

Bailey checked her notes. "Dave and the painters had the most opportunity. It should be easy enough to find out if they were seen when Desiree was killed or you were

230

kidnapped. I wonder if the painters do their drinking at The Comet?"

"Why would Dave kill Desiree? He was in love with her," Lia said.

"Maybe we're looking at this all wrong," Terry said. "We're assuming the thugs dumped you because they'd been discovered, before they were able to achieve their purpose."

"And?" Lia asked.

"What if they dumped you because they didn't need you anymore." He stabbed his index finger in the air. "What if the fact of the abduction was the point?"

"What would that accomplish?" Lia asked.

Terry stroked his chin. "I don't know . . . I must ponder this. Perhaps a threat to assure her compliance at a later date?"

"To what purpose?" Bailey asked. "Lia, what all *did* they accomplish during your abduction?"

"Besides terrorizing me? They kept me from getting home on time, but Peter was already there."

"They lured Peter away from the house," Bailey pointed out. "Was anything disturbed when you came back?"

Lia shook her head. "Not that I could tell."

"And they didn't get your wallet or your phone." Bailey said.

"All they got was Desiree's necklace. He was going to take my wallet and cell phone, but Brainard interrupted them, so they took off and dumped me."

"The amethyst? What would they want with that?" Terry asked. "It was pretty and all, but hardly worth the risk."

"I don't know," Bailey said, "but let's think this through."

"But the driver said he would shoot my shoulder, that I wouldn't need it for what they wanted me for. It sounded like they were going to rape me."

231

"That would be an excellent way to encourage your compliance, wouldn't it?" Terry said. "Or maybe that was just going to be a bonus. They targeted you. If they just wanted to rape someone, there are easier ways to do it than with a cop boyfriend in pursuit."

"Let's get back to the amethyst," Bailey said. "It's the only thing we know for sure that was accomplished out of everything that's happened. Nothing was taken—that you know of—when you had the break-in, and both break-ins at Desiree's and the one here showed they were looking for something small."

"How do you know it was small?" Lia asked.

"I saw the mess. They got into everything. You don't look for a Volkswagen in a breadbox.

"Now, you found the necklace back in Julia's hoard under the bush. What do you want to bet Julia stole it before that goon broke in and shot her. Therefore, he would not have found it when he broke in, and Desiree would not have been able to tell him where it was if she wanted to," Bailey said.

"So he's trying to scare the location of the necklace out of her and shoots her by mistake?" Lia asks.

"Or he's insanely angry about it being lost, and she can identify him," Terry said.

"We need to find out more about the necklace."

"Do you think the landlady would know anything?" Bailey asked.

"Doubtful. She strike you as the type to let us haul off all Desiree's stuff if she knew there was something valuable there?"

"Dave knew Desiree better than anyone. He might know where she got it. Who's up for a trip to The Comet?" Lia asked.

"How do we know Dave isn't our perp?" Terry asked. "You could be walking into the lion's den."

"He told me to keep the necklace. Why would he do that if he wanted it?"

"Better you have it than be outbid at auction," Terry said.

"I don't know . . . but that's one reason to go into the bar, to see how he reacts when I ask him about it."

Dave set three ginger-ales on the bar before they could order.

"On the house."

"What did we do to rate special treatment?" Bailey asked.

"We raised over a thousand dollars for Three Sisters."

Lia winced. "But we got your bar shot up."

Dave shrugged. "It was my idea to hold the service." He glanced around to assure no one was listening. "The publicity I'm getting from the stand-off is worth ten times the cost of repairs. I'm leaving the bullet holes. People are driving in from all over the Tri-state to see them."

"I'm glad you see a bright side to it. Now I don't have to feel awful about it anymore. Can I ask you a question?"

"Sure, shoot."

Lia absently touched the spot on her chest where the amethyst had lain, forgetting for a moment that it was no longer there.

"The necklace, the one you told me to keep? Do you know where it came from?"

Dave rubbed his chin while considering Lia's question. "Desiree never wore it in here and she never mentioned it. The first time I saw it was on you. Why do you want to know?"

"Just curious. I wanted to know more about it, give it a story, " Lia said.

The trio conferred over their ginger-ales as Dave went about his business.

"Alfonso said he'd never seen the necklace before," Bailey said.

"But he said it was worthless," Lia reminded her.

"He still might know where it came from," Bailey said.

"He tried to buy it. Maybe he said it wasn't worth anything so I'd think fifty dollars was a good deal," Lia said.

"Could Alfonso Vasari be our man?" Terry asked.

"If he is, he has help. The guys who attacked me were younger."

"How do you know they were younger?" Bailey asked.

"The way they talked, like a couple of young idiots."

"Were they familiar to you at all?" Bailey asked.

"Geezelpete! How was I supposed to tell with a pillowcase on my head?"

Terry looked at his watch. "It's five-thirty now. I imagine Vasari closes at six. I don't know if we'd make it."

"We need to think about this. The sensible thing to do is tell Peter our theory and let him pass it on to Brent. They're the professionals," Lia said.

"Peter and Brent have guns, too," Bailey said.

"Bah," Terry said. "Faint heart never won lady fair."

Bailey looked at Lia. "You want to win lady fair? She's not exactly my type."

Lia rolled her eyes.

"Of course," Bailey said, "we could snoop around the back of the store after everyone's gone."

"What good would that do?" Terry asked.

"Aren't the cops always going through garbage?"

"What would we be looking for?" Terry asked.

"I don't know . . . Lia, didn't you throw out that towel you used to wash up after you maced everyone last night?"

"Well, duh. It reeked." Lia wrinkled her nose at the memory.

"Maybe your attacker did, too. When is garbage collection in Clifton?" Bailey asked.

"That would be Thursday. But even if it was Alfonso, he wouldn't have washed up at the shop, would he?" Terry said.

"You think he wants to go home to his wife smelling like pepper spray?" Bailey said.

"Good point. But I still think it makes more sense that he would wash up at home. So, are we going to skulk around sniffing trash?" Terry said.

"Well?" Bailey asked. "Are we? Or are we going to hand this brilliant idea over to Peter and Brent?"

"Depends. We've got to figure out where Alfonso lives, and when his garbage goes out," Terry said.

Bailey looked up, noted that Dave was at the other end of the bar, then whispered. "We should check Dave's garbage, too."

"Why would we do that? He said he never saw the necklace on Desiree," Terry said.

"What else *would* he say if he was behind it? And why would Alfonso admit to knowing about it if he wanted to get it from Lia?" Bailey said.

"Excellent question," Terry said. "Perhaps our friend behind the bar was not so smitten with the lovely Desiree as he claimed. Perhaps he set up the memorial service to give him a chance to take the necklace."

"He did offer to help you search through her papers," Bailey said to Lia.

"True." *Because he needed to plant the designated agent form.*

"Cheezit! Here he comes!" Bailey whispered.

"How are you folks doing down here?" Dave asked, eyeing their empty glasses. "Can I interest you in some nachos?"

"We were just leaving," Lia said. "But thank you."

"Sorry I couldn't be more help," Dave said.

Lia waited until everyone was in Terry's truck. "Are you both nuts?" she exploded. "Crazy people are waving guns around and you want to go digging through their garbage?"

"While taking appropriate precautions, of course," Terry said, affronted.

"Right. More guns," Lia snarked. "I've been shot. Have either of you ever been shot? No? Well, it doesn't feel very good. I'm going to share what we think with Peter and Brent and let them take care of it. You two can do what you want, but leave me out of it."

"Well, er . . ," Terry mumbled.

"How about this?" Bailey offered. "Terry and I will put on our rattiest clothes and take my truck. We'll pretend we're trash-pickers. Dave might recognize us if we're not careful, but Terry's never met Vasari, and he only saw me one time. He won't recognize me if I tuck my hair up."

"And what are you going to do if you find anything?" Lia asked. "Once you take it, how will you prove where it came from? DNA's not as easy to get as everyone thinks."

"What if we just sniff the bags, and if we think we have something, we back off and call Peter. Would that work?"

"Your necklace? You think they were after your necklace?" Peter asked.

He and Brent were sitting in Lia's living room. Peter was off duty and wasn't even supposed to be in on this conversation. He had a beer. Brent eyed it enviously. Lia said she wouldn't tell, but Brent refused to drink on duty. Brent shrugged and took another bite of the vegetable and brown rice casserole Alma sent over so Lia wouldn't have to think about cooking. Viola sat alert at Brent's feet, waiting for something to fall off his fork. Brent cringed, knowing that Viola's hair was, at that very moment, gluing itself to his slacks.

"It's the only thing that makes any sense." She showed them the calendar and took them through the sequence of events.

"But why?" Peter asked. "Amethyst was a big deal a hundred years ago, but now it's common, and even antique pieces aren't worth much." When Lia and Brent looked at him, he shrugged. "I'm getting an education from these old robberies. Want to know what a Pre-Revolution spittoon goes for?"

"What does the necklace look like?" Brent asked.

"I never saw it," Peter said. "She always wears stuff like that under her shirt, except on special occasions." He looked pointedly at Lia.

Lia bit her lip, thinking. "It was an oval . . . about two inches long, set in a whitish gold prong setting . . . not white and not yellow. Pale blonde. The stone was faceted, but the cut was unusual. It was flat on the bottom, like a cabochon. The face of the stone wasn't flat. It rose to a shallow peak, and had facets. It was sort of the the reverse of the usual cut, except the point on the face of the stone is barely noticeable."

Lia was on her second portion of Alma's casserole by the time Peter found a website with diagrams of lesser known gem cuts on his laptop.

"That one," Lia said, pointing. "The rose cut." She leaned in close to Peter to read the page, ignoring the frisson this gave her.

"It says it was first used in the Middle Ages, and it's only used now to repair antique jewelry. That means my necklace could be a thousand years old, from the crusades. Wouldn't that be amazing? That would make it valuable, wouldn't it?"

Peter frowned. "Somewhere in that pile of cold cases, they mention a rose cut something or other, but I don't think it was an amethyst."

"Do you think there might be a connection?" Lia asked.

"I don't know, but it's all I can come up with right now," Peter said.

"What's the next step?" Lia asked.

"The next step is, you go back to working on your murals and try to forget about this for now," Peter said. I'll review my case files and see if there's a connection."

"I'm heading up to The Comet to talk to Mr. Cunningham," Brent said.

"Why would you want to do that? He already said he knew nothing about it." Lia asked.

"Sugar, not being a professional interrogator, you might not notice obvious signs of duplicity. I just want to make sure Mr. Cunningham is on the up and up."

"I'm coming with you," Peter said.

"As long as you remember I'm in charge," Brent said as they walked out the door.

"Men," Lia said to Honey, "First they can't get enough of you. Then they're off, chasing after some dusty old rock."

"Like I told Lia earlier, I don't know anything about the necklace. She's the one who told me it belonged to Desiree." Dave shrugged and went back to polishing a beer glass. The set of his shoulders told Peter that the bar owner was unhappy about the necklace. He wondered why.

"Is there anyone else you can think of who is likely to know where she got it?" Brent asked. Peter stood beside Brent, observing the interview.

"Desiree wasn't the sort to get close to another woman, and I doubt she would tell a date where she got her jewelry." Dave said.

"Why is that, do you suppose?" Brent asked.

"She wouldn't advertise that she bought her own jewelry. At the same time, she wouldn't say some other guy had given it to her. She'd want the guy she was with to feel like he had all of her attention, even if he knew it wasn't true. Her habit was to be mysterious."

"So the jewelry becomes the elephant in the bedroom, so to speak?" Brent asked.

"Something like that."

"You think a man gave it to her?" Peter asked.

"Unless she found it in a thrift store or on eBay. Desiree made a hobby of finding vintage dish-ware and funky clothes. That necklace looked like it was outside her budget, so I don't think that's likely. If someone in her family had given it to her, she'd have shown it off."

"She seeing anyone in particular, lately?" Peter asked.

Dave grunted. "She saw lots of people. I didn't keep track."

"If you could come up with some names, that would be very helpful," Brent said.

"You can ask the other detectives, they have a list."

"Just out of curiosity," Peter said, "you encouraged Lia to keep the necklace instead of putting it in the auction. Any reason why?"

Dave shrugged again. "Why not? Lia saved Julia. She did a lot of work, rescuing Desiree's things and making it possible for me to give Desiree a send off. Besides, have you seen her? Lia's hot."

Brent stepped hard on Peter's foot. "I see your point," he said to Dave.

Peter gritted his teeth and said nothing.

"I'd say the lady's love life was a sore spot with her former boss," Brent said as they sat in Brent's Audi A4, comparing notes.

Peter grunted, too familiar with the feeling.

"Do you get the sense our investigation is coming uncomfortably close to Heckle and Jeckle's turf?" Brent asked.

239

"Screw them. They've had weeks to pursue this. They latched onto the simplest solution and stuck with it, then shuffled the file to the bottom of the pile when it didn't pan out. You have a perfectly legitimate reason for looking into Desiree."

"Could get noisy later on," Brent warned.

"So we'll share. We'll just wait a bit before we do."

Brent dropped Peter back at Lia's.

When she let him in, he nodded at a pillow and comforter stacked on the end of the couch.

"I guess that's for me."

"I'm sorry, Peter, I just can't be with you right now. I'm not going to pretend I didn't enjoy being with you last night, but that was sex. It didn't change anything. You can stay, but you and I are still on hold. I don't want to confuse all of this with my feelings for you. It's too much right now. It would be too easy to ignore the fact that we haven't resolved anything."

Peter wanted to hold Lia and shake her and tell her last night was a hell of a lot more than sex, that he knew she felt it, that it had resolved a whole hell of a lot for him, that there was no way he was going to let her go now. Wisely, he thought about his childhood in the Kentucky forests, waiting patiently for small animals to lose their fear of him.

"Okay," he compromised. "I'll sleep out here, but if you start having bad dreams, I'm coming in."

He camped on the couch, Viola curled on the floor next to him, his fingers buried in her fur.

# Chapter 27

Peter woke to Viola nuzzling his face. Three more pairs of canine eyes stared at him from the side of the couch as if he were the source of all things wonderful. They watched as he sat up and scrubbed his face with one hand, then twisted his back to pop out the kinks. *I suppose now they expect me to juggle.*

Peter pulled his jeans on and wandered towards the back of the apartment, lured by the sound of Lia bustling around the kitchen. The dogs followed on his heels. "Why are they following me? Did you refuse to feed them?"

"They must think you're a soft touch," Lia said, pouring a cup of coffee and setting a bowl on the table at his usual place. "Have you been sneaking them biscuits when I'm not looking?"

"I plead the fifth." He let the dogs out in the back yard, then stared down into the bowl of shredded carrots. "What the heck is this?"

"This is breakfast," Lia said, pouring him coffee, "unless you want to root out the stale Pop Tart that may be hiding in the back of my cabinets."

Peter sat down, gamely picked up a fork and poked through the shreds. "What, exactly, is in here?"

"Carrots, apple, lemon juice, olive oil, curry . . . ."

So far, Peter thought, it didn't sound too bad. "What are these little round things with the white tails?"

"Lentil sprouts." She watched closely for his reaction.

"Umm . . . sounds wonderful." He plunged his fork in, gamely reminding himself that it was food, and someone, somewhere, ate it and didn't die. He took a mouthful. Chewed. Chewed some more. Swallowed. Took a sip of coffee.

"Well?" Lia asked.

"It tastes like carpet, wrapped in an enigma and drowned with lemon juice."

"Give it here," Lia sighed. "I think there's a bagel left from yesterday."

"Sorry, Babe. I can't help it if I was raised on Frosted Flakes and bacon. Forgive me?"

"I'll just wait a few years until you start feeling like crap and gaining weight. Then we'll talk."

Peter gratefully snagged the last blueberry bagel and popped it in the toaster. He watched with fascination as Lia consumed her bowl of carrot and lentil salad with a gusto usually reserved for triple chocolate ice cream. He wondered if she was putting on a show, just for him. No one could be that enthusiastic about lentil sprouts, could they?

She emerged from her bowl of forage. "What's on your dance card today?"

"I'm going to hunt up that reference to a rose cut stone and see where it takes me. Brent is running Eric Flynn. You?"

"After I take the dogs out, I'm going back to the convalescent center. I haven't made up my mind about Scholastic yet. At least I have the weekend to think about it. Are you coming back tonight?"

"That's the plan."

"You might as well leave Viola here, then."

Lia was sitting at the park with Bailey and Terry when Eric called. She scowled at the number on the screen and hit 'reject.' Terry raised his eyebrows at Bailey and neither commented.

"Cynth, what the hell is a spinel?" Peter and Cynth were reviewing the stack of 27 like crimes, searching for any references to a rose cut. It was after lunch when Peter finally found it.

"Beats me," Cynth said, not looking up from the file she was scanning. "Animal vegetable or mineral?"

"Mineral. It's jewelry. I'm assuming it'a a gem of some kind. This listing of jewelry stolen from Hatch lists a '20 carat, oval, rose-cut spinel pendant in a gold prong setting, valued at $4,000. '" He pulled up Google on his computer and typed "spinel" in the search bar. "'Rarer than rubies, but often mistaken for them, undervalued despite their scarcity. . . .' Rubies means red, so that couldn't be Lia's pendant."

Cynth left her seat, read over his shoulder. One graceful but deadly hand rested lightly on his back. Cynth was inclined to casual touching. Today it was a distraction. He leaned forward, away from the contact.

"Down at the bottom," Cynth said, pointing. "Looks like you can find spinel in any color you want. Doesn't it list the color in the report?"

"Nope."

"Pictures?"

Peter shuffled through the file. "Nada."

"Do you want to see if the insurance company still has photos, or shall I?"

"I'll do it, though I can't see why anyone would create so much havoc over a $4,000 piece of jewelry, even with inflation." Hopefully they would email him a jpeg and he could forward it to Lia. He set the file aside and tossed the remains of lunch - a stack of napkins, empty Wendy's wrappers and a few cold fries mired in congealing ketch-up - while Cynth stacked the rest of the files.

Peter wandered over to the soda machine to stretch his legs, bought a Pepsi to sustain him for what he expected to be a long afternoon of phone calls. As he bent down to retrieve it from the machine, a heavy hand fell on his shoulder.

"Hey, Dourson, can't you hang onto your girl? We hear Brainard got shot because someone grabbed her, right in front of you. That's got to be pretty embarrassing, especially now that Brainard is telling everyone he figures he's got an in with her, since he got shot on her behalf."

"Brainard," Peter gritted out, "got wounded because he thought being a cop would be a piece of cake after Iraq and didn't bother to wear his vest. Lia isn't impressed by stupidity. If she was, she'd be hanging all over you two."

"If she doesn't like stupid, what's she doing with you, Dourson?"

"Speaking of stupid, did you close Willis yet?"

"Hey, Peter, what are you doing with this pair of pencil-dicks?" Cynth asked, joining the fray.

Peter snorted.

"Your mother know you talk like that?" Heckle asked.

"Who do you think taught me?" Cynth said cheerfully.

Heckle and Jeckle headed on down the hall. Peter heard one of them hiss "dyke" under his breath.

Cynth grabbed Peter's arm. "Let it go. I hear plenty worse from the neanderthal contingency."

By late afternoon, Peter had a jpeg featuring a purple spinel. He shot it off to Lia's phone, then gave her a call.

"You should have called me," Brainard told Lia from his hospital bed. "Those creeps would have never laid a hand on you if I'd been there when they showed up."

"I'm just glad you were there. I'm sorry you got hurt."

"You know what they say," Brainard deepened his voice in a bad John Wayne imitation, "All in the line of duty, ma'am." Lia mentally rolled her eyes.

A pretty young nurse bustled in, neatly stepped between Lia and Brainard. "Time for your meds, Paul." She shot Lia an evil look while Brainard downed his pills. "How are you feeling?" she cooed. "Are you in any pain?"

"Not as long as I'm looking at you," he said, flashing her a grin and a wink. "You'll stop back in before your shift is over?"

"Maybe," she said with a coy tilt of her head. She smirked at Lia and sashayed out. Lia rolled her eyes, for real this time.

"Gotta flirt with the nurses," he explained, "if you want the good meds."

*Uh huh.* "Do you know how long you'll be here?"

"I imagine they'll kick me loose in a day or two. I'll be on medical leave for at least two weeks, with nothing to do but twiddle my thumbs."

"I imagine you'll think of something," Lia said, regretting that she'd felt obligated to visit the man.

"Will you come see me?" He put on a sad-puppy face.

"I, uh, I'm really busy with a mural and a part time job right now." Her phone beeped. She pulled up a text from Peter. She read 'See jpeg. Is this it?' "Wow, looks like I'm late for a meeting. I'm so glad you're feeling better." She started to squeeze his hand, then thought better of it. The man would mistake any compassion for attraction. She jumped up. When she was a safe distance away, she gave him a quick wave and ducked out.

Lia sat at the nearest waiting area, pulled up her email and opened the picture. There, resting on black velvet, was Desiree's necklace. She called Peter.

"That's it," she told Peter. "It was stolen? Twenty years ago? How did Desiree get her hands on it?"

"That's the question, isn't it?"

"Goodness, brother, isn't that interesting?" Brent said when Peter tagged him with the news.

"What's even more interesting, the lady happened to work for a jeweler."

"Why don't we play dumb and see what Mr. A. Vasari has to say about Desiree's little trinket?"

Alfonso Vasari smiled when Peter and Brent entered his store. He waved them back to the counter. "Good to see you, Officer Dourson! You ready for me to make another gift for your lady?"

"Not today. We're hoping you can help us with a little information," Peter said.

"I understand from Lia Anderson that she showed you a necklace recently that belonged to Desiree Willis."

"Was that her name? Nice girl, cared about Desi. You must mean the amethyst."

"Was this it?" Peter pulled the photo of the spinel out of the inside pocket of his jacket and showed it to Vasari.

Vasari tapped the photo thoughtfully. "Could be. It was cut like this. Why are you interested in a cheap necklace?"

"How cheap was it, Mr. Vasari," Brent asked.

Vasari stuck his lower lip out and shrugged. "Who knows? Fifty dollars? A hundred? Hard to tell without looking at it under a loupe. It's an old cut, and the right buyer might be interested in it as an antique. Beyond that . . . ." He made a 'pfffft' sound.

"Did you ever see Desiree Willis wearing the necklace?" Peter asked.

Vasari shook his head. "First time I saw it, it was on your Miss Anderson."

"We were thinking she got the necklace here," Brent said.

"I've never sold anything like that here," Vasari said.

"Where would you buy a necklace like this?" Peter asked.

"Estate sale, maybe? But Desi, she doesn't have fifty dollars to spend on old jewelry."

"Now where do you suppose she got it?" Brent asked.

"Pretty girl like that," Vasari gave the two detectives a meaningful look, "where do you think she gets her jewelry? But she wouldn't tell an old man like me about it."

Vasari looked over Peter's shoulder and gave a nearly imperceptible shake of his head. Peter turned to see a dark, curly head ducking into the back. He looked at Brent, gave a microscopic jerk of his chin. Brent gave an equally microscopic nod. He pulled his phone out of his pocket and looked at it as if he'd received a text.

"Excuse me, Mr. Vasari, looks like I need to attend to this."

"Who was that?" Peter asked.

"Who was who?"

"The guy in the back."

"Oh, him. That's my son, Lonzo. He comes around sometimes to beg money. He says borrow. But borrow means he pays it back, no? Why do you want to know about Desi's pendant?"

"Someone went to a great deal of trouble to steal it recently. We're wondering why."

Vasari's eyebrows rose in surprise. "Desi's necklace? It was pretty, but not worth much. You sure they were after it?"

"It's all they took," Peter said.

Vasari frowned at this.

Brent returned through the back of the store, escorting the sullen young man Peter had seen. "I thought we should have a little chat with Lonzo. You don't mind, do you Mr. Vasari?"

"We help any way we can, don't we, Lonzo?" Vasari said.

Brent jerked his head, urging Peter closer. Then Brent took a deep breath and exhaled audibly. Peter got the hint. He leaned and smelled the faint aroma of pepper spray mixed with the sweat on Lonzo's skin.

"Lonzo, where were you, night before last?" Peter asked.

"Playing Assassin's Creed with my cousin, Fredo. Why do you want to know?"

"Will he back that up?" Peter asked.

"Sure, why not? You want his number?"

"Do you know where we can find him now?" Brent asked.

"Sure, he's at work."

Brent took this information down, then stepped aside to make a private call. When he was done, he nodded to Peter.

"Gentlemen, I think it would be beneficial to continue our conversation with young Mr. Vasari at the station."

Lonzo's eyes widened in horror before he could school his face. Then his expression toughened, his eyes shuttered. His father frowned and nodded to him.

"You go. I'll send Vincent."

"Who is Vincent?" Brent asked.

"My brother, the attorney."

Peter stood next to Brent in the little room behind the one way mirror in the interrogation room while the punk who kidnapped Lia consulted with Vincent Vasari, the family lawyer. Vincent Vasari was a criminal attorney with an oily manner that had always gotten under Peter's skin.

Peter clenched his fists, then forced himself to relax. Right now he was allowed to attend the interview due to the connection with the necklace. If he misbehaved, Roller would sideline him.

Despite Peter's outward calm, Brent knew he was steaming. He knew it before they'd even got Lonzo to Brent's car for the drive to the station, so he'd opted to sit in the back with Lonzo and tossed Peter the keys to his beloved Audi, keeping Peter busy and as far away from the aromatic punk as he could get in the little car. Brent mourned his car and the possibility that the smell of pepper spray would emerge from the leather when he finally enticed Cynth into the back seat. He'd have to make sure the kid paid for ruining his favorite fantasy.

"We need grounds to pull the old man in," Peter said. "If this loser grabbed Lia, Alfonso was involved somehow. Damn Roller for putting Heckle and Jeckle on him. They're probably reading *Hustler* in the parking lot while Alfonso destroys evidence."

"They do not inspire confidence, do they?"

Peter snorted like an angry bull. "We may have Fredo on ice, but keeping them separated is pointless since they're using the same lawyer. You know Uncle Vincent will tell Fredo everything Lonzo says before we can even walk in the room."

"Nothing we can do about it, brother."

Vincent Vasari rose from his chair and opened the door, signaling his readiness for the interview to begin.

Once everyone was seated, Vincent Vasari spread his hands wide, palms up, affecting confusion. "Gentlemen, why are we here? Lonzo states he has been told nothing since Detective Davis took him into custody."

*Sure spent a hell of a long time conferring for an innocent man.* "Lonzo, we're concerned about your body odor," Peter said.

"Huh?" Lonzo shoved himself out of his chair, half-stood. Vincent put a hand on his shoulder and urged him back in his seat.

Peter walked around the table, behind Lonzo. He leaned over and gave an audible sniff. "You've got pepper spray coming out of your pores. You've been maced recently."

"That's a lie!" Lonzo said.

Vincent leaned over and the pair whispered.

The lawyer folded his hands. "Me, I smell nothing. But my client admits he and his cousin, Fredo, have been on a nacho kick lately, and have been extreme in their pepper usage. Perhaps that is the source of this unfortunate misunderstanding."

"You won't mind if we verify that, will you? We'd like to have a lab tech test his skin for the residue," Brent said. "That will clear up this misunderstanding, then."

"We most certainly do mind. What, exactly, do you believe my client has done, Detective?"

"Two nights ago, two men in a dark blue van abducted Lia Anderson in front of her home," Peter said. "Ms. Anderson discharged her pepper spray at that time."

"Then she incapacitated her abductors, did she not?" Vincent asked, guilelessly.

"The man who took the brunt of the spray was conveniently wearing a motorcycle helmet with a visor."

"Ah, I see. And do you have this helmet? Or have you taken my client into custody due to his fondness for nachos? I assure you my client does not own a van, dark blue or otherwise."

"A few minutes after they abducted Ms. Anderson, these same men shot and wounded a police officer," Brent stated.

"And do you have this gun?"

"Where were you two nights ago, punk?" Peter gritted out.

"I told you! At Fredo's!"

Vincent held a hand up and Lonzo quit speaking. "My client was visiting his cousin Fredo Vasari, at which time he played the game, Assassin's Creed for more than three hours and ate several platters of nachos, washed down with beer. Since he had been drinking, he camped out on Fredo's couch. He was there from eight in the evening till the following morning. All of which, Fredo will be happy to verify."

"That's quite handy, counselor, since that means they alibi each other," Brent said. "Is there someone who isn't family, to vouch for his whereabouts?"

The pair put their heads together and conversed. "Quite possibly one or more of the neighbors saw them. He isn't sure."

"You may volunteer the sample, or we will get a warrant," Brent said. "One way or another, we will have it."

"On what grounds will you get a warrant?"

It took until nine that evening to interview Fredo and put together the line up. Lia stood in the little room, facing away from the window as each man in the line up repeated the sentences, "The windows are down. Fumes are coming off your helmet." and "I gotta hold her, don't I?"

Lia listened intently. Some of the men stumbled over the lines and were told to repeat them with an angry inflection. Two of the responses sent chills through her.

"Three and seven," she said.

"Are you certain?" Brent asked.

"Three was the driver. Ask him to say, 'We've got company.'"

When he did, Lia nodded. "It's him. I'm certain."

"Seven was the one who grabbed you?" Peter asked, eyeing Fredo and wishing him dead.

It was enough for the skin swabs and search warrants. It was not enough by itself to charge them, the DA being unwilling to prosecute on such flimsy evidence.

"Get me something, for God's sake," Roller roared. "I've got a man down because of these creeps. The helmet, the necklace, the gun, fingerprints! You've got less than 24 hours before I have to cut them loose. Start fresh tomorrow morning. Do your jobs!"

# Chapter 28

**Sunday, June 15**

Cynth conducted the tech end of the search and noted several hours of Assassin's Creed on Fredo's game console, exceeding the critical window of opportunity.

"Easy enough to get your cousins to cover for you," Cynth said. "The Vasaris took God seriously when he said 'Go forth and multiply.' They have cousins to spare and they all look alike."

Fredo's neighbor in the next apartment reported hanging on the wall due to all the racket they made two nights earlier.

Fingerprint techs could not match Fredo or Lonzo with the van. The only fingerprints on the duct tape were Peter's.

Patrol cops searched dumpsters and trashcans along likely escape routes.

They found nothing.

The lab reported that pepper oil, processed for weapons use and in the same concentration as Lia's pepper spray, was indeed on the swabs taken from the two men.

It would not be enough to hold them.

Peter and Brent drove by the Clifton home of Alfonso Vasari. Heckle and Jeckle were nowhere in sight. Peter suspected they were keeping an eye on the store, sitting at a side walk table in front of the cafe two doors down while hiding the latest issue of *Penthouse* inside a copy of the *Wall Street Journal*.

Peter watched a gardener edge the walkway to the flag-stone Tudor house. "Vasari's covering for them, I know it," he said.

"You know it and I know it," Brent said, "and we can't put a foot on the man's property. I bet that necklace is less than 50 feet away from us as we speak."

Another gardener rounded the corner of the house, riding a mower. Peter eyed the tall, thin man. Something about his perfect posture was familiar. The man wiped sweat off his forehead, shoving the ball cap just enough to reveal a sliver of red hair.

"Do you see what I see?" Peter asked Brent.

"I see a pair of gardeners in front of a house. What of it?"

"Check out the one on the mower."

Brent watched as the mower advanced across the lawn and down the driveway, up a set of portable ramps into the back of the truck. Peter knew the minute Brent caught on.

"Sweet bleeding Jesus."

"Yeah."

"Is she doing what I think she's doing?"

"You mean snooping? Why else would she be there?"

"This is highly irregular."

"Damn straight. We've got less than two hours to find something on the Vasari punks, and I don't dare leave, in case Bailey runs into trouble. Lia would never forgive me if I let anything happen to her."

"Can we pretend we didn't see her?"

"Did you have anywhere specific you needed to be?"

"No, dammit. I'm out of ideas."

"So we sit."

Lia used her fan brush to feather pink into peach on a luminous cloud.

"You're awfully chipper for looking like someone ran over you with a wheat thresher."

Lia smiled down at Alma from her perch on the ladder. "It's your casserole. Fixed me right up."

"Oh, my casserole is good, but I don't think it's *that* good. Peter hasn't been home much lately. You patch things up with him?"

"Not officially, but I think it's only a matter of time."

"I'm so glad those awful men are in jail. My heart was in my throat when I saw on the news that you'd been kidnapped. That nice young reporter was standing in front of that van, talking about it. I don't know how they got there so quick. How is the investigation going?"

"I haven't talked to Peter or Brent today. I'm doing my best not to think about it." She climbed down from the ladder, set the jar of paint aside and stood back. "What do you think?"

"It's wonderful! It's all pink and gold and pearly in the clouds, and there's violet, too. I feel like I'm sitting outside, looking at the sky and God is behind those clouds, smiling down on me."

"That's lovely, Alma, Thank you."

Lia's phone beeped. She checked the screen, disconnected yet another of Eric's calls and returned her attention to Alma.

"What's left after this?" Alma asked.

"Not much. I may just let it all sit for a few days, and see what I think about it when I come back. I'd like to look at it with fresh eyes."

Eric disconnected his phone when it went to voicemail. He'd already left Lia three messages. He had to talk to her, had to know what she was thinking, had to convince her not to report him, no matter what it took.

There was only one way. If she wouldn't take his calls, he'd have to confront her, somewhere they'd be alone. He knew just the place.

Bailey finished loading the mower into the back of Jake's truck. Yesterday she'd called Mrs. Vasari, pretending she was looking for new customers. When the woman said Jake the Rake already had a contract for her yard work, Bailey offered to make an estimate to see if the woman would switch services. Of course, she never planned to show for the appointment.

She knew Jake slightly, and had offered him free labor for the day if he would take care of Vasari's lawn earlier than scheduled and take her along.

Her main goal had been to check Vasari's garbage. It had been a long shot and it hadn't paid off. There had to be something else she could do to help Lia. Bailey grabbed a bag of mulch and headed for the beds by the stoop, trying to be philosophical about losing a day's income and getting behind on her own clients.

As she spread mulch around the bushes, she noted a series of cast iron turtles. Too cute for her taste, and a bit surprising considering the sophisticated jewelry the man sold. Still, they were better than garden gnomes or even worse, porch geese wearing Bengals shirts, though those had finally gone out of style, thank God. Nowadays, people went in for resin statues of squirrels, which were slightly better.

She paused on her knees to grab an elusive thought. Something about the squirrel. One of her clients had one, and it had a compartment for an extra house key, in case you locked yourself out. She took another look at the trio of turtles and dragged her bag of mulch over by the decorations.

Bailey glanced over her shoulder. Jake was now edging the other side of the walk, facing away from her.

She picked up the smallest of the turtles, eyed it for a seam that would indicate a lid. No dice. Same for the second. The third turtle gave a slight clink as two parts shifted against each other. The top did not lift off. She tried twisting the pieces and the iron doo-dad came apart in her hands. Sunlight hit the oval spinel inside, sparking off the gem's facets and making Bailey blink.

Peter checked his watch. It was after five. They had less than an hour before Lonzo and Fredo would be cut loose. He and Brent had been chewing the case apart while they kept an eye on Vasari's house. The bottom line was, they had nothing beyond Lia's ID of her attackers' voices and the chemical match of the pepper spray. Peter was certain the pair would come up with a fairy-tale to explain the pepper spray away. They'd probably say they'd had a misunderstanding with a young lady whom they either couldn't identify or didn't want to embarrass.

He tapped a rhythm on the dashboard of Brent's Audi, venting his nervous energy.

"Would you quit that?" Brent said. "You're giving me an ear worm. That's the worst version of the *William Tell* Overture I've ever heard."

"Sorry. I suppose our only option is to stick to these guys like glue once they get out."

"We'll be walking a fine line, brother. With a lawyer in the family, I imagine they'll scream harassment at the first opportunity. But I'm with you."

Johnny Cash sang "Ring of Fire" from Peter's pocket. He glanced at the readout on his phone, but didn't recognize the number.

"Dourson."

"Peter, it's Bailey. I'm at Vasari's house."

"What the hell do you think you're doing lurking there? Brent and I have been watching you for the last forty-five minutes while you skulk around, pretending to do yard work. Do you have any idea what kind of trouble you could get into?"

"Peter, I found it."

"How do you think Lia—"

"I said, I found it. The necklace. Do you want it or don't you?"

"Whoa . . . where? You didn't touch it did you?"

"No, I didn't touch it. I assume you need a search warrant. It's hidden inside a lawn ornament. Do you want me to send you a picture of it? Will that be enough? What do you want me to do?"

"Send me the picture. How much longer will you be there?"

"Jake's going to be done any minute now."

"Can you get him to stall while we get the paperwork? If you're working in the yard, no one is likely to try to retrieve it before we can serve the warrant."

"Jake drives a hard bargain. You're going to owe me, copper."

~

Peter sweated bullets, waiting for the warrant to show up in Brent's email. Bailey went back to work on the already mulched beds while Jake sat on the tailgate of his truck and took a break.

All he needed was ten minutes, no, seven minutes, to print the warrant on Brent's portable thermal printer, knock on the door, serve the paper and grab the necklace. Then he could call it in and have the Vasari cousins charged.

The entire system, from District Five to the DA to the Hamilton County Jail and finally to a sympathetic judge waiting at home to sign the warrant, was on alert, waiting for the call. Everyone wanted to keep Brainard's shooter in custody.

While they were waiting, a trio of officers met down the block to assist in searching the premises for the gun and motorcycle helmet.

The warrant came through fifteen minutes before the Vasari cousins were to be released. Brent served the warrant to an appalled Mrs. Vasari and led the team into the house, followed by the distressed matron. Peter lingered outside on the pretext of shooing Bailey and Jake off the property.

"Jake says, since he could lose clients over this, he figures he's entitled to stay and watch." Jake, burly, bearded and burnt red in a sopping wet "Jake the Rake" tee shirt, nodded.

"Whatever. Do it from across the street, then. You can't be on the property."

Peter donned neoprene gloves and proceeded to 'search' the outside of the house, starting with the mulched beds and the cast iron turtles. The necklace lay inside, the chain coiled underneath the purple stone. He placed the necklace in a plastic bag and marked it, tucked it inside his jacket.

He called the jail with four minutes to spare.

"Sorry, we can't hold the Vasari cousins any longer. Their lawyer is here to pick them up," the sergeant said.

Peter sputtered.

"You'll have to talk to Roller."

Peter disconnected and called District Five.

"What's this bullshit about not holding the Vasaris after I got the necklace they took off Lia during the abduction, sir?"

"You retrieved the necklace from the residence of Alfonso Vasari, is that correct?"

"Yes, sir."

"I'll contact Hodgkins and Jarvis and have them bring in Alfonso Vasari for receiving stolen property, but unless and until you find Fredo and Lonzo's fingerprints on that stone, or Alfonso chooses to tell us where he got it, you have nothing that connects the necklace with them. Has Vasari shown up yet?"

"Not yet, sir, but I believe he's on his way."

"Arrest his wife for receiving stolen property. When he arrives, you can arrest him as well. Keep them separated. We can add other charges later."

"I suggest you send the stone on into the lab and we'll print it immediately. That's the best I can do."

"Respectfully, sir, those punks could be in the wind by the time that happens."

"Punks have rights. Suck it up, Detective."

Hinkle volunteered to run the spinel to the lab. Mrs. Vasari professed no knowledge of the necklace. Brent informed Mrs. Vasari she was under arrest and put her in the breakfast nook with a police officer on her. Peter tamped down his anger and joined Brent in the search for the gun.

Lia was humming on her way to the car, a silly ditty she'd made up about Julia. She carried a box full of supplies she no longer needed for this project. The hours of painting cleared her mind and she didn't have to worry about getting to Scholastic during rush hour. She shook her head, enjoying the way her hair swished around her shoulders after being confined by a hair pick all day. A free evening lay before her, a treat, like a hot fudge sundae. Maybe she'd toss the dogs in the car, run up to Putz's Creamy Whip. A hot fudge sundae for her and baby dishes of soft serve for the furred ones.

She balanced the box under one arm while she pulled her keychain out of her pocket. This dislodged the hair pick she'd stuffed there. It fell onto the pavement.

"Damn." She set the box on top of her car and knelt down, fishing the pointed dowel out from under her car. Her body still ached from the tumble it had taken during her abduction and she groaned as she pushed herself up off the asphalt. She unlocked her ancient Volvo, leaving the keys in the lock as she slid the box of paint into the back seat. When she stood up, she felt a knife against her throat.

"Don't move. We have your keys and your pepper spray. We're all going to take a little drive." Lia recognized the voice of the van driver. The smart one.

"What do you want?" Her throat, tight with fear, could barely push the words out.

"Shut up and get in the car, or I'll give you a dose of your own medicine."

Lia's mind raced. It was suicide to get into a vehicle with an assailant, but how could she duck two assailants with the knife against her throat? What could she do? If she dropped away from the knife, could she get away before they maced her? If they maced her, they'd toss her into the car and she'd be even worse off than she was now. She froze while she considered possibilities.

He gave the knife a quick jab under her chin, just enough to nick her. "In. Now!"

She obeyed.

Eric watched in disbelief as two men forced Lia into the back seat of her car. What should he do? Call 911? They'd be gone before the police could arrive. For one insane second it occurred to him that his troubles might be over if he just let them go.

He gunned his engine and, tires squealing, rammed into the rear quarter-panel of the Volvo.

Lia heard tires squealing. The crash sent her Volvo rocking violently. Abruptly, the knife vanished from her neck. She twisted around and recognized Fredo from the police line-up, grinning at her with her mace aimed in her face.

"Feel lucky?" he asked, smirking.

She shied away, looked out the back window. Lonzo had his gun pointed at the driver of the other car. He pulled the trigger and hopped back in next to Lia. Fredo jumped the curb onto the grass and drove out onto Belmont Avenue, the car limping from the misaligned rear wheel.

"Yeah!" Fredo yelled, pumping his fist.

"Shut up," Lonzo said.

The shot slammed Eric against the car seat. He bounced and slumped forward, waiting for the shot that would blow his head apart. It didn't come. Lia's car struggled over the grounds in a drunken path. He stared stupidly at his bloody shirt, struggling to stay conscious, struggling to think past the burning in his chest.

*Phone.*

He dragged it out of his pocket, stabbed 9-1-1 with a bloody finger.

"What's your emergency?" The operator said.

"Armed carjackers," he wheezed, "took a woman . . . Lia Anderson . . . Black Volvo 240 . . . license plate VZP-795 . . . heading east on Belmont . . . towards Hamilton."

"Sir, are you all right?"

"They shot me."

He passed out.

Hinkle caught the call and tore up Hamilton Avenue, lights flashing and siren wailing, hunting for Lia's Volvo.

The ambulance pulled into the Belmont Convalescent Care Center parking lot, waved on by a crowd of people at the other end. The crowd parted to make room for the ambulance. Eric lay on the pavement where one off-duty nurse was compressing his wound with a pad made out of her sweater and the other gave him CPR. They had bloody grocery bags wrapped around their hands, an emergency version of universal precautions.

The EMTs took over, popping Eris onto a stretcher and into the back of the ambulance.

A patrol car pulled up and two officers got out. One began moving people away from the crime scene, the other approached the EMTs.

The EMT in the back of the ambulance shook his head. "We're doing our best, but I think we're gonna lose him."

"Shit, it's hell getting a statement out of a dead man," said one of the officers as the ambulance launched its siren and drove off. "Let's look at the car, see if we can figure out what's what."

"Excuse me, officer." It was one of the nurses. She had removed the contaminated bags from her hands and turned them inside out to contain the blood.

"There's something you should see. When we found him, his phone was on. He was following someone on GPS. We thought it might be important."

"Thanks, we'll check it out."

The bloody iPhone lay on the passenger seat. Officer Thurston pulled on a pair of neoprene gloves, picked up the phone and hit the wake-up button. The GPS tracking app was still running. A red dot sat less than a mile away on the map, past the end of Belmont Avenue.

"What do you think it means?" he asked his partner.

"Turn right, Fredo. Can't you go any faster?"

"Relax. We're almost there."

Lia felt the prick of the knife under her chin as her car ran over a bump on the narrow, wooded lane. *Shit, shit, shit. LaBoiteaux Woods. Not good.*

"You got the necklace. What do you need me for?" Lia demanded.

Lonzo pressed the knife a little harder. "We just spent the night in jail because of you, bitch. We figure you owe us. Now shut up."

"You won't get away with this."

Lonzo grabbed her hair and twisted with his free hand, making her cry out. He laughed.

"We will if you don't testify. And we're going to give you a taste of what will happen to you if you don't tell the police you made a mistake."

Sirens screamed in the distance.

"What do you think, Lonzo?"

"Can't be for us. It's too soon."

The sirens trailed off. The little bit of hope that had budded in Lia's heart died. If they were looking for her, they were headed the wrong way.

Fredo stopped in front of a saw-horse barricade at the end of the lane. A sign posted on the barrier read "Closed for repair."

*Damn.*

Fredo left the motor running and moved the barrier aside. He got back in and turned into the parking lot for the LaBoiteaux Nature Center, a rustic one story building that Lia knew was filled with ancient stuffed examples of local wildlife. She thought, absurdly, of a moth-eaten raccoon she'd seen there as a child. It had given her nightmares.

The parking lot was empty. Lia's last hope, that there would be maintenance men on the premises, fled as Fredo drove over the weeds growing through the cracked asphalt. He parked in front of the building. The same snarling raccoon sat in the window. An owl with spread wings stared through the blinds.

"End of the line, sugar," Lonzo announced cheerfully as he dragged her out of the back seat by her hair. "Hands where I can see them. Make me a happy man and maybe I won't cut you up so much."

"What about me?" Fredo whined. "She's gotta make me happy, too. Can I have her before you cut her? I don't want to mess up my shirt."

More sirens, this time growing louder.

"Shit, Fredo, why didn't you put the barrier back? Quick, in the woods."

They dragged Lia into the trees as the first patrol car blew into the parking lot, slew around and screeched to a halt broadside to the building, red and blue lights flashing silently on the roof.

"Take her," Lonzo said, thrusting Lia at Fredo. She stumbled as he grabbed her arm, twisted it up behind her back and forced her behind a large tree.

"What are you going to do, Lonzo?"

"I'm going to give these cops something to think about." He pulled his gun out of his waistband and waited for the first head to appear.

The doors on Lia's Volvo hung open. Hinkle stared at the abandoned car, at the woods, and thanked God that he always wore his kevlar, and that the gun shot victim had been tracking Lia. He wondered if he'd ever learn why someone had Lia on GPS. Detectives rarely shared such details with street cops. Two more patrol cars screamed up, followed by a third, forming a line across the parking lot.

Hinkle got out, staying low behind his car and duck-walked to the next patrol car.

"What do you think?" he asked Thurston. "They can't be too far ahead, but which way?"

"Hundreds of acres out here. We might need a chopper and dogs."

"Maybe we can get him to show himself," Thurston's partner, Williams, said. He grabbed a bullhorn out of the truck. "This is the police. We know you're in there. Come out with your hands up."

A bullet blew out the light bar on Thurston's car.

"Not so far ahead, then," Hinkle said.

A patrolman approached Peter and Brent in the Vasari living room. "We've got a situation. Carjacker pinned down at LaBoiteax Nature Center, trading fire. They have a hostage. Her name is Lia Anderson. They say you needed to know."

Peter looked at Brent. Brent shrugged, tossed him the keys to his Audi. As Peter bolted out the door, Brent called, "Don't you get bullet holes in my car, dammit!"

Peter flipped on the Audi's grill lights and hit the siren. LaBoiteaux Woods was a straight shot up Hamilton Avenue from Ludlow. He cursed the need to pass through the Northside business district. It would cost time he couldn't spare. He blew past District Five, down the inclined viaduct towards Knowlton's Corner. He barely slowed at the five-way intersection, zipped into the oncoming lane to pass the line of vehicles stopped at the light, and played chicken with cars that had nowhere to go on the two-lane thoroughfare.

Peter listened to radio chatter as the the business district ended and the road widened, past Millionaires Corner and up the hill. The stand-off continued at the LaBoiteaux parking lot. So far, they only knew they had one unidentified gunman taking cover in the woods behind Lia's car. Peter bet it was the Vasari cousins. That no one had seen Lia and the other carjacker worried him.

Just below the top of the hill, he turned off his siren and pulled into the LaBoiteaux Apartments. The apartments backed up to the west side of the woods, a few hundred yards from the nature center. There had to be a path from the apartments to the trails behind the nature center. If there wasn't one, he would make one.

Peter took precious seconds to grab Brent's kevlar vest out of the trunk and pull up a map of the LaBoiteaux Woods trails on his phone. He pulled to the south end of the parking lot behind the apartments and jogged across an open field featuring an abandoned tennis court. On the far side, he searched for a break in the woods to indicate a path.

He heard gunfire.

Lia counted the shots. Five, so far. How many shots did Lonzo's gun hold? She wished she knew more about fire-arms. Peter once told her that newer pistols could easily hold 15 rounds, but you could get magazines that would hold 50. Lonzo was grinning. He couldn't be running low.

The chorus line of officers behind the wall of patrol cars held their fire, though they had their guns out and pointed in Lonzo's general direction, arms and pistol butts resting on the roofs of their cars.

Lonzo kept them pinned down. Every so often, an officer would attempt to sneak out from behind the cars and Lonzo would shoot, like he was attempting to pick off duck silhouettes at the county fair. This could go on for hours.

Fredo pressed against Lia's back, holding her against a tree, bark biting into her cheek, her shoulder screaming from the way her arm was twisted behind her. Her cheek was clammy from him breathing on it. She thought he still held her kubotan in his other hand.

But his attention was drawn into the tense stand-off and his grip on her wrist had eased. There had to be something she could do while he was distracted. If only she still had her kubotan. She'd like to give them a stiff shot and - Shot! How could she have forgotten? Her kubotan only held three shots of pepper spray, and she had forgotten to load a replacement cartridge.

It was empty.

Fredo was still stronger than she was. She mentally inventoried her pockets. So many things could be used as weapons. If she could find a substitute for her kubotan, she might have a chance. Then she remembered her hair pick, a five-inch, pointed wood dowel. She'd originally bought dozens to tool copper foil with school children. She'd shoved it in her hip pocket after she picked it up off the asphalt earlier.

Could she sneak her free hand back and pull it out? He was standing so close, maybe he couldn't see with her twisted arm in the way. If she could keep the rest of her body still enough, maybe he wouldn't notice.

She considered stomping on his instep to make him step back, then discarded the idea. No leverage from her position. It would only make him mad, and it wouldn't give her enough time to dig out the pick and ready herself for an attack.

London fired off another shot. Fredo whooped and bounced against her. She used his movement as cover to position her free arm closer to her pocket and proceeded to inch her hand back, mindful of the narrow gap between their bodies.

The tips of her fingers slid into her hip pocket. She felt around until the tip of the hair pick was positioned between her index and middle fingers and slowly began working it out of the pocket.

"What's with the squirming, hot stuff?" Fredo breathed into her ear. "I think you like me on you." He gave her pinned shoulder a bump for emphasis.

Her shoulder screamed as he applied pressure to the twisted joint.

Pick now firmly in hand, she jabbed the make-shift weapon into his outer thigh, hoping to hit the nerve located there.

"Bitch!"

Fredo's leg contracted in pain and he lost his balance. He windmilled and fell as Lia stumbled away. He remembered the pepper spray, hit the plunger. Nothing happened. Lia got her legs under her and ran hard towards the rear of the nature center, away from Lonzo and his gun.

"What the hell is going on?" Lonzo yelled.

"Bitch stabbed me."

"Get her back!"

Lia raced out of the trees, behind the building, across the rear lawn to the trailheads, veering onto the first path she saw. Down the trail, heart pumping, adrenaline pouring through her veins as she heard feet thudding on the trail behind her, as she pushed harder and harder. The trail dropped away in a series of steps. She tripped, but kept running and somehow regained her balance.

What to do? Climb a tree? No suitable trees around. Duck into the woods? She'd make too much noise, he'd find her. If she could round a curve in the trail, maybe she could duck behind a tree, but she'd need a better lead and bigger trees. Fear spurred her on.

The feet were closer. She didn't dare look back.

The pain of a sudden stitch stabbed Lia in the side. She stumbled and Fredo was on her, sending her to the ground.

She screamed.

"How about it?" He panted, grabbing her hair, twisting, pulling her head up as he straddled her back. "We're all alone here. This could be fun."

Winded and furious, Lia realized she was still holding the pick. She jabbed at his thigh. He caught her wrist and laughed, a derisive grunt. With a quick twist he had her hand open and she felt the pick fall away. She struggled and bucked against him as he pinioned her wrists over her head.

"Honey, you're more fun than the mechanical bull at Bobby Mackey's. Now lay still for a moment, or I'll have to beat the shit out of you. You can buck later, I promise."

"No way in Hell, asshole," Lia spat out. She yanked her elbows down, attempting to pull her hands away. Fredo held fast.

He wrapped one large, knobby hand around her neck, squeezing her larynx, the tips of his fingers drilling into her skin. He leaned over and drawled into her ear.

"As long as you're still warm, I don't really care if you're dead or not."

Lia stilled.

Peter stood in the woods fifty feet from the nature center, working out his best move. The shooter, likely Lonzo, was on the far side of the building. There was a large, grassy expanse behind the center. He could work his way through the trees around the open yard and come up from behind, get the drop on Lonzo, but that would take longer than he liked. Every second increased Lia's danger. He could hug the back of the building, but he might be seen. Fredo could be anywhere. He decided to risk it. He unsnapped his holster.

Lia screamed behind him.

Peter pounded down the trail hugging the west side of the park, searching for the cross trail linking it with the others. He scanned the woods for signs as he ran. If he missed the turn-off, it could cost Lia her life. *Shit, Dourson, you're always a day late and a dollar short when Lia runs into trouble. If you don't make it this time, you won't be able to live with it.*

He found the cross trail, followed it to the first fork, turned back towards the nature center. The trail forked again. *Which way, which way?* He strained his ears to hear over the thundering of his heart. *Last time, both options were wrong.* He picked out a thrashing sound, and grunts . . . ahead, to his left. Peter took off again, rounded a curve. They were lying on the trail. Lia's struggles ceased as Fredo pinned her to the ground, whooping gleefully.

All thought left Peter's head. He dove forward.

Fredo's hand ripped away from Lia's throat as his weight flew off her back. She flipped over to see Peter grappling with Fredo, the men rolling and trading punches beside the trail. She pushed herself up off the ground and stumbled around, searching until she spotted a fat branch. She limped over to it and picked it up. It was two inches in diameter and over four feet long, trimmed during a tree removal and left on the ground to rot by a park worker. She turned towards the grunts and thuds of battle.

Fredo was on his back, trying to grab Peter's gun out of its holster while Peter struggled to restrain him. Lia approached, branch in hand, until she stood by the pair.

"Dammit, Lia, get out of the way!" Peter ordered, pausing, his fist in the air, panting. Fredo made another grab for the gun.

She stepped on Fredo's hand, coming down hard. He screamed. She eyed him cooly. Holding one end of the branch in both hands, Lia shoved the other end against Fredo's throat, pinning his head to the ground. Fredo's eye's wheeled like a spooked horse. Still standing on his hand, she transferred weight to the branch.

All movement ceased.

Fredo's eyes goggled.

"If you so much as twitch, I'm going to lean on this branch and shove it through your throat," she gritted out. "But don't listen to me. Go ahead, punk. Make my day."

"I had him," Peter grumbled. He hauled a now compliant Fredo up and shoved him back against the nearest tree, pulled his hands back around the trunk and cuffed him.

Lia sat on a stump. Her shoulders sagged as the adrenaline faded out of her system. She still held the

271

branch, thumping it absently against the ground. Each time she did so, Fredo flinched.

"You did, but I wanted him. I'll let you have the collar. Will that do?"

"Okay then, Miss Sassafras."

"God, Peter." She rubbed a temple.

Shots sounded.

"It's not over yet, Babe."

Peter pulled out his phone and called Hinkle. He knew from the radio chatter on the drive up that the officer was on site. The stand-off continued. "Keep him busy," Peter said. "I'm coming. I'll send you a text when I need you to hold your fire." He pocketed the phone.

"You're *leaving* me?"

"You'll be okay. Just keep that log pointed at his crotch. If he gives you any trouble, give it a good shove."

Lonzo was so caught up with his personal shooting gallery, that Peter was able to slip up on him.

Peter assumed a shooting stance ten feet away with his gun trained on Lonzo's back, then shouted, "Freeze! Drop your weapon! Now!"

Lonzo whipped around, firing wildly, bullets spraying. Peter fired twice, catching Lonzo in the chest and shoulder. The gun tumbled out of Lonzo's hand as he fell. Peter advanced, kicking the gun out of reach. He stood over Lonzo, gun pointed at his head, while the young man screamed in pain.

"Did you have to shoot me? I'm hurt! Call an ambulance!"

"Oh, for the love of . . . ." Peter muttered. He leaned over Lonzo. "Shut up, punk. I was aiming at your head, and it's a damn shame I missed. It would be an even worse shame if you tried to take my gun back here where no one can see us."

Peter saw fear and understanding in Lonzo's eyes. Satisfied, he yelled to the team in the parking lot. "It's over. Come get him."

# Chapter 29

**Monday, June 16**

Peter sniffed the air when he walked into Lia's kitchen. "What are we having?"

"Chili."

"You're making three-ways? Brent and Cynth will like that."

"I'm making chili con carne. Chili with beef. Not chili with spaghetti and oyster crackers. No shredded cheese, either."

"Sacrilege. You'll be run out of town. What happened to lentil sprouts? I thought that was the wave of the future."

"Yeah, I did too. Then I got my blood work back from Dr. Jackson today. I found out I'm type O neg."

"And this is meaningful because?"

Lia sighed. "I've been reading about the Blood Type Diet. Lentils are toxic for type O's. I can't have them anymore."

"You can't have lentils?"

"No lentils, no avocados, no dairy, no peanut butter, no olives, no mushrooms except portabella . . ." Lia continued to tick off forbidden foods.

"Is there anything left?"

"There's beef. I can eat beef. Beef hearts, beef liver, I can have beef any way you can dream up. I can even eat beef testicles. Yum. "

"A diet where you can still have burgers can't be all bad."

"No burgers. I can't eat wheat, so no buns."

"How are you going to manage that?"

"I don't know." Her lower lip trembled. Peter took her in his arms, amused at her distress. She sniffed into his shirt.

"It means no more pizza," she groaned. "And that's not the worst of it."

"What could be worse than no more pizza?"

She looked up at him, a lone tear spilling down her cheek.

"Peter, I can't have *coffee!*"

"That necklace has an amazing history." Cynth said smiling warmly. She was sitting in Lia's living room drinking Red Zinger. Lia didn't know how she felt about seeing her. She hadn't talked to the computer detective since the blow up with Peter. Brent kept looking at Cynth with an odd expression while Cynth appeared unaware of any vibe.

Peter sat next to Lia on the couch, arm around her shoulder, perfectly relaxed. Boy Scout that he was, Peter could not be so casually affectionate in front of another woman he'd been sleeping with. Bailey was right. There never was anything to begin with, not on Peter's side. But she'd be having a chat with Cynth. As if reading her thoughts, Cynth winked at her.

Brent continued the story. "The trinket that caused all this trouble is a spinel mined and cut in the late 19th century belonged to Evelyn Hatch, a famous medium who used it to stimulate her visions. Evelyn knew all the occultists. She ran with the Golden Dawn, William Blake,

Evangeline Adams, and Madam Blavatsky. She even met Aleister Crowley, and had the sense to say he gave her the creeps. Rumor has it the necklace was given to her by a secret lover who could not bring himself to leave his wife's millions."

"Why would he give her such an odd stone?" Lia asked. "Why not give her an amethyst?"

Cynth explained, "Mystics claim spinel renews energy and helps one keep one's beauty, as the 'stone of immortality.' The gift was very romantic if you were into Victorian Age occultism.

"Spinel has always been around. Until recently, stones were classified by color alone. Spinels come in all colors, but most old spinels were classified as ruby since so many of them are red. Spinel was first recognized as a unique gem in the 1850's. They are rarer than rubies, so rare that few people know about them. Since no one knows about them, nobody wants them. The few nerds who do know about them tend to treat them as inferior stones, which they aren't. Lack of good PR has always kept prices down.

"When Evelyn died, her heirs kept it as a curiosity and a memento of Grandma's occult leanings and wild years. Fast-forward several decades. Methods of gem identification became more sophisticated and new, rarer varieties of gems were discovered. Gemologists often tested old spinel to assess whether it might really be taaffeite, discovered in 1945, or musgravite, discovered in 1967.

"Alphonso Vasari fenced jewelry and antiquities for the ring of thieves Peter and I have been hunting. When they brought the necklace to Vasari as part of the haul from Judge Hatch's home, he told the gang that the necklace was an amethyst and played down its value. He said it wasn't worth selling and they let him keep it.

"Are you saying my stone isn't a spinel?"

"It's a musgravite," Brent said, "and at 20 carats it's the largest known, faceted musgravite in the world. Vasari knew what he had, but he was stuck. The only way he could sell it would be to cut it into smaller stones, which he couldn't stomach, and which would never return anything like the stone's real value. He yearned for the stone to take it's place as the world's largest faceted musgravite and kept it for years hoping that some day the path would be clear for the stone to be what it was, even if he couldn't take credit for discovering it."

"How did you learn all this?" Lia asked, fascinated.

"Vasari told us—Alfonso, that is," Brent said. "It was his last chance to claim the stone, so he spilled the beans. He figured he didn't have much to lose, and he'd rather be known for stealing a historically significant gem than for being a crooked jeweler. With the statue of limitations up, nobody could prosecute him for the theft, though he will go down for aiding and abetting Lonzo's shenanigans."

"What about the rest of the gang?"

"It no longer exists," Brent said. "Alphonso was the youngest of the gang. He took over for his father when the old man was ready to retire. The rest of the members have died or are next to dead in nursing homes. A couple have left the country and are out of reach. Alphonso said the younger generation lacked the discrimination and skill to do the worthwhile jobs. He cited Lonzo as case in point. He started his jewelry manufacturing sideline to make up the difference in his income while he waited for the right time to reveal the musgravite."

"Why did he give it to Desiree if it was so valuable?"

"He didn't. Lonzo did. He'd been chasing Desiree, and she was putting him off with comments like "Give me jewels and I'll think about it."

"She told me he was after her, but she didn't want to wreck her job because she really liked working there. So Lonzo didn't know what it was?" Lia asked.

"Alfonso never told Lonzo about it. He didn't trust him because Lonzo was keeping bad company and always looking for a quick score. Alfonso kept it hiding in plain sight on his workbench, masquerading as a simple amethyst pendant where he could look at it every day. Then Desiree Willis admired it and Lonzo didn't see the harm in using an old amethyst pendant to seduce her.

"When the old man realized the stone was gone, he accused Lonzo of taking it and threatened his life if he didn't get it back. But Lonzo never told his father it was Desiree he'd given it to. I think that's another reason Alfonso caved so easily. He was truly fond of Desiree. It was a real shock to the system to find out Lonzo killed her. He kept muttering about his serpent's tooth of a son."

"Why did Lonzo shoot her?" Lia asked. "Why didn't he just ask for the stone back?"

"He said he did, and Desiree said she didn't have a clue were it was and didn't care. Apparently they'd had a falling out, so when she caught him in her apartment looking for it, she kept changing her story to torture him. First she said she flushed it down the toilet, then she said she threw it in the trash.

"Lonzo was threatening her with the gun, trying to get the truth out of her, but instead of being intimidated, Desiree attacked him. He says the gun went off by accident, though since she died while he was committing a felony, it's still murder."

"I'm sure she didn't know where the necklace was because Julia had stolen it," Lia said. "It would be just like her to mess with him about it if she were angry."

"It's unlikely she had any idea what it was worth, but Lonzo convinced himself that she not only knew, she manipulated him into giving it to her and hid the stone from him."

"Brent, How much *is* it worth?"

"I defer to Officer McFadden."

Cynth scanned her notes. "Musgravite is currently valued at $35,000 per carat. . . . At $35,000, 20 carats comes to $700,000. Since large gems are worth more per carat than smaller stones, the value of this stone is easily in the millions."

Lia grew faint.

"Unfortunately," Brent said, "since the necklace was stolen, it's not yours. However, you can expect a nice finder's fee from the insurance company. I imagine you'll come out of this quite nicely, once the stone goes to auction and the value is established. You could wind up with a quarter of a million dollars or more."

"Not quite enough for me to aspire to being a kept man, but enough to hang around for," Peter deadpanned, giving Lia's shoulder a squeeze.

"Yes, dear," Lia simpered. She patted his knee, then dug her middle finger into a convenient pressure point.

"Ow!"

Cynth winked at Lia.

"So this whole thing had nothing to do with Eric?"

Brent rubbed the back of his neck. "Not precisely."

"I don't understand. Either he was involved or he wasn't," Lia said.

"Eric . . . Eric was no killer, but he was a voyeur, and he had issues. I don't know if he ever would have harmed Desiree, though you don't know what would have happened if he'd confessed his feelings and Desiree rejected him," Brent explained.

"We went over to his apartment today and had a look around," Peter said.

"Do I want to know what you found?"

"Hundreds of little foil dolls, for one. We also found an alarm clock that had a spy cam hidden in it. The spy cam couldn't 'see' Lonzo shooting Desiree because it was in the next room. But Julia here . . . " He scratched behind Julia's ears. Lia could hear Viola grumbling until Peter resumed stroking her. "She activated the camera by jumping on the bed while they were arguing. It caught their voices, so there's no doubt Lonzo shot her."

Lia's mouth formed an 'O'. "There was a clock that disappeared from Desiree's bedroom—a little, blocky, black, plastic thing?"

"That's the one."

"Eric knew we were cleaning out Desiree's apartment. If I hadn't told him, it would have still been there. Maybe we would have solved it sooner."

"Doubtful. You had to know the specific order to push the buttons to activate it, and the slot for the memory card was out of view. Heckle and Jeckle didn't notice the cam. At that time, there were no grounds for anyone else to get involved. Likely, the clock would have been sold at your auction."

"Then Eric knew? He had proof? Why didn't he go to the police?"

"We can only postulate," Brent said, "since the man is dead. One of Eric's video files has Desiree in a 'tete-a-tete' with Vasari the Younger—I want to make clear right now that I volunteered to view the videos to keep Peter's virgin eyes from being blackened when you found out about it. My own purity is of such caliber that it was at no risk of being sullied. Therefore, it was no sacrifice . . . ."

Lia and Cynth looked at each other and rolled their eyes.

"Meaning, as IT specialist, analyzing the videos was on my turf, but Officer Davis insisted on horning in."

"Just doing my civic duty. It is entirely possible that despite the fact that Eric was tracking her every movement, he never made the connection to Vasari. All he had was a voice. The constabulary, meaning us, do not look kindly upon his brand of romance. It's probable he felt going to the police was more likely to put him in prison than catch Desiree's killer. But he clearly knew that Lonzo was looking for something, and when you took Desiree's possessions, he may have realized that you might be in danger."

"He was *protecting* me?"

"I don't like it either, Babe," Peter said. "But he did interfere when Lonzo and Fredo grabbed you at Belmont."

"What about the dolls? He left me dolls. What was the point of that? Wasn't he obsessed with me like he was with Desiree?"

Cynth sat forward. "We don't know, Lia, but finding the dolls let you know someone was watching you, didn't it? Maybe this was his way to put you on alert without revealing himself."

Lia frowned. "Now I feel bad."

"Don't," Cynth said. "He may have done the right thing in the end, but he also put you in danger. He could have sent a copy of the files to the police anonymously, but he didn't."

Peter looked pointedly at Julia, who had wormed her way between him and Lia and was now fending off evil looks from Viola.

"All that's left is the dog." He tugged on a lock of Lia's hair. "That's your department. Will you keep her?"

"She is adorable, but she's caused enough trouble. Dave Cunningham and his brother, Ed, are fighting over her."

"The guys from The Comet? Is this about Desiree?"

"Dave figures Julia saved his life. The band is writing "The Ballad of Julia", which will end with her single-pawed rescue of two dozen hostages. Ed wants her for the band mascot."

# Epilogue

"What's in the bag?" Lia asked Peter when she met him at the door.

"Mysterious things," he answered, leaning over and giving her a friendly peck on the lips.

"No, really." She reached for the bag, but he held it out of reach.

"Uh-uh-uh," he admonished.

"Peterrr," she whined.

"It's a cootie kit."

"Uh huh." She gave him a skeptical look.

"I consulted an expert."

"And just who is this expert."

"Why, your favorite New Age juju guru. Bailey, of course."

"I see." Lia stuck her tongue in her cheek.

"We're going to do a cootie clearing. This is very serious. We need the right atmosphere." He removed a CD from the bag. "Special cootie-clearing music. If you would be so kind."

Lia took the CD and popped it into her stereo.

"Ooooooooommmmmmmm," the stereo intoned. "Ooooooooommmm." Lia raised her eyebrows as the chanting continued. Peter pulled the coffee table into the center of the living room and dropped a pair of Lia's new throw pillows on the floor. "You sit on that side."

He reached into the bag and withdrew what looked like a miniature pair of cymbals bearing Hindu lettering around the edge and connected by a leather thong.

"And this is?"

"They're a kind of cymbal, called tingshas. You can use sound for purification. He held the thong in both hands with the bells hanging level, a few inches apart. A tug on the thong, and the bells swung together and tapped, chiming in a high, clear note that provided a counterpoint to the Oms on the stereo. Peter remained motionless as the final, faint vibrations faded away.

Lia was charmed.

"Would you like to try?" Peter handed her the bells. "Let the sound die out before you tap them again. You can do that while I set up the rest."

Lia straightened her back and assumed a meditation posture, legs crossed. She tapped the bells together as Peter pulled a square plastic container out of his bag.

"Tupperware? That doesn't seem very juju to me."

"Oh, ye of little faith," he sighed, popping the top off of the container to reveal a multi-colored silk bundle. Peter set the bundle in the middle of the table and gently peeled back the cloth to reveal a pressed glass bowl containing rose petals in the center of a silk scarf printed with an intricate mandala.

Lia was fascinated despite herself. "What's with the bowl of rose petals?"

"The rose petals are for purification purposes. The bowl was my grandmother's."

"Oh, really?"

"And the bowl has been wrapped in silk to absorb negative energy."

"Uh huh."

He withdrew a feather from his bag and laid it on the table.

"What's that?"

"It's an eagle feather."

"It is not. It's a duck feather."

"Shhhh. Don't let it hear you. You don't want to damage its self-esteem. Tap your bells. Don't speak."

"Yes, sir." She ducked her head to hide a grin as she tapped the bells.

Peter withdrew an abalone shell the size of an ash-tray and set it beside the 'eagle' feather. Next he pulled out a cigar-shaped bundle of dried herbs tied together with criss-crossed string, and a lighter. Peter lit the end of the bundle, tilting the tip of the down so the flame fed on the herbs. He blew out the flame and set the smoldering smudge stick in the abalone shell. Smoke curled up in sinuous arabesques. Lia could smell sage, lavender and cedar.

Peter smiled at Lia, mischief in his eyes, as he dipped his fingers into the bowl of rose petals and lifted a delicate chain up until Lia's opal emerged from its flowery bed. The opal dangled and swayed, flashing colors. He held it over the abalone shell and the smoldering smudge-stick, using the feather to wave smoke over the necklace and chain while Lia continued tapping the bells together. When he was satisfied, he set the feather down.

"Is it pure yet?" Lia asked, as serious as a neurosurgeon removing a brain tumor.

"One last step."

Peter withdrew a five-inch long rod that looked like a small, steel microphone with holes in the bulbous end.

"And this is?" Lia asked.

"A holy water sprinkler. We are now moving into the exorcism portion of our program."

Lia fell back on the floor, giggling. The giggles turned into full throated laughter until tears ran down her cheeks. She shook her head, speechless with mirth.

Peter leaned over her, supported by one hand on either side of her head, looking down into her face. "Are you making fun of my holy water sprinkler?"

"Oh, Peter. I love you."

"You do?"

"Yes, I do."

"Be my girl again?"

"I thought you'd never ask."

He kissed her, and she kissed him back. Her opal could wait.

# The Ballad of Julia

Julia the Beagle
Loved the lovely Desiree
Till a bad man came and shot her,
Desi's young life bled away

At The Comet they were cryin'
Over ashes cold and gray
Former lovers were a sighin,'
Swore to make her killer pay

Orphaned Julia was lyin'
By the urn, and she did bay
For the owner Dave to come
And take her home that day.

Paul the preacher he was preachin'
'Bout the circle without end
Desi's papa came a-calling
With his favorite Remington.

"You sinners killed my daughter
with your wicked, evil ways.
I will send you to perdition,
For your trespass you must pay."

Your life will now be over,
But I give you one more chance
If you give your life to Jesus,
You might see that Pearly Gate.

One by one they came a-prayin'
At the hostage taker's feet.
While his gun it was a-pressin'
On Dave's temple slick with sweat.

Julia, she was a dog
And like a dog, knew mean
She heard the voice she hated
Break through her slumberin'

Every dog knows right from wrong
And this was wrong as it could get
So she girded up her dog loins
Her tiny brain was set

Big-eyed Julia was no dummy,
An orphan needs a home
And that wasn't gonna happen
If they blew to Kingdom Come

She identified her target
As she slit her buggy eyes
And crawled beneath the tables
Desi's papa was not wise

To the loyal dog's devotion
Until the bitter end.
When she peed upon his foot
And sent him into conniptions

Dave saw his chance and took it
He grabbed the loaded gun.
Then a SWAT team blew the doors in
And it all came tumbling down

# Author's Notes

The Comet and Blue Jay are Northside fixtures. LaBoiteaux Woods Nature Center is also real, though I simpli-
fied the landscape for the sake of the story. Belmont Convalescent Center and A. Vasari are figments of my imagination. Scholastic Scoring Systems is also fictional, pat-
terned after my own experience grading short answers on
standardized tests.

# Acknowledgments

In no particular order, Thanks to Paul Ravenscraft, for writing the memorial tribute; Dave Cunningham, for allowing me to use The Comet as a pivotal location in this book; Desiree Willis, for having a sense of humor and egging me on as I stained her reputation; Eric Flynn, for being a good sport; She-Who-Refuses-to-be-Named, for fighting the good fight against my random capitals and vanishing quotation marks; my Beta Readers, for their invaluable feedback. I am also thanking The Comet All Stars in advance for recording "The Ballad of Julia the Beagle," though I haven't asked them yet.

The following members of my mailing list have dogs who were the original thieves of many items in Julia's treasure trove: Joyce Hoffman, Christine Lowe, Donna, Charlotte Gaal, Sherry Pace, Ruth Peltier, Susan Dierker, Marilyn Calhoun and Jessica Townley. Thanks also to Margaret Moore and John Cunningham for their lentil suggestions.

# About the Author

Carol Ann Newsome is a writer and painter who lives in Cincinnati with two former street urchins named Shadda and Chewy. She and her tribe can be found every morning at the Mount Airy Dog Park.

## Books by C. A. Newsome

A Shot in the Bark
Drool Baby
Maximum Security
Sneak Thief
Muddy Mouth (October 2015)

Carol loves to hear from readers. You can contact her at carolannnewsome@netzero.net . Join Carol's mailing list at CANewsome.com if you would like to be notified about future releases in the Lia Anderson Dog Park Mysteries series.

$19.00

9/15

T 578702

CPSIA information can be obtained at www.ICGtesting.com
Printed in the USA
BVOW06s2145140915

417972BV00012B/94/P

9 780996 374200